Simon Lewis was born in Wales in 1971. His short fiction has appeared in Pulp Fiction compilations *Techno Pagan*, *Skin* and *Random Factor*, and in the *Big Issue*. He divides his time between London, India and China.

Acclaim for *Go*:

'Lewis blends the pace and disposable wit of Elmore Leonard with Alan Bennettish realism in a satisfyingly round plot . . . highly accomplished and enjoyable'
The Times

'*Go* drags you halfway around the world and expects you to keep up – but you are happy to do it'
Observer

'There are few contemporary British writers that are both funny and breathtakingly brilliant, but Simon Lewis is one of them. This is a book you really must experience for yourself. Alone. And soon'
Billy Liar Magazine

'Read of the week . . . An entertaining read from a promising young writer who puts an often amusing spin on subject matter it's all too easy to be cynical about'
The Big Issue in the North

go

SIMON LEWIS

CORGI BOOKS

GO
A CORGI BOOK : 0 552 14717 6

Originally published in Great Britain by Pulp Books,
an imprint of Pulp Faction

PRINTING HISTORY
Pulp Books edition published 1998
Corgi edition published 1999

Set in Bembo by
Phoenix Typesetting, Ilkley, West Yorkshire

Corgi Books are published by Transworld Publishers Ltd,
61–63 Uxbridge Road, London W5 5SA,
in Australia by Transworld Publishers,
c/o Random House Pty Ltd,
20 Alfred Street, Milsons Point, NSW 2061,
in New Zealand by Transworld Publishers,
c/o Random House New Zealand,
18 Poland Road, Glenfield, Auckland
and in South Africa by Transworld Publishers,
c/o Random House (Pty) Ltd,
Endulini, 5a Jubilee Road, Parktown 2193.

Reproduced, printed and bound in Great Britain by
Cox & Wyman Ltd, Reading, Berks.

In no particular order:
Sarah Swann, Gin and Rob, Rizla No-stars,
Charles, Nicky, Gags, Ed, Jonathan, Elaine, Foluke,
Jenna, Wang Bin, Jing Wen, Qian Fan, Brent, EJ,
Layla, Nina, Louise, Thorbjorn, Bill, Du, Jo and
one more: Benoit.
Cheers.

part one

gorgonzola city

one of the boys

Imagine having to run an obstacle course in the early hours of the morning while rancid cheese is poured into your ears. That was what my job was like. Piece-of-shit job that it was, it provided a necessary supplement to the loose change I got off the dole – I mean, I liked to eat as well as smoke. I collected glasses, Friday and Saturday nights, at 'Dazzlers', a club in Deptford. The sort of place I'd have crossed the street to avoid after one look at the entrance. The garish light puking over the pavement through the open doorway, the spangly silver sign, the dickie bows of the heavies – to me it all said gorgonzola city.

A Saturday in the summer, Seventies night, just gone eleven. A knot of half-cut people lined up before the door. Normally, I'd have got a twinge of satisfaction at breezing past a club queue, exchanging a few words with the bouncers and swanning on in there, but working that place had no credibility attached to it at all.

Marlowe, security man and hard case, a Volvo of a human, was vetting a punter, patting him up and down, as I squeezed into the entrance.

'How's it going?' I asked him.

'You're late,' he said. He jerked his neckless head towards the inner door with a twitch of his shoulders, meaning go on through. Marlowe communicated with his body as he couldn't breathe and talk at the same time. I watched him work a moment. Perhaps he didn't like the punter's pony-tail, taking it as an insult to his own poor showing on the hair front, because he was really giving him the once over; he looked inside the bloke's fag packet, in his wallet and down his white socks.

Through the door was a corridor, painted black, with a fishtank stuck inside a recess. A fishtank, for fuck's sake. Gel, the manager, reckoned it was a class touch when he had it put in six months back. Then all the fish – cheap little black ones mostly, with a few flash numbers for variety – started dying off. They had a life expectancy of about ten days, and every other night there'd be a new casualty going belly up. So one of my extra duties, on top of leafleting, fly-posting, cleaning up and massaging Gel's ego, was to nip off down the pet shop and buy new fish.

I told him it was all the smoke in the air. It wasn't good for the fish, he'd have to get a new tank with a closed top. But it wasn't the dying fish that convinced him, finally, to go for a closed tank. It

go>> simon lewis

was seeing punters dipping glasses in and drinking the water after he'd turned off the cold taps in the loos.

Opposite the tank was the cloakroom where Hell was caged. She'd have made it all worthwhile, if only she'd have fucked me. Every night, she was the best looking woman there. She had long, curly black hair, brown eyes and a wide mouth. Her face was the way faces should be. All faces, ideally, would look like hers. She usually wore lots of black eyeliner and a pissed-off look. Italian designers could not have improved on the styling of her aero-dynamic body. She was dressed in a black fishnet top that halted just above her pierced belly button. Below it I could see the tantalizing top half of an exotic tattoo.

I always tried to talk to her, anxious to point out that I hated it here, too, to set up a common bond.

'All right, Hell?'

'Yeah.'

I looked at the book, *Introduction to Tarot*, flattened on the counter before her.

'Will you read my cards for me then?'

'I don't need to read any cards to tell you your future, Lee. It's bleak.' But she was almost not sneering as she said it, so I was making progress.

After Hell's den, the corridor branched off, one way led to a door marked 'Staff Only', beyond which lay the cave where Gel planned his inept campaigns, the other leading to the fountain of

13

cheese. I headed for the door, knocked once and opened it.

Gel had a pointy face the colour of used sheets in a geriatric ward, and eyes that asked you how much money you made. He talked the kind of rhyming slang you could only get out of a book, like he once said he had to go sausage a gregory, meaning cash a cheque.

He sat behind his desk, talking to Danny, who was perched on one end. Danny was a different proposition. A short, stocky man with coke-bottle glasses and a stammer, technically he was only head of security and promoter, but really, he ran the show, or at least prevented it crashing and burning.

I wove past boxes of flyers and broken lighting equipment towards them. The heart of the club, the cave, the place from which everything else grew, had the style and glamour of a prison cell. Its windowless walls were white, the ceiling low, the lighting so harsh it made you look like a zombie.

'Glitter,' Gel was saying, 'glitter is the future. I know this firm, right, they'll come in, and they've got this fucking machine, right, hello, Lee, this fucking machine right, like a vacuum cleaner but in reverse, which'll spray your walls with glue and glitter, make it look silvery, fucking everywhere. Fuck black, I'm right fucked off with black. Looks like a fucking dungeon here.'

'That's a g–great idea, Gel,' said Danny, 'great idea. But it's not one, I feel, that the k–kids are ready for. We've got a strong identity going, and we muck it about at our peril.'

'But we have to change with the times.'

'Yes, Gel, but the kids are c–c–conservative. They don't want it to change, they like what we offer, that's why they come.'

'Do you want to see the walls changed, Lee?' said Gel.

Because I was the youngest person working there, Gel often sought my opinion, treating me as a yoof culture consultant, a hotline to the kids.

'No, Gel. It's like Danny says, I'm fundamentally a conservative. I don't want things to change.' I didn't give a shit what colour the walls were, but I felt that tactically it was a good idea to support Danny, because I was about to ask him a big favour. They were both looking at me, so I gibbered on, 'Plus I like black, it gives the place a dangerous feel. Like, teenagers are always wanting to paint their walls black, and their parents don't let them.'

'So they come here,' went Danny, 'and they know they're in an environment where p–p–parental values don't matter, and they can be as naughty as they like.'

'Yeah,' I said, nodding, 'that's it.'

'See,' went Danny, 'it's a subtle psychology thing.'

Gel looked broody a moment. 'It'll cost a lot to change it over,' he went. 'Maybe I'll wait till next year. I'll see what other people think.'

'That's the way,' said Danny. 'Why don't you go and get things going out there? You're needed.'

Gel liked to play a set himself, and Danny let him, but only for an hour, right at the start. Gel slapped his hand down on the desk.

'Let's get this arty farty into gear,' he went, and headed off. Arty farty meant party; I think he made that one up.

'You should be getting to w–work and all,' said Danny to me.

'I want to ask you something.'

'What can I do you for then?' he went.

This was it.

'It's like this. I want to ask your permission for something.'

'Oh yeah?'

I had a little speech planned, but in the end I junked it and headed straight in there.

'I want to start dealing some speed.'

Danny didn't say anything.

'I know you've got dealers already, but no-one's doing whizz, yeah? Not on a regular basis. It's all Es. So I won't be treading on anyone's toes. I'll give you a cut, of course, whatever's standard.'

Danny drummed his fingers on the desk at about the pace my heart was going. He looked concerned. Fuck, I thought, I've blown it. I had two ounces at home, waiting on his word. I'd already mixed it – chucking in a bit of guarana and baking soda – and wrapped it. I didn't want a lot of expensive origami packages sitting around.

Danny looked at his big square nails.

'W–w–w–'

'Yeah?'

He paused, fixing me with glaring eyes, magnified by his glasses.

'We'll see. You've got a c–car, yeah?'

'Yeah.'

'Right. You're giving me and Marlowe a lift home. We'll have a b–b–businesslike discussion. Now get to work.'

I headed into the club, where a scattering of villians, wasters, wannabes, dreamers, dickheads, dossers, disco dollies, downright alcoholics and students were limbering up for the night's entertainment. Half of them were about fourteen, the others about forty-five. They stood around in little gangs, like in a playground, and cast speculative glances at each other. A few girls were dancing, making sure everyone else was watching. Gel was playing some awful shite. Like the Seventies weren't bad enough the first time around. I had fuck all to do really, just wander around hating it, picking up the plastic glasses and wondering what Danny was going to say.

I thought about how much I was clearing – twenty quid a night, cash in hand – and how much more I'd be making if I was dealing on the side.

Maybe two hundred. I wouldn't do it without Danny's permission, though. I'd seen what happened to people who did that, and cleaned up afterwards on one occasion. Next to the cave was a room, bare except for a few broken chairs, some old newspapers and a dark stain on the carpet that just wouldn't come out.

As the night progressed the place got crammed and clammy and the punters more frantic. The work got more gruelling; I was constantly pushing through the crowd, my left hand holding a telescope of glasses, my right raised to bat people aside. To them I was a piece of mobile furniture, worth barely a glance. Every night at the club was identical to every other. I heard some guy say to a girl, 'Get your coat, you've pulled,' which I heard him say the week before. Or maybe it was someone else.

When they put the lights on at two it was like a bomb had gone off; there was rubbish everywhere, the crowd lemminged for the exits and a few casualties lay still against the walls. I blagged myself a drink, then propped up the bar and lit a fag, enjoying the silence and the emptiness.

A sweaty Gel came up, and I told him what a good night it had been. He gave me two crushed tenners, the way you'd lend money to a junky, and pissed off.

'Oi, Mr Big.'

Danny. He came up with Marlowe in tow. Marlowe had changed into casual gear and was carrying a bag. The guy moved like a robot, you'd think he'd been knocked up in a garage. It was a mystery to me why Marlowe was such a favourite with the ladies – couple of times I'd left and clocked him fucking some girl in the alley round the side.

We went outside, where the sudden cold was a relief. A gaggle of party people clustered round the hotdog van. A guy was handing out flyers for another club, and the ground was littered with them. It stressed me out that neither Danny nor Marlowe had said anything. My crap car, a Fiesta, was parked down the street, and I really wanted it to start first time.

Danny got in the back, sweeping aside a collection of empty crisp packets, and Marlowe folded himself into the passenger seat, an arrangement which surprised me.

'Where do you live?' I asked.

'Take us to Camberwell,' went Danny.

'That's a bit out of my way.'

'It's just this once.'

The car started, second time, and I steered it out into the road and slotted some decent music into the stereo.

'What's this shit?' asked Marlowe, and I reached over to change the tape.

'Let the boy listen to what he wants,' said Danny. 'Good night?'

'They're not good or bad,' I said, 'I just get them over with.'

19

Danny laughed. 'You hear that, Marlowe? Good one, k–kid.' He leant forward and tucked his head between the seats.

'I get the impression that you're not entirely h–happy, working at the club.'

I had to negotiate a turn so I had the chance to think before I replied. 'I like the club. I just think the job I do isn't challenging enough.'

'You feel that you're not r–realizing your full potential?' went Danny.

'Yeah, that's what I feel like.'

'Not realizing your full potential,' said Marlowe, gnashing each word like toffee.

'You know the club is losing money?' went Danny.

I didn't.

'Why don't you run it?' I asked. 'You'd turn it around easy.'

'Truth is,' he said, 'I'm m–m–more interested in my other business concerns.'

'And what are they?'

'A b–bit of this, a bit of that.'

'A bit of the other,' said Marlowe, and we all laughed, like we were mates.

All this conversation was great, but I was wondering when they were going to get to the point.

We headed into Peckham, making swift progress. I liked driving at night with the streets so empty. I put my foot down and whipped the car round a night bus.

'You're a good driver,' said Danny. 'What do you reckon, Marlowe?'

'He's a good driver.'

Danny settled back in his seat and we stayed silent till we reached Camberwell. I wondered whether I should bring up the issue at hand, or if that was bad manners.

Marlowe looked round at Danny, then said, 'I'm hungry.'

'There's a bagel place near here that's still open,' I went.

'Nah,' said Marlowe, 'I want a cheese-and-onion pasty. It's got to be a cheese-and-onion pasty.'

'There's an all-night garage in a sec, just on the right,' said Danny. He sat up straight again.

'So about me selling whizz in the club,' I went.

'Just here,' said Danny, pointing to a garage, 'this one.'

I slowed down and pulled into the forecourt.

'Park by the front,' said Danny.

'You can't,' I went, 'they move you on.'

'P–p–park by the front.' I parked by the front. Marlowe grabbed his bag and got out, leaving the car door open, and lumbered over to the bit where you shout at the man behind the glass.

Danny laid his hand on my shoulder. 'Leave the engine running.'

'What's going on?'

I didn't believe what I saw next.

Marlowe pulled a gun out of his bag and

shouted at the startled cashier, 'All the fucking cash, now!'

'Fuck's sake!' I went.

'Keep your head down,' barked Danny, pushing hard at the back of my neck. 'They've got cameras.' I ducked down, sticking my head under the steering wheel. I was suddenly very cold; the night air rushed through the open door. I felt Marlowe land on the passenger seat.

'Move then!' shouted Danny.

I ground the car into first as Marlowe slammed the door shut. I kept my foot down and the car screeched out of the forecourt into the street.

'Go! Go! Go!' shouted Danny.

I was lucky; there were no cars coming. I bombed down the road, hardly knowing what I was doing. The engine roared. I let my foot off the accelerator, slipped it into second and stamped down hard. I was heading back the way we'd come. I discovered I was shouting, 'Fuck, fuck, what the fuck?'

'Turn around,' shouted Danny. 'Now!'

I hit the brakes and the car skidded and Marlowe slid over the seat towards me. We were side-on in the road, and the night bus I'd overtaken earlier was charging down on me. I could see the driver's pale face. I was into reverse before I knew what I was doing and the car bucked back onto the pavement. The bus roared past, a blur of red.

'What's going on?' I shouted.

'I saw a cop,' yelled Danny. 'Fucking –' I was in first and back on the road before he got to finish his sentence '– get a move on!' I threw a glance in the rear view but didn't see any traffic. I headed past the garage and tensed up, waiting for a siren to explode. I went straight into third and the engine howled till I got up some speed. I felt better the faster we were going.

'Left. Left now!' went Danny. I hit the brakes and threw the car off the main road into a narrow turning that led into a dark estate.

'Next right,' said Danny. I made the turn – just – mounting the pavement and clipping the wing mirror on a railing. I sped through the narrow streets, the houses flashing by. I got some security from the darkness. I could feel Marlowe and Danny coiled up and alert. Still no sirens. I was focused on the pool of light thrown by the headlights.

We went past a load of turn-offs and I figured Danny had directed me into the estate because there were so many roads to hide in. All the streets here looked identical, variations on a few elements: streetlights; squat, concrete, low-rise housing, straggly trees. We didn't pass any people, which reassured me, then I wondered how many had seen my earlier manoeuvres, and I started thinking I'd have to ditch the car.

'Left here,' went Marlowe. I turned into a short cul-de-sac.

'But it's a dead end,' I went.

'Park there,' he said. 'Just there.' He pointed at the kerb.

'But they might be chasing. Someone might have seen us.'

'J–J–Just do it,' said Danny.

I stopped the car and it stalled. It was still in third. We were parked outside a house with one ground-floor window illuminated by a telly. Suddenly it was very quiet. I started shaking. My hands had been clutching the steering wheel so tight they hurt. My skin was filmed with sweat.

'That'll do nicely,' said Marlowe. 'This is where I live.'

I was silent for a second. 'Where you live? This is where you live?'

Marlowe turned and looked at me. 'Fancy a bite?' he said.

In his right hand he still held the gun. In his left he had a cheese and onion Ginsters pasty. He'd already taken a couple of bites. He began to crack up, going, 'huh, huh, huh, huh,' and spitting crumbs. Danny patted my shoulder.

'Marlowe's brother works nights', said Danny, 'at the garage.' I blinked. I took my hands off the wheel. Danny cackled. I put my head in my hands.

I chuckled once, twice, then felt it swell up from my chest, pure hysteria.

'You fuckers. You fucking – fuckers. Fuck's sake.' I was crying.

'K–k–kid,' said Danny, 'you did brilliant.'

We were laughing so hard the car was rocking.

'You can sell what you f–fucking well like. Consider yourself one of the boys.'

two

wicked curves

A month later, Friday night, Eighties night, around ten. I strolled into work. The club wouldn't be open for half an hour, but I liked to get in early now, have a chat with the staff, mooch around, share a beer with Danny maybe. I'd started to look forward to it, even. The place was tolerable before the music kicked off. And even after it started, things weren't so bad now. Someone must have had a word with someone, because I didn't seem to have to do any work any more. I picked up the odd glass every now and again and took it to the bar just for a bit of variety, for old times' sake. Nobody asked me to do it. And at the end of a night Gel gave me twice as much money as he used to. It was almost embarrassing.

I headed past Marlowe. I think he considered me a mate now – his nod was a centimetre deeper.

Hell was in her cage, hanging up her coat, a green leather number. Her bag, a brown hippy-type sack thing, sat on the counter. She usually came in early;

it gave her time, she told me once, to get some quiet reading done.

Tonight, I told myself, it was going to happen. Tonight.

At the sight of Hell, my legs became weak, my bones turned to rubber, the blood pounded in my face; I felt like I was going to be sick. In black jeans cut low to her hips and a black crop top, her curves were in full effect. The sight of her smooth midriff, punctuated by the dimpled full stop of her belly button, did not help my concentration any. I focused on her jingling silver bracelets.

'Hi.'

'Oh, hello Lee.' She started unbuttoning her bag.

I rested my hips against the counter and placed my right arm up on the metal strut at the side of the opening, a manoeuvre designed to exude casual confidence and show off my new watch, which sat big and chunky on my wrist. How expensive it looked, nearly as expensive as it was. These days I was pulling in so much cash – a few hundred a week – that I could afford to treat myself. A shining steel diver's watch, it was water resistant to a hundred metres and featured glow in the dark hands and a unidirectional bezel, whatever that was.

I had flash gear on and my new mobile bulged in the back pocket of my jeans. I knew I was looking good. I was sharp. I was confident. As I'd been telling myself for the last two minutes, I was super-cool. Yeah.

I felt about fourteen.

'How's it going?'

'Good,' said Hell, rooting round in the bag. She looked up. Her eyes were a deep, bottomless brown, like when you hold a bottle of Coke up to the light.

'You all right, Lee?' She smiled, revealing slightly crooked teeth, white and glossy like the most expensive kind of paper.

'Yeah, I'm good.' I smiled back.

'Can't find my fags,' she said, and started rooting again.

'I wanted to ask you—'

'Here they are.' Hell pulled out a packet of Silk Cut. Her fingers were tipped with bitten nails, and the end of the first and index fingers of her right hand were stained a woodland brown.

'Yeah, I thought, um . . .'

I'd rehearsed the line a couple of times in front of the mirror, and I reckoned I'd got it down – let the words pop out and float, casual, like it was just something you say.

'Would you, would you, you know, like, like to go out with me? Maybe.'

The words plopped out and sank. They curled up and died. Hell looked at me like I'd admitted I ate babies.

'What?'

'One day. I'm just asking. Obviously. You don't have to.'

I braced myself for the brush off.

'Lee!' Danny strode in through the door. 'Lee!' I took my arm off the strut and turned round.

'G—g—good to see you,' said Danny, loud. He strode up swiftly and lowered his voice. 'Marlowe said you did a great job the other d—day.'

'Well, it wasn't much. I just did what you told me.'

'Exactly.' He extracated himself from his black bomber jacket.

What I'd done was chauffeur Marlowe, plus a sports bag, up the M1 the previous Sunday. No-one told me where we were going or why or how much I was going to get paid. It was a little favour, Danny said. After a couple of hours, we stopped at a service station and Marlowe got out, taking the sports bag. I stayed in the car. Ten minutes later he got back in, minus the bag, and told me to drive him back to London. And that was it.

'And you didn't ask questions,' said Danny. 'That's an important talent.'

He held the jacket out to Hell. Through the corner of my eye I saw her hand reach out and take it, and I heard her step back to the racks in her cage.

Danny delved in his jeans pocket and pulled out a fat leather wallet.

''Cause you know what they say about curiosity,' he said, counting out ten tenners. 'C—c—curiosity gets cats fucked over.' Danny folded the notes together and passed them over. 'Token of my appreciation.'

I slipped the money into my back pocket, wondering what Hell was thinking. 'That's very kind of you.'

'L–listen. There's something else you can do for me.'

'Yeah?'

He jerked his head back towards the entrance. 'Come outside a minute.'

I glanced at Hell as I turned. She had her back to me and was filing her bag away in the shelves at the back of the cage.

'So, see you then, Hell,' I mumbled. I wasn't sure if she heard.

Danny led me out into the street and down the dead-end alley at the side of the club. As usual, there were a couple of big bins at the side and it stank of piss. And there was a car there. Not just any old car. A silver Merc. It was dark down there in the shadows, but this vehicle seemed to glow with an inner light.

'Got a little favour, Lee. I want you to drive this.'

I stepped around to the front of the sleek car. It was a class act. There were even little wipers on the headlights. Danny stood at the side.

'I want you to take this to a reservoir, Lee, and get rid of it.'

I looked up sharply. 'Get rid of it?'

'Yeah.'

'Just get rid of it. And I'll give you three hundred quid.'

'Three hundred quid?'

'Three hundred quid.'

'I don't know, Danny.'

'What don't you know, Lee?'

'You mean ditch it? Ditch this?'

'Like I said. You take it, tonight, to this reservoir and dump it.'

'It's beautiful.'

Danny took a set of keys out of his pocket, stepped forward and unlocked the driver's door.

'Here, get in.'

I eased myself inside. It was like getting into a hot bath. I felt instantly at home. I could have lived in it. It was everything I didn't have and always wanted. It smelt of money and power.

Danny bent down to talk to me through the open door.

'Lee, how much money you clearing a week, selling your gear? A couple of hundred? Enough to buy you, what, new clothes, records?' He paused. I closed my hands over the steering wheel and the padding yielded under them like it wanted me.

'It's pocket money. Have ambitions Lee. Th–think high. Think big. You're y–y–young and fresh and full of ideas. You want to go places, get somewhere. I look at you, Lee, and I see a young man full of raw t–t–talent. W–would you say that was true?'

31

I was looking at the space-shuttle spread of hi-tech on the walnut dashboard. 'Yeah.'

'You do this for me, Lee, and after, there'll be other things you can do. You'll make some powerful f–f–friends. You'll make a lot of money. You'll go a lot of places.' I let my left hand fall and rest on top of the shapely gear stick.

'You do it tonight, all right? After work. It's not far, this place. I'll draw you a map inside.' He dropped the key in my lap and slapped the roof. 'G–good lad.' Danny strolled off, leaving me tucked tightly into the sexy thing. I stayed there a minute, bonding with the machine, then got out with the same sense of loss I felt when I climbed out of bed. The clunk when I closed the door was deeply satisfying. I held the black oblong keyring in my hand and spun the key round as I headed back into the club.

'Lee,' Hell called out as I approached her cage.

I shuffled to a halt. 'What? Look, I'm sorry, all right—'

'OK.'

'What?'

'OK.'

'You busy tomorrow?'

'No. No I'm not.'

'Right.' I nodded my head, curt, businesslike. 'How about I meet you outside here, one o'clock. Fancy coming for a drive?'

Hell smiled. 'I know just the place. I'll make us a picnic.'

I spun the key, caught it and held it in my closed fist. Supercool.

The thing about Hell was that she was actually quite nice. She was intelligent, artistic, well-informed, enthusiastic, sane and she could tell a joke. And she had a lot to say for herself. Yes, she had a lively, interesting personality. And the tits! The arse! The legs!

And here she was! With me! Alone!

We were in the middle of a circle of standing stones in a field somewhere outside London, right out in the middle of nowhere. The grass was green, the birds were singing, there were trees and bushes and flowers all over. Not the sort of location I'd have chosen, but I was more than willing to go along with her idea – I'd have been happy to sit and eat veggie rabbit food, and chat, and steal furtive glances at her tits, in a war zone.

Hell was wearing a purple T-shirt and a black skirt with tassels along the bottom, like my granny used to have along the bottom of the sofa. It was a long skirt, but when she was in certain positions, when she reached across for an apple, say, and I ducked my head down, I got to see quite a lot of her legs.

Hell was lying down on the rug and pointing her

33

snub nose up at the sky. Her long black hair was spread around her face like a wiggly halo. She hummed softly. It was one of those moments when you could just be there and enjoy the fresh air and the sky and the green stuff, and you didn't feel the need to talk. For me, this was a great relief. I didn't have to keep scouring my mind for suitable things to say.

I was lying beside her on one elbow, resting my face. All the smiling, the nodding, the eyebrow raising, had made my facial muscles ache.

My new pager bleeped. I rolled around, pulled it out of my pocket and fumbled with the buttons. Chelsea drew nil-nil away.

'Who is it?' murmured Hell.

'Business.'

A silver chain attached the pager to my belt. I admired the way it glinted in the light, then I slid the thing back and enjoyed the view. About twenty metres away, on the grass just inside the hedge, the Merc sat waiting.

In my mind I ran over a special moment on the drive down. We'd been behind this pottering Nissan Micra on a country lane, doing maybe forty, if that, in third. I though we'd never get past it, then we cleared a corner and I could see the road ahead for maybe fifty metres. It was going to be tight, but I went for it, straight off, no hesitation. I hit the pedal hard and the car shot off like a rocket. In half a second the Micra was a fading memory. We swerved back into lane, sweet as a Brazilian striker's side step. The car didn't break a sweat. I could see Hell was impressed. Beautiful machine. It was a moment that made me tingle inside.

Now she said, 'It's not really your car is it?'

I turned my head and saw Hell on her side, looking up at me, smiling. Tactically, I felt that now would be a good time to tell it like it was. Girls respect that. I'd be honest. Well, more honest.

'It's a mate's.' I paused. 'I wanted to impress you.'

'You didn't have to.' She rolled around, raised herself up on one arm and looked me in the eye. 'I wouldn't care what car you drove, Lee.'

'No?'

'No. Or what job you did or how much money you earned or how many gadgets you had.'

'No?'

'No. You care too much about that stuff. That's sort of why I brought you here. I wanted you to realize something.'

'Oh yeah?'

'I see you now, and you're this big-shot dealer strutting around, and you're all pally with Danny, and it's funny.'

'What?'

'You're caught up with the little things, Lee. And people get so caught up in the little things – money and all that – they forget what's really important.'

'What?'

'You come somewhere like this, somewhere

beautiful, somewhere sacred, and you realize that, well, all that's just . . . details. It's other stuff that's important.'

'What other stuff?'

'You know . . . just being. Look at the birds, Lee, and the flowers, and the stones. They don't care about being big shots.'

I had a limit, even with her.

'Hell, what are you talking about? You tell me to look at the birds? Well I am. I'm looking at that one.' I pointed up at a big, nasty-looking bird with blunt wings, a bomber of a bird, circling in the air above us. 'That bird got to be a big bird 'cause it eats little birds. All that other stuff, that comes after. When you're a big bird.'

'But Lee, Lee, it's not being a big bird that matters. Little birds are just as good. They're just as happy. What it's about, Lee, what I'm trying to explain, is that we're all one, we're all part of the, the—'

'The cosmic energy flow?' I said. It was a phrase she'd used earlier. I knew that, to stand any chance at all, I was just going to have to agree. If she said the world was flat, then it was flat, and would remain so till I was lighting a post-shag fag.

'Yes!' She seemed pleased. 'The ancients knew that. That's why they put these stones up: to remind us.'

'Yeah. Right.' I nodded my head, trying to look convinced.

We looked at the lumps of rock for a bit. There were five of them, they were about as high as I was, and they were five metres apart. Hell told me they were an ancient temple that marked a sacred site. Personally, I thought that if a bunch of primitive people wanted to lug some stones to a field and set them up, then that was their lookout. Civilization had moved on a bit since then.

'The people who put these up,' went Hell, 'they knew things we don't.'

Yeah, right, I was thinking, if they were so clever, how come they never invented anything?

'I feel like I can really recharge here, you know what I mean?' said Hell.

'Yeah.'

'You can feel the energy here, can't you?'

If energy was what she was after, we should have picnicked under one of the parade of pylons in the distance. I was working hard, looking for an opening. I was, like, energy, energy, I've got a lot of energy; if you've got the time I've got the energy.

'Oh yes,' I said.

'And the, the magic.'

Magic, magic, let's make some magic together. I think you're a magical woman, Hell. Want to look at my wand?

'And the sense of peace.'

Sense of peace, sense of peace – I couldn't do anything with that.

'It's the sort of place that wakes you up, don't you think?'

'I'm awake now, Hell. I'm wide awake.' I leant towards her and time slowed right down. Fuck me now. Oh God, please. I'll do anything. Just fuck me. Please please please. Fuck me now.

WEE!WEE!WEE!

The car alarm went off. It sounded like the end of the universe. I whipped around in time to see the big bird flapping away from the roof, where it had decided it wanted to sit. The big flappy bastard.

'Shit, shit, shit!' I stood up. So did Hell. She covered her ears.

'Turn it off,' shouted Hell, 'turn it off.'

I ran across the grass, fumbling the car key out of my pocket.

WEE!WEE!WEE!

Jesus, was it loud.

I stuck the keys into the door and unlocked it. But the noise didn't stop. Hell came over.

'Make it stop!' she shouted.

I opened the door, slid into the front seat and stared at the dashboard. Dials and digital displays stared back. I hit some buttons.

WEE!WEE!WEE!

'Do something!' shouted Hell.

'I'm trying, all right? How do you stop this fucking thing?'

Hell grabbed the key off me and went round to the back of the car.

'What are you doing, woman?'

'When my Dad's alarm got stuck, he opened all the doors and it went off.'

'What are you talking about?' I swivelled round, and in the back windscreen saw the boot rise up.

WEE!WEE!WEE!

Hell screamed. Like what we really needed now was more fucking noise.

'I've got it!' I shouted. 'The thingy, on the key, the infra-red thingy! Press it! Hell?'

I watched her run away screaming from the car, out the gate and down the track. 'Hell!'

I got out and stared after her. She was going for it, full pelt; she turned a corner.

'What the fuck?'

WEE!WEE!WEE!

I walked round to the open boot and felt my face go white. Not as white, though, as the face of the dead man who was lying curled up there, looking as surprised as I was, staring with big dead eyes, naked but for a pair of red-and-black polka-dotted boxer shorts. No, white and black; they were stained by the goo that had oozed out of the three little holes in his chest.

WEE!WEE!WEE!

>>>gorgonzola city

groovetastic

That night, I slunk up to the club around eleven. Some of the queuing punters, the regulars, recognized me and said hello. The source of my new popularity – forty wraps – was tucked in my trainers. I could have shifted more, but I wanted to make sure I left with nothing, there was always the risk of being stopped on the way home. I moved down the line like a royal at Wembley, nodding and shaking hands, but my heart wasn't in it. I was knackered. I'd spent most of the afternoon walking over fields and hitching, and the evening at home pulling my hair, scratching the skin at the base of my nails, or pacing in tight, worried circles.

Marlowe gave me his nod, and I smiled back weakly, then strolled past him and along the corridor, to Hell's cage. A queue of five people, coats and jackets bunched in their arms, lined up before her counter. I moved around them to the front and peered past the first in line, a middle-aged man with his frilly orange shirt open to reveal a froth of pubicky hair.

'Hell.' She didn't look at me. 'Hell.' She was still wearing the clothes she'd had on earlier. There were grass stains on her skirt. She looked more beautiful than ever, unfortunately.

'I'm busy,' she said, and slid a pink slip across the counter. The man took it, and she scooped up his fifty p. He moved off towards cheese central and I slipped into his place.

'Hell, listen, I'm sorry. I'm sorry, all right. I can explain, Hell.'

'I don't ever want to see you again.' There was a catch in her voice. She looked at me straight and I got her eyes, full power. 'I don't know if I'll ever forget that.'

'Oi, mate.' The next guy in line spoke in my ear. I turned and glared at him and got a blast of after-shave. He glared back.

'I'm not interested in your excuses,' said Hell. She looked past me at the guy behind. 'Can I take your coat, sir?'

He tried to push a leather jacket past me. I put my hands on the struts on either side of the counter to block him, lowered my head and hissed at Hell.

'Hell, the car keys. I need the car keys.'

'What?'

'The car keys. You ran off with the fucking car keys.'

Someone in the queue tutted loudly.

41

'Well, I haven't got them,' said Hell. 'I don't remember having them. You know it took me ages to get home? I had to walk to—'

Her face fell. 'You mean you left it there?'

'I'm fucked, Hell. I'm fucked.'

The man behind tapped me on the shoulder. 'You will be, mate,' he said, 'if you don't move it.'

'Yeah,' added the girl behind him.

'That's not my problem, is it?' said Hell.

'Yes it is,' I went. 'It is your problem.'

'I'll give you a fucking problem,' said the man behind, and he started trying to push me aside.

'All right, all right. Fuck's sake,' I scuttled off, and headed for the cave.

'Lee.' Danny, swivelling in the swivel chair, greeted me heartily. Gel looked up briefly from behind the desk, where he was hunched over an A4 pad, his arm curled protectively round it, like the square kid who doesn't want his work copied.

I dodged my way further into the room. Danny stood up, put his arm around my shoulder and steered me into the corner, by the table with the fax machine, as far away from Gel as you could get in there. We parked our arses on the table. I was very conscious of the weight of his fat, snake of an arm curled around my shoulder.

'How did that l–little bit of business go?'

I pretended briefly to wonder what he was talking about.

'Little bit of business? Oh fine, yeah, absolutely.'

'It all w–worked out?'

'Yeah, no problem.' My tone was matey, casual. 'Took it to a reservoir, like you said, and I parked it on the edge, and then jammed the accelerator and watched it go glug glug all the way to the bottom. Like you said. Shame. It was a lovely vehicle.'

I remembered to look him straight in the eye, not to lick my lips, to keep my voice slow, not to put my hand over my mouth, or do anything I wouldn't normally do. I'm a good liar, having put in a lot of practice down the dole office.

'And nobody saw you?'

'Nobody saw me.'

'Excellent.'

Danny reached inside his jacket and pulled out a wodge of tenners bound with an elastic band.

'P–payment as agreed.' He handed it over and I tucked it into my back pocket.

'Lee,' Gel called over, 'has groovy got an E in it?'

'No. Unless you put two in', I went, 'at the end.'

'That's a g–g–good one,' said Danny, loud. 'Like it. Jee are owe owe vee ee ee. Yeah. Groovy.' Gel went back to his labours and Danny lowered his voice again. He applied pressure with the arm around my shoulder, pulling my head down and drawing me closer.

'That little thing you did, that was appreciated that was. Appreciated by a lot of p–people. Some of them quite important p–p–people. You just made yourself a lot of friends, Lee.'

43

'Oh yes?'

'Oh yes. Powerful friends. Influential friends.'

Gel slapped his hand on the table and called over. 'Tell me I'm stupid. Tell me I'm wrong. Superfly. It's two words, isn't it?'

'One, I'd say, Gel,' I went.

'What the fuck's that?' said Danny. 'I'll tell you what that is: that's a fly that wears his underpants outside his t–trousers. It's two.'

'That's what I thought,' said Gel.

Danny turned his head and lowered his voice again. 'Are you a good guy, Lee?' he said, his voice low and urgent.

'I like to think so.'

Danny paused. The light reflecting off his specs put a gleam in his giant eyes. ''Cause there are some n–n–nasty characters out there. I want you to know that you're on the right side. You're working with the good guys here. I just want you to under-stand that.'

'You've made that very clear.'

Danny didn't move any further away. I could feel his hot breath on my face.

'G–good guys are g–good to their friends. That's the thing about g–good guys. They look after each other. But when someone who acts like a g–good guy turns out to be a bad guy, the g–good guys get annoyed. They don't like him any more. And you know what happens to bad guys?'

'What?'

'They get it in the end.'

'I'm a good guy, Danny, you know I am.'

'How do you fancy playing with the rest of the gang, Lee? The g—good guys.' He jostled me with the arm around my shoulder. 'Eh?'

'Good guys?'

'There's s—s—something I want to let you in on, Lee. A piece of work you can do for me. And for your new f—friends. An important piece of work. Very well paid. Driving, Lee. That's all. Driving s—someone from somewhere to s—somewhere else.'

Gel slapped his hand on the desk to get our attention, and stood up.

'How about this,' he went. We turned to watch him. He held his pad in the air with one hand and read off it, putting on the zany accent he used when he spoke into a mike. 'The supertastic Seventies sound is brought to you by the number one guys, groovee – two ees – Tony Marconi and Super fly Andy Pee. So get on down you groovetastic Seventies funky funsters, and check out the number-one hip and happening hotspot in town, Dazzlers down Deptford way, blah, blah, the address, nine till early, wear what you dare, six quid, four before eleven and concessions, are owe ay are, check it out you groovee – two ees – funksters. And a picture of a platform boot. What does that say to you?'

'That says Seventies,' I went. 'All over.'

'Right, Lee,' said Gel, 'I'm going to get the

45

fucking printer to do us a bunch of fucking posters. Next week I want you to go round New Cross with a bucket of fucking wallpaper paste and slap them up. Give you a monkey. Be discreet. I don't want you getting banged up for the night. If the police ask who you're doing it for, you say a bloke in a fucking pub asked you, all right?'

'S—sorry Gel,' said Danny. ''Fraid Lee can't do that.'

'What?'

'He's working for us next week.'

'Is he?'

I looked at Gel and I looked at Danny. They both looked at me.

'Er – yeah,' I went.

Gel put down the pad. 'Right, well. Time to get the arty farty into, er. Right.' He tapped his thigh and, silently, without looking at either of us, got up and left the room.

'Good lad,' said Danny.

'I've got to know the details,' I said.

''Course you have. There's a meeting tonight. Come and sit in. Any time you want to pull out, you pull out, no problem, no problem.'

Danny swung his arm around the back of my head, letting me go, and moved away, over to the desk. 'M—meet me by the pinball machine in half an hour.'

'Right.'

I couldn't get out of the cave fast enough.

46

'Lee!' Hell called over. She stood smoking a fag among the coats in the cage. No-one was waiting. I walked over, and she lowered her head to whisper across the counter. I lowered mine, too. I could hear Abba's 'Super Trooper' in the background; Gel had started his set.

'What are you going to do?'

'I don't know,' I said.

'We could go to the police,' she said.

'I was driving the car for Danny, Hell. I didn't know what was in it, honest. I just told him I'd got rid of it. He's not going to be happy with me if I report it. Or with you. And I don't think it's a good idea to piss him off.'

'So if we don't go to the police, what?'

'Then it gets discovered, and we're accessories.'

'How will they know we were there?'

'Our fingerprints are all over it. I've got a record, so mine are on file. Even if you haven't, they'll still find you. We didn't clear any of the stuff up, did we?'

'So we can't go to the police, and we can't not go to the police?'

'Right.'

'So what are we going to do?'

four

get away

I sat in the driver's seat of a stolen Austin Montego,
listening to my Walkman, catching some rays
through the open sunroof. It was a beautiful day;
the sun was shining and the sky was blue and cloud
free. I was parked in a lay-by in the country. To my
right, I could see a hedge, then a field, across which
were spread a bunch of black and white cows, just
standing there looking unrealistic. Behind them
was a wood. The horizon beyond that was a
wobbly line, with little blobs – trees – on it, the way
horizons are in the country. To my left, I could see
the road, and then another hedge, and then another
field, and then more cows, and then another
wobbly horizon.

It seemed like recently I'd been spending a lot of
time in the countryside. And I'd decided that, once
you were used to it – to the lack of straight lines or
easily accessible consumer goods, to just how boring
it was – it wasn't so bad. A regular dose of green

stuff, I'd decided, did you the world of good. It was quite relaxing.

At that moment I was remarkably relaxed. Considering.

My mobile, in my lap, started ringing. I stared down at it like it was about to explode. Three rings, then nothing. That meant they were on their way. Right.

I sat up, slipped off the headphones, and shoved the Walkman into the glove compartment, on top of someone else's crap tape collection and tin of disgusting mints. As I shifted in the seat I realized it was damp with sweat. My bum was numb from having been sat there for an hour already.

I looked in the rear view at the second car, a brown Sierra parked twenty metres behind me. The guy in there was wiggling about in his seat. So he'd got the message, too.

They were on us before I had time to get worked up. A blue transit van swung round the corner behind me. I watched it stop in the road, then I was down fiddling with the two wires hanging from the dash, trying to start it the way Danny had taught me. My hands were shaky with nerves and it took me a few seconds to make the connection. I almost pissed myself with relief when the engine kicked off. I looked back and saw Marlowe running towards me dressed in a tracksuit, carrying a red sports bag. Marlowe running was quite a sight. He

49

reminded me of the Terminator, but he'd be sussed long before he hit the rebel base, he just wasn't realistic enough.

The other guy, also in a tracksuit, was running for the Sierra with another, identical bag. I never got his name – not that he didn't tell me, I just forgot it.

The transit sped off down the road. I leant across and opened the passenger door and Marlowe threw himself into the car, which dipped under the weight. He was panting and smiling at the same time. He dumped the bag on the back seat.

'Fucking move it then,' he shouted, unnecessarily loud.

I heard the Sierra rev up, and it flashed past me. I slipped into gear and steered the car onto the road.

'How did it go?' I asked.

'S'move,' said Marlowe.

'I'm moving, all right, I'm moving.'

'No,' he said, 'it was smooth, all right? Smooth. Everything went smooth.'

A couple of hundred metres down the road we came to a little crossroads. The transit headed straight on. The Sierra turned left. I turned right.

We were onto an A road now, and I got up some speed.

'Easy,' went Marlowe, 'don't want to get stopped.'

'No police then?'

'Naw. No sign.'

I held the car at fifty.

'Easy?'

'No bother. Country places, they haven't got a fucking clue. We walked in there, they took one look at us and they were shoving the cash in bags before we'd got the shooters out. Fuck, I do like it, Lee. Fuck I like it. It's a fucking rush.'

'You get much?'

'Fair to average. What you'd expect. Funny thing, Lee. That building society. I've got an account with them.'

'No way.'

'Competitive rate of interest,' said Marlowe. The tone of his voice – each syllable like a banging rock – made the subject sound sinister and wrong.

'You shopped about then?' I said, not taking my eyes off the road ahead.

'Oh yeah. I'm very careful with my money. I won't invest with just anyone.'

He paused, and I glanced across. He wrinkled his brow and peered like he was reading the words off the windscreen. 'They got my endorsement.'

'Personally,' I went, 'I don't trust any of them.'

Marlowe looked genuinely shocked. 'That's an immature attitude,' he said.

'Why's that, Marlowe?'

'Say you got a Rio.'

'A what?'

'A grand. You put that under the bed, and after ten years, what have you got? A Rio. You put it in

51

a bank or a building society, and after ten years, what have you got? At an interest rate of ten per cent, you got, you got a lot more than you had when you started.'

He settled back into the seat with a grunt, and was silent. I took in some scenery.

The next two hours were not good. I was wired right up – I was queasy and needed a dump, and the last thing I wanted was Marlowe's conversation. We did, or rather Marlowe did, the outrageous cost of water rates, the injustice of the council tax, what road signs meant, the mysterious extinction of the dinosaurs, the necessity of a good pension plan, the thieving cunts that British Telecom are, the advantages and disadvantages of strong Indian food, and how stocks and shares were a better bet than the gee-gees.

By Slough I'd had enough.

'Do you want to listen to some music?' I asked.

'Yeah. None of your shite, mind.' Marlowe reached forward and twiddled the plastic nipple of the radio, running through the stations. We got violins, and he leant back with a grunt.

'You want classical?' I looked across.

'I love a bit of that. Mahler, whassim – Bach, Dvorjak. Love a bit of that.'

'What?'

'I work out to it. Gets me going.'

Some poncey announcer told us we were going to listen to someone's third something, and

Marlowe closed his eyes and settled back into the chair, head against the headrest. He didn't move again till we got to Deptford. Total systems shutdown.

We were due to go back to the club first, where Danny was waiting. When we picked him up, he'd tell us where we were going next, to join up with the rest of the crew. Then the take would be counted and we'd all get pissed together, me and my new friends.

I parked on the street about twenty metres from the club's entrance, next to the alley.

'I'll get him,' said Marlowe. 'Wait here.'

'I'll leave the engine running then, shall I?'

'Yeah.'

Marlowe got out of the car and slammed the door. I watched him walk up the street to the entrance and buzz the buzzer, running through my seven times table in my head, trying to keep my breathing slow.

A dark figure in jeans and a hooded top, with the top pulled up over a balaclava, stepped out from the alley, pointing a gun at Marlowe with both hands. Marlowe didn't even notice. The figure stepped quietly up to the car, let one hand drop down and opened the passenger door. I watched the figure swing the gun around till it was pointed at my head. Marlowe still didn't notice. The figure slid inside, into the passenger seat. The gun was pressed against my forehead. Marlowe remained oblivious, staring

53

at the club door. The stupid fucker.

'Drive then,' said the figure in the passenger seat.

The club door swung open, and I saw Danny's pale face pop out of the shadows behind. 'Help! Danny!' I shouted, my face twisted in panic. The figure smashed me in the cheek with the butt of the gun.

'Drive!'

I put the car in first. Marlowe turned and looked blank for a second, then his face creased up as he shouted, 'Oi!'

I saw Danny push past him and come bursting out of the door onto the pavement. I pulled out into the street. Danny started running for the car, but I was accelerating, and he was fifteen, twenty metres behind.

I changed into second, and in the rear view watched Danny and Marlowe run out into the road. They slowed down as I sped up and we pulled further and further away. They stopped, and I watched them getting smaller.

'What did you have to hit me for?' I said.

'What did you have to shout for, you idiot?' said the figure.

'It wouldn't have worked if they didn't even fucking notice, would it?'

The dark figure squirted me with water from the black plastic Colt .45 water pistol. It got me in the ear, some splashed into my eye, and I swerved and nearly crossed over into the opposite lane.

go>>> simon lewis

'Mind!'

The figure put the gun down on the dashboard, pulled the hood down and took off the balaclava. Hell shook out her long black hair, and it bounced over her shoulders like breaking surf.

'See?' I said. 'Easy.'

'I was waiting for hours.'

'You got a rush off it, though, didn't you?'

'Not really.'

'I thought you were great. You were brilliant.'

Hell took a packet of Silk Cut out of her pocket and lit two off the dashboard lighter. She slipped one in my mouth and I sucked hard, trying to get some sort of nicotine hit off the thing.

'I don't know why you even bother to smoke those,' I said, 'they don't do anything.'

'Get this car off the road,' said Hell. 'Now.'

'Relax. I've got it all sorted out.'

I drove a couple of miles, and turned into a strip of waste ground behind an abandoned warehouse, down by the river, between Greenwich and Deptford. It was bounded by high walls and filled with litter, on the edge of an industrial estate. I drove across the waste ground and parked in an old doorless garage at the back. I reckoned we'd be safe there.

We got out of the car, Hell carrying the bag. 'I'll count this and split it,' she said, and walked out of the garage and over to a busted armchair standing on the ground outside. She sat down primly, and took two Safeways' bags out of the front pocket of her hooded top. She began taking wads of cash out of the bag and put them into the shopping bags.

I opened the boot of the car. A smell like off beefburgers wafted out at me. The body from the Merc was curled up inside. This car had a smaller boot and it took me ages to get him inside; he was frozen solid.

Dressing him in my clothes wasn't easy either. His feet, fortunately, were the same size. I couldn't get my earring in his ear, that was the only thing. But I reckoned that wasn't going to matter.

I pulled him out of the boot and hoisted him over my shoulder. I'd got the hang of shifting him now, but I still nearly fell over with the awkward weight. I stumbled round the car to the front and dumped him in the driver's seat. He fell forward and his head rested on the steering wheel. I shoved his feet inside, trying really hard not to wonder who he was. I took off my watch and put it on his arm, then put the pager in the pocket of his jeans. I couldn't get them buttoned up and I wasn't going to have another go now. The whole time I managed to avoid looking him in the face, but I could see his expression vividly in my mind; it said, 'What the fuck are you doing?'

I stood back. Oh no. Suddenly I wasn't coping fine; suddenly I felt like I was going to be sick. The brick garage walls wobbled. No. No. I forced myself to go round the car and back to the open boot and take out the can of petrol there.

I opened it and sloshed it over the inside of the car. I made sure I got plenty on his face and hair. The smell of the petrol was heady, it made me dizzy. I felt like giggling. Enough. I chucked the empty can into the back seat and walked over to Hell. I fumbled my fags out and lit one.

'All done,' I said. For a minute I watched her, looking at her long fingers, tipped with divinely bitten nails, deftly flicking through the notes. She whispered the numbers as she counted, and she wet her lips a couple of times with her sharp pink tongue.

She looked up. 'Six grand,' she said. 'Here's yours.' She handed me a shopping bag.

'Let's go then.'

She headed to the entrance. I walked back to the garage with the butt of my fag, chucked it into the car and started running back. I'd hardly gone a few strides before the whump of the explosion tickled my neck. I didn't look back, but I could hear the crackle of the burning car as we walked quickly out into the street.

I turned to Hell. She was walking slowly, head down, jaw tense with determination. She was beautiful. 'Fancy coming to celebrate with me? I thought we could go for a drink or something. A meal.'

She didn't look up. 'I don't think so, Lee. We're coming up to a crossroads. I go left, you go right, OK? Let's get out of here.'

57

We moved quickly, in step, a forced march. We were both silent as we approached the crossroads. My head was full of things to say, but they didn't reach my mouth. I forced myself to go over the plan, looking for flaws.

I could see the headline in the South London Press: BODY FOUND BURNT IN CAR; FOUL PLAY SUSPECTED. Stuff about how it had been shot then set on fire. Danny would hear about it, I hoped, and he'd assume that the unidentified body was me, that I had been the victim of some gangland double-cross.

Maybe the police would eventually work out the identity of the guy in the car from dental records or something, but by then it wouldn't be news, would it? For the plan to work, for Danny to get off my back and stay off it, I had to leave the country. Maybe never come back, or not for a long time. Keep my head down. But that was OK. What did I have here, after all?

Hell and I reached the crossroads. We stopped and looked into each other's faces.

'Goodbye, Lee.'

I said it. 'I love you, Hell.'

'You just want to shag me.'

'Yeah, but . . .'

'Goodbye, Lee.' She looked impatient. She wanted to get going.

I was hit by a sudden twinge of despair, thinking that I'd never touch her nipples, or the back of her neck behind her hair, and she would never look at me like I looked at her.

'I'll see you again.'

'Goodbye, Lee.'

'Goodbye.'

She turned one way, I turned the other. I walked down the road and resisted the impulse to look back. Fuck. Left the Walkman in the car. I tried to look forward to the good long holiday I reckoned I deserved.

part two

holy cow

five

flip flop

Dressed only in red-and-blue striped cotton trousers, patched on both knees, Lee lies in a lazy arc, sunk deep into his hammock on the porch outside his tourist home. The canvas rises around his sides, cradling him in a split cocoon. His right leg pokes out like the leg of an emerging imago, the foot planted on the ground.

He rocks himself gently back and forth, unconsciously swaying to the slow rhythm of the deep, hoarse Darth Vader-style breaths coming from inside the concrete hut.

Lee's eyes are half closed and he thinks of nothing; his mind is as vacant and featureless as the cloudless sky above him. Only blood moves through his body.

The schlup schlup of approaching flip-flops disturbs him. He turns his head to the left, the most effort he has made for an hour, and watches Sol spring up the two steps onto the porch, carrying a large, square-shaped plastic water bottle. The tall

>>holy cow

black man moves with jerky enthusiasm and adolescent clumsiness, as if he's still getting used to the length of his limbs. He wears a lungi wrapped around his waist and his chest is bare. His firm, fatless physique is better developed than Lee's. A cluster of short curly hairs form a rough heart shape between his big brown nipples.

Lee raises his left hand in greeting, then lets it flop back again onto his tanned, hairless chest.

Sol holds up the empty bottle. 'There's no water. The tap's gone dry again.'

'Oh,' murmurs Lee. This, he feels, is not a problem. Lee figures he doesn't need to wash because he goes swimming in the sea sometimes. He doesn't drink the tap water, will only drink mineral water. But it's a problem getting rid of all the blue plastic bottles. There's maybe a hundred under his bed. He means to burn them but knows that he'll probably never get round to it. Gradually, over the months he's been here, he has found it harder and harder to do anything that doesn't directly fulfil his own needs, and this chore seems epic in its scope.

'The fishermen are fighting again,' says Sol, and ducks under the hammock at the point where it's tied to the wooden upright of the porch, the only easy way to access the door. He goes inside.

Lee thinks this might be worth getting up for, and struggles out of the hammock. He stumbles a little as he hauls himself upright, the sudden change to vertical making him momentarily disorientated. He moves to the far-left end of the porch.

From here he can see the other two tourist homes. The nearest is occupied by a group of Dutch students, the other by an Israeli couple. Both also have hammocks slung on their porches. The squat buildings stand on scrubland, blotted in places with dark patches: the marks of fires. Behind the huts the ground rises steeply. Strips of pink toilet paper hang snagged on the dense foliage on the hillside. In front, Lee can see the sea, which starts abruptly, as at the side of a reservoir, about fifty metres away. A road follows the shoreline and terminates before a rocky headland. A small restaurant stands here, and a wooden shed, and a jetty protrudes into the water.

Five thin, dark men stand on the jetty. All wear lungis around their waists, the material tucked up between their thighs in the local fashion. Two have small towels wrapped around their heads. They are clustered around a naked man lying on the ground and beating him with palm-tree leaves. From this distance the scene is comic. The big green leaves, nearly as large as the men, flap up and down. They could be fanning him. Surely, thinks Lee, they can't do any damage with palm branches; perhaps they're just larking about.

Sol comes out and stands beside Lee, holding his camera. It's an expensive camera, German, with lots of numbers on the rings round the lens, and mysterious to Lee in its operation. It's the only thing of worth Sol seems to own; all his other possessions are cheap and locally made, even his toothbrush and wallet. Sol takes his photography very seriously; he seems happiest behind a lens. Sol fiddles with the lens and fires off a couple of photos. Good to have a hobby, thinks Lee, the thought drifting up and quickly dissipating.

'Hey,' says Lee, 'check the sunset.'

The sun, a red circle set in a blush of pink and orange streaks, is beginning to dip below the sharp horizon line of the sea.

Lee considers himself something of an expert, a connoisseur, of sunsets; since being here he has missed few. They are the only events that give his life a timetable; sunset means it's time to begin thinking about food and the night's entertainment.

'You should take a picture.'

'I don't do sunsets.'

Sol's remark strikes Lee as superior, its tone seeming to suggest that sunsets are somehow beneath him.

'No, right, you only do water buffalo and beggars and women with pots on their heads. You should take pictures people want to see. Palm trees, beaches, your mates having a laugh, topless women. Yeah, now there's a good use for your telephoto.'

Sol turns, points the camera at Lee and clicks.

'That's all you want to see, maybe.'

Sol lowers his camera and they stand together,

watching the setting sun. In the fading light the sea is steely grey, shot through with rippling lines of black. The fishermen stop beating the naked man, drop their branches and wander towards the little restaurant. The man lies still. Lee reaches into his pocket and gets out a packet of Gold Flake – to him the least intolerable of the cheap local cigarette brands – and a tiny box of matches with a picture of a light bulb on the front. He gives Sol a cigarette, takes one himself and strikes a match. They lean together to light their cigarettes, and in the silence that follows both become uncomfortably aware of the breathing coming from inside the hut.

Innnnnnnn and ooooooooout. The rhythm is so slow, and so loud, it doesn't sound human; it could be a sleeping rhino. The white wax-paper matchstick burns down quickly.

'The problem with topless women,' says Lee, punctuating with flourishes of the cigarette, 'is you can't talk to them. Where do you look? How are you supposed to concentrate on what they're saying?'

'Still not getting any then?' It's a rhetorical question; Lee knows Sol knows he isn't, and sees the question as a taunt. The two men are in unspoken competition, and Sol is winning, a fact Lee puts down entirely to the colour of Sol's skin. Lee believes the girls who find him attractive, mostly blonde northern Europeans, are simply succumbing to the lure of the exotic.

'I'm still chasing that Israeli girl in Anjuna.'

'Forget her. They only fuck their own. Go Spanish, or Dutch, or Swedish. French.'

'French? What are you saying? Now I'm no racist – I'd be quite happy to let my sister, if I had one, marry a coloured gentleman like yourself, or an Arab or a spic or whatever – but the French?' Lee puts on a comedy French accent and spits out the words, 'Croissant. Baguette.' He shakes his head. 'French?'

Sol grins. A grin is never far from his wide mouth. 'I never know when you're pissing about, or when you really mean what you say.'

Lee shrugs. 'It's all bullshit.'

Sol's expression becomes serious. He nods his head towards the door of the hut.

'Is he any better?' he asks.

Lee lowers his voice. 'He's been working on his shrine. It's the breathing I can't stand. It keeps me awake at night.'

'He'll be all right again soon,' says Sol. He begins to play with his camera, clicking the lens rings round and around.

Lee grinds the half-smoked cigarette into the wood of the porches upright. His voice rises to its usual volume. 'You hungry?'

'I could be.' Sol shrugs. 'Food. Yeah. That would be something to do.'

'Let's change, right, go up into the village, right, and then eat, right, and then we'll head for the party.' He drums a fast beat with his palms on the upright. 'Party party. Good?'

'OK.'

Lee leads the way into the hut.

'It's going to be a mental party,' he says.

The hut is about four metres long on each side, with uneven plaster walls painted blue and prickled with the stubs of joss sticks. The floor is covered with a fine tracery of sand. There are windows in the right- and left-hand walls. Each windowsill holds a splurge of melted candles and a plastic water bottle with the top cut off, half full of butts.

Three iron beds with thin mattresses are evenly spaced along the right-hand wall. The first, Sol's, is covered with folded clothes and has a deflated rucksack beside it. The second, Lee's, is scattered with tapes, underwear and other objects hidden underneath the rumpled sheet. The heaped plastic bottles under the bed look like a giant mutant crystal. Clothes on the floor form a trail to an empty kit bag hanging on the end of the bedstead.

The bed furthest from the door is shrouded in a mosquito net, a sagging cube of white fabric, secured at the four top corners by lengths of red string, three stretching taut from the bars on the windows, the fourth attached to a nail driven into the wall by the bed. Inside the net a figure sits cross-legged and very upright on the mattress, his form ghostly and vague through the gauzy material. Before him a lit candle rests on a book. The sound of his slow, harsh breathing fills the room, and seems completely out of proportion with his thin, short body; it's as if all it contains are two giant lungs. With each out breath the candle flame flickers and the broad shadow it projects on the wall behind the figure quivers.

In a niche in the wall beside the bed, a Swiss Army knife, three juggling balls, a set of postcards, a conch shell and stone figurines of Krishna, Ganesh and Shiva, all smeared with red powder, stand around a brass joss-stick holder. Three lit sticks inside discharge spirals of heady smoke.

Lee switches on the light. The bare bulb hanging from the ceiling, its wiring taped to the wall, dispels the shadows. He shuffles around the room, picking up T-shirts from the floor and sniffing their arm-pits. Thoughtfully he considers the fourth, sniffs it again, then puts on the third. From the middle bed he picks up a can of deodorant and sprays liberally.

He removes a quarter-ounce brown lump of charas from a hole in the wall and tucks it into his pants. He picks up his green canvas wallet, sealed with velcro, from the bed, and slips feet blotchy with ingrained dirt into a pair of blue flip-flops.

'Ready,' he says.

Sol, standing by his bed, is changing into a pair of baggy, blue cotton trousers.

Lee glances at the few notes in his wallet.

'How much money do you owe me?' he asks Sol.

Sol pauses in the act of tying a knot in the string that fastens the waistband of his trousers. 'I had . . . three lemon sodas, walnut strudel, a beer, three chocolate bars—'

'Call it a hundred,' says Lee.

'Ninety.' Sol reaches under his mattress and pulls out a paperback-sized black-and-white cotton shoulder bag, fastened with a shell button.

'Look at us,' says Lee, 'we're haggling over twenty p here.'

Sol takes out a hundred-rupee note and hands it to Lee, then slides the bag back under the mattress. He puts on a black T-shirt.

'You should hide your stash somewhere less obvious,' says Lee. 'Anyone wants to rip you off, that's the first place they'll look.'

'Where have you got yours, then?'

Lee grins. 'That would be telling.'

Sol puts on a green canvas waistcoat and transfers canisters of film from a side pocket of his rucksack to its many zipped pockets.

'Sol,' says Lee, 'you're not going to take pictures at the party?'

''Course I am.'

'Can't you just come off shift for, like, a night? Just go out and enjoy yourself.'

The harsh breathing stops. The figure speaks. His voice is low and measured, deeply serious.

'You have interrupted my meditations.'

'We live here, too, Paul,' says Lee.

'The energies have gone wrong now.'

'What energies?' says Lee, wearily.

'I'm going to have to purify the space now,' says Paul.

Paul pulls the net up from where it's tucked under the mattress and climbs off the bed. A thin young man in black dungarees, his pale complexion is basted pink by the sun. His eyes are blue, his eyebrows blond, his hair – about three inches long all over – is spiky, unkempt and dyed dark red with henna. A spot of red paste is smeared in the centre of his forehead. His face is gaunt and his cheeks hollow, as if the skin was being sucked by some inner force. His movements are slow and deliberate.

'How are you going to do that?' asks Lee.

'I'm going to juggle.'

Paul takes the three balls out of his shrine. Lee and Sol watch him juggle. He's not very good. He drops one after a few throws, bends to scoop it up and starts again.

'Paul,' says Lee, 'me and Sol are going to go and eat something.'

Paul lets the balls hit the floor. Thump. Thump. 'I'll come, too.' Thump. 'But I won't eat. I'm fasting. Are you going to go to the party afterwards?'

'Yes,' says Sol. Lee stares hard at him, mouthing the word 'no' with an exaggerated movement of his lips.

'I'll come with you,' says Paul.

'I thought it wasn't your thing,' says Lee.

'I want to go.'

'I'll give you a lift,' says Sol, and returns Lee's stare.

Paul strides straight out of the room.

'You're going to need some money,' says Sol.

'Yes. Money.'

Paul comes back in, reaches into his net, pulls out a bum bag and negligently clips it round his waist.

'How about putting some shoes on?' says Lee.

'I want my feet to be in touch with the ground,' replies Paul.

'Fuck's sake,' murmurs Lee, and turns around to follow him out. Sol, the last to leave, fastens a heavy padlock on the door.

Outside, the naked man has disappeared from the jetty.

The motorbikes are parked at the side of the hut. Lee straddles his red Enfield and Paul climbs onto the back of Sol's black Rajput, putting one hand around Sol's waist. Paul had a bike of his own until a week ago, when he took it out and forgot where he left it. Its loss doesn't seem to bother him, but it will bother the man they hired them from when they're due to return them. Paul will lose his deposit, a hefty sum, but Paul doesn't seem to care about money any more, doesn't seem to want much to do with it. A few days ago Sol stopped Paul giving away the contents of his wallet to a small child asking for a school pen.

They ride along the rough road away from the jetty, through a palm grove, where more tourist homes sit between the trees, and into the village, a single rough street, lined with wood and concrete buildings: a general store, a second-hand bookstall, a few off-licences, a chemist, a boutique, a green-grocer for the locals, but most of them restaurants.

The Welcome is full, the Shiva is a bit too dirty, you have to wait ages at the Happy Seafood and Lee has argued with the owner of the Sai Ganesh, so they plump for the Vishnu, which has hard wooden seats but does a great prawn and chips, which both Sol and Lee order. Sol persuades Paul to have a lemon soda. When it arrives he puts the straw in the glass and watches it rise and drop out onto the table. He puts it back in again, watches it fall out, puts it in again, watches it fall out.

'Paul,' says Sol, 'you have to let it settle.'

Paul leaves the straw lying on the table and stares hard at the necklaces of rising bubbles in the drink.

From their table under the coconut-matting roof at the side of the road, Sol and Lee watch village life passing as they eat; dreadlocked Europeans on motorbikes, lumbering oxen with painted horns, pulling carts full of straw, gangs of Israelis in their tie-dyes, cows and hippies wandering around or standing looking vacantly about them. Ragged children play tag and pigs root around in the scrub between the buildings. Sol takes pictures between mouthfuls. A man with a snake wrapped around his shoulders comes up and asks if he wants to take his picture; Sol says no. A boy with a thin metal rod asks if they want their ears cleaned, showing them a dirty scrap of paper typed with the words 'certified ear-hygiene specialist'. Lee shoos him away.

Darkness falls, and strip lights strung up in palm trees along the road flicker into life. The red fairy lights wrapped around the wooden beams of the restaurant are switched on.

Lee is struck by a sudden sense of deep content-ment. His life is an easy routine of pleasure. Get up whenever. Lie on the beach. Get stoned. Eat. Get pissed. Sleep. His days are soft focus, a blur. He has no idea what day of the week it is. There's nothing he has to do. He has no responsibilities. There's nothing to worry about, no decisions to make. It's like living in a warm and cosy bubble; life should be like this all the time. It occurs to him that today is the first day in months that he's been aware of the date.

'Hey,' says Lee, grinning, 'think of all those people at home with their trees and their logs and their presents and their shit weather.'

'Nothing on telly but ads for kiddies toys,' says Sol.

'Exactly. Mary fucking Poppins. The fucking Queen.'

'I always hated it at home,' Sol looks down at his remaining chips, 'all that family shit on TV.'

'I love it here,' says Lee with emotion.

'Listen to you. Maybe you should go round in one of those T-shirts,' says Sol. 'I heart Goa.'

Lee clasps his hands together to try to kill a mosquito flying reconnaissance around his head.

Paul jerks his head up suddenly. 'Don't.' His tone is severe.

'It's just a mosquito.'

'It's a soul.'

Lee raises his eyebrows at Sol and goes back to his food, staying alert for any more signs of the buzzing insect. It's his ambition to one day kill a mosquito the way he has heard the Indians do it. You wait till they have landed and are jacking you up, then squeeze the skin on either side of them really hard; then, apparently, they can't pull out, fill up with blood and explode.

A tall, tanned girl in a sarong and a crop top with a Japanese slogan passes them in the street. Lee knows her vaguely but can't remember her name. He remembers that she's from north of the river. Camden, Archway, somewhere like that. Lee reckons he's met more north Londoners in Goa than he ever met in south London. Lee flicks his eyes over her and concludes that, though she has a good body, her nose is too big and her eyes are too small. He's about to ignore her, then chides himself that just because she's not attractive doesn't mean he shouldn't talk to her. After all, she might introduce him to some pretty friends.

'Hi,' says Lee. 'How's it going?'

'Good.'

'You going to the party later?'

'Yeah.'

'Join us for a smoke?' asks Lee.

'Hey, you know about the aum?' Paul leans forward and stares hard at her. 'The first letter is the first letter of the Sanskrit alphabet. The second is the middle letter. The last letter is the last letter. Ay. You. Em. The beginning, the middle, and the end.' He sits back in his chair and pops the straw into his drink. It stays there. 'It's the sound the universe makes as it breathes.'

'Really?' says the girl.

Paul stands up. 'I have to go and piss.'

'So, yeah, see you around guys,' says the girl.

'At the party,' says Lee.

'Yeah.' She walks on down the street. Paul leaves the restaurant and walks round the side of the building.

'We've got to get rid of him,' says Lee.

'He's our friend.'

'He lives with us. He's a grown-up. He can make his own bed, you know?'

'He's just got a lot of shit to work out in his head.'

77

One day he'll wake up and he'll be like he was before.'

'What if he doesn't? What if he's just flipped, gone, out there? What if he never comes back?' Lee puts down his fork. 'Are we going to be looking after a nutter for ever?'

vehicles of the gods

Lee doesn't see the cow until it's right in front of him.

One second he's bombing down the road, looking at the palm trees, and the bike roaring beneath him is the sound of freedom and the wind is tousling his hair and massaging his face and in his head Steppenwolf are singing 'Born to be Wi-ild' — then there's this black thing side on to him, looking at him with liquid eyes, and there's a thump and a crunch and he's tumbling over the handlebars and he can see the grainy tarmac rearing towards his face in slow motion. He just has time to wonder if his life is going to flash before his eyes and then it all goes red. And then it goes black.

The first thing Lee becomes aware of is noisy, repetitive beats, all around.

Rckrckrckrckrckrckrckrckrck.

Tzztzztzztzztzztzztzztzztzztzztzztzz.

Drrrrdrrrrdrrrrdrrrrdrrrrdrrrrdrrrrdrrrrdrrrr.

With a sudden burst of elation Lee thinks, Yes,

>>>holy cow

79

we've arrived. A voice swims towards him and brushes his cheek. 'Are you hurt? Lee, can you move all right?' He's aware of someone shaking his shoulder.

'The party. Are we there?' Lee opens his eyes. He can see the big friendly face of Sol, huge above him, and behind Sol he can see the frilly tops of palm trees, like black cut-outs against a night sky bluer than it ever gets at home. He starts to hurt and he remembers where he is.

The noises he can hear are just frogs and creepy-crawlies making a racket, like they always do, and with this realization Lee's mind shuts them out.

He sends his consciousness around his body for an emergency check-up. Legs? Pain in left thigh. Arms? Fine. Hands? Hurting. Chest? Raw feeling on left side. Cautiously he flexes muscles. Nothing is broken. Just friction burns, painful friction burns. He looks about.

Behind Sol, Paul is crouched, bending over a dark shape humped in the road. Beside him lies Lee's Enfield, its front wheel slowly revolving. Sol's Rajput stands next to it, guarding its fallen companion.

'My bike,' says Lee.

'Are you hurt? Can you get up?' Sol's brow is crinkled with concern. He's wearing his camera around his neck, and he begins to twist the rings.

Lee raises himself onto his left elbow. He winces. Ow.

'Fucking wandering everywhere,' says Lee. He licks his dry lips. 'Getting in the way.'

'You're OK? Nothing broken?'

'I'm pissed off,' says Lee.

'But you're not really hurt?'

Lee looks at the palm of his right hand. It's got itty bits of dirt stuck to it. He looks down at his left side. His T-shirt has ridden up, exposing an ugly dark scrape. It reminds him of what a wall looks like when you start to take the wallpaper off.

'Only I think we'd better get out of here fast.'

'What?'

Paul raises his head. 'It's so beautiful,' he moans to no-one in particular, and puts his hands on the side of his face and drags them downwards, pulling the skin.

'You know what they're like about their cows,' says Sol.

'What? Fuck's sake, Sol, I'm hurting here.'

'Come on. Get up.' Sol stands up abruptly.

Lee gets to his feet very slowly, his face running through its full set of grimaces, feeling outraged at not receiving the level of sympathy he believes is his right. One of his flip-flops has come off and lies upturned on the road. The moon, low on the horizon, is nearly full, and in its light everything is a shade of blue, as if seen through a tinted filter, except for a soft red and yellow glow in the sky just above the horizon, in the direction they've been travelling. The party.

Lee looks at the cow. It's only little, small even for an Indian cow, so slender it resembles a deer. Its spindly legs are stuck out straight, and its fleshy nose glistens with saliva. Its loose skin sags on its bones like baggy clothes.

Paul reaches down very slowly and touches its stubby little horns.

'It leapt out in front of me,' says Lee, 'I didn't have a chance.'

Paul looks up at him. He mouths the word softly. 'Killer.'

'How do you know it's dead?' says Lee.

'It's not moving, is it?' retorts Sol.

'Maybe it's just stunned. Its eyes are open.'

'Their eyes are always open,' snaps Paul. 'When have you ever seen a cow with its eyes closed?'

'They have to be able to close their eyes, don't they?' says Lee. 'Everything does. Otherwise eyes get dirty.'

Paul blinks rapidly.

Lee gropes with his foot for the flip-flop. 'Maybe we should put a mirror in front of its mouth, see if it's breathing.'

Paul slips his hands underneath the cow's head and cradles it in his arms. 'There, there,' he whispers. 'There, there, there, there.' He sways back and forth, stroking the bristly hair on its head.

'Lee,' says Sol, exasperated, 'it's dead and we've got to get going.'

'What are you talking about?'

'I heard this story,' Sol whispers urgently, 'from this guy. He was on this bus, right, it hit a cow, and villagers chased the driver and beat the crap out of him. Lynched him.'

'That's whatjamees, Hindus,' says Lee. 'They're Catholics here, aren't they?'

'Lee. They're Indians. Indians love cows. Get your bike up and let's go.'

Lee takes a step forward and cries out as new, sharper pains slice through him. He stands still, breathing hard.

'Come on,' says Sol.

'I'm fucking hurting,' shouts Lee. 'All right? Fuck.'

Lee takes the three steps to his Enfield. Ow ow ow. He bends down over it and groans.

'I'll help you get it up.' Sol dashes over, raises the bike with a grunt, and holds it while Lee straddles it. The pain in Lee's left side is throbbing like a beat. When he hoists himself into the seat, a jabbing pain in his thigh is laid down over it. He grips the handlebars and his raw palms sting.

'You OK?' says Sol.

'Maybe.'

Sol watches as Lee tries to start the bike. The engine gives a farting noise, then nothing. He raises himself on the seat, wincing, and kicks down on the throttle. The only noise this time is Lee's whimper as the pain kicks in.

'Let me do it,' says Sol.

83

'I can start my own fucking bike.' Lee tries again, savagely kicking down, and lets out a roar. The bike sits silent under him.

'Fuck,' says Lee, 'it's fucked. '

'Try again.'

Lee tries again. Nothing.

'I must have got fucked up by the cow.'

'You can ride on mine. We'll get the three of us on it. It's not far now.'

Lee sits back on the seat, hands palm upwards on his hips. 'I can't leave my bike here, can I?'

'Fuck your bike. We've got to get out of here.'

'If I ditch it, I lose my deposit, don't I?'

'You can pick it up in the morning.'

'Yeah, by which time the locals will have found the cow. If I come back for it, I'm in trouble, aren't I?' Lee sits silent for a moment. Sol looks down and runs his hand across the back of his neck.

'We'll have to hide the cow,' says Lee. Sol looks up sharply and Lee catches his eye. Lee shrugs and raises his hands, shaking them to try to make the stinging pain go away. 'We'll have to hide the cow, then come back for the bike tomorrow.'

'All right. But let's get out of here, yeah?'

Lee gets off the bike, feeling better now that he's decided what to do; he feels strong and in command. Lee and Sol walk over to the cow.

Paul looks up at them, still stroking the cow's long head. His face is broken up with distress.

'Cow killer,' he says. 'Murder man.'

'Paul.' Sol's manner is stern. 'Get out of the way.'

'Bad. Bad, bad.'

'Paul.' Lee stands over him. 'Get out of the way, now.'

'You did a bad thing,' says Paul.

'Please,' says Sol.

'Cow killer.'

'Paul, leave the cow alone.' Sol puts his hands on Paul's shoulders and tries to pull him up. Paul shrugs him off, then lowers the head, gets to his feet and steps aside. Muttering to himself, he watches Sol and Lee walk around the cow. They look at it from all angles and frown, like art critics appraising a talentless sculpture. Lee crouches down by its head and looks into its eyes. He prods it between its long ears. Its short fur is soft and fuzzy. He pinches an ear. The skin feels silky smooth.

Sol raises his camera and takes a photo, and for an instant the night is lit up white.

'What the fuck are you doing?' says Lee.

'Good picture,' says Sol.

'Fuck's sake.'

Lee stands up and grabs the cow's two front legs. His hands can almost reach completely around them. He tightens his grip slowly and gives the legs an exploratory tug. The cow's body shifts; its neck extends and its mouth drops open. Its thick, pink tongue lolls out. It looks a lot more dead than it had before.

85

Sol bends and picks up the cow's back legs, holding them just above the hooves.

'On three,' says Lee. He observes Sol's expression of distaste. 'Imagine it's a sack of spuds, all right? One, two, three.'

The body is surprisingly heavy, and Lee shuffles and grunts as they hoist it up. Lee faces Sol, the legs of the cow held to the side. The body sags low between them, head lolling, horns scraping the tarmac.

Paul, watching, holds his head in his hands and moves it violently from side to side. He starts to moan.

Lee and Sol stagger off the road and into the scrub around. As Lee steps backwards the cow's head swings around, banging into his shins. Lee looks behind him to see where he's going, and to avoid catching the cow's eyes, which glint in the moonlight.

The stretch of scrub beside the road divides two sets of paddy fields. It's about fifteen metres across, scattered with a few palm trees and dense with knee-high bushes, their branches either thin and prickly or thick and hard. Lee and Sol make a lot of noise as they crash through it.

'Mind,' says Lee. Sol is walking faster than him, and Lee is stumbling. Fifteen metres more from the road the scrub and trees are denser. It's darker here, the canopy of palm leaves above cutting off most of the light.

go>>> simon lewis

They hear Paul begin to wail.

'That's all we fucking need,' says Lee. 'All right, that'll do.'

Sol drops the cow's back legs. Lee drags it further, the undergrowth crackling under the weight, and dumps it. He begins pulling twigs and leaves off the shrubs around.

'It's such a shame,' says Sol, half to himself. 'Their cows are beautiful. Not like the mutants we have at home, you know, with giant tits and that.'

'Can't believe my bike's fucked,' says Lee, scattering the body with foliage. 'How am I going to get around?'

'I can still see it,' says Sol.

'We need big leaves,' says Lee, and begins foraging around the base of the palm trees for fallen leaves. He picks one up. It's surprisingly heavy, and Lee remembers the fishermen on the jetty earlier that day. 'Give me a hand, then.'

Paul's wailing begins to sound like words.

'I wish he'd shut up,' mutters Lee. 'What's he saying?'

Sol steps forward and begins collecting branches.

'Something about vehicles of the gods, I think.'

'We'd better get out of here before he attracts attention,' says Lee.

Paul starts shouting. 'Cow killer! Death to the cow killer! You're doomed! You're all fucked up!'

Paul's voice begins to recede; he's running away down the road.

'Cow killer! Co-ow ki-ll-er. No, no cow, no more, no, no, no more! No more!'

Lee looks at Sol. 'Great. Now he's lost it completely.'

acid pigs

Lee is dancing. Around him the whirl of limbs and torsos, the bobbing faces, are an animated abstract composition. He closes his eyes and feels the spots and stripes on the red curtain of his eyelids pulse in time to the music. He's getting there. He wills his thought bubbles to pop and the heavy bass beat takes control and jerks him like a puppet; he feels like a cartoon character getting electrocuted, face all eyes and teeth, limbs spasming out in all directions, a jagged blue glow around his 2D body. The pain in his side, in his palms, in his thigh, is still there, but it's not pain any more, just another kind of buzz.

He feels a tap on his shoulder. Lee opens his eyes, stops and turns around, and reality lurches back into place as Sol points a camera in his face and takes his picture. The flash makes him blink.

'All right Sol? Happy Christmas.'

Sol plants his feet wide apart and bends down to shout into Lee's ear.

89

>>holy cow

'For an injured man, you dance good.'

Lee feels himself spiralling down to earth and is annoyed at the interruption. 'I'm fucked,' shouts Lee. 'Got some ket.'

Lee first tried ketamin a couple of weeks ago, and has become an enthusiastic convert. He likes the way it makes him feel floppy and useless, disconnected. And you can buy it at the chemists!

Sol snorts. 'They give that to soldiers to keep them fighting.' It strikes Lee that Sol's attitude towards drugs is irresponsible. His disapproving tone might one day cause someone to have a really bad time.

Lee is standing on a flat terrace, one of a series carved in steps into a steep hillside. He has driven past many of these distinctive cubist hills. Mostly they're used to grow rice. Through the dust cloud sent up by all the pounding feet he can just make out the beach at the bottom of the hill and the blank, black sheet of the sea beyond, darker than the sky.

'Paul's here,' shouts Sol.

'Yeah?'

'I heard he's freaked out completely.'

'So, who hasn't?' shouts Lee.

'No, I mean really.'

'Yeah?'

'Yeah. Someone told me he's ripped up his passport. On a dancefloor. Threw all the little bits over himself.'

'Wow.'

'We should find him.'

'But—'

'He might do something stupid. Come on, Lee.'

'OK, OK.'

They shoulder their way out of the crowd and onto one of the narrow earthen stairways that wind around the terraces.

It's about 2 a.m. and the party is just getting serious. This is Lee's fourth, or fifth, or maybe seventh party here, and easily the biggest he has been to. In the last few weeks the place has filled up with revellers – earnest round-the-worlders stopping over, shower-gel ravers, bargain-break E heads, European über hippies, even some quite old people – and all for this. Everywhere he turns Lee can see people, thousands of them, expending their energy, and it's like looking at a nest of disturbed insects, a frantic clamour of activity with no clear purpose.

Sol and Lee head down towards the beach, a grey strip spotted with yellow dots – the lanterns of the chai mamas, the local women who sell tea and cakes. The path is thronged with bodies and moving anywhere is difficult. Periodically Lee has to remind himself what he is doing. He keeps wanting to just flop out, let himself be carried off by the atmosphere, sucked back onto a dancefloor. He focuses on Sol's back. Follow, he tells himself, follow.

Sol is so responsible, thinks Lee. Always aware and a little detached. He never just lets things go.

It's a mystery to Lee why Sol is here at all. The man's not tuned in to the place. He says he's bored of lying on beaches all day, of parties, of druggy conversations. Occasionally Lee feels that Sol is only interested in studying and documenting. A worrying thought, as it makes Lee wonder if he himself is the main subject.

Lee has stared so long at Sol's back that his vision, he feels, is beginning to go skew-wiff. Everything looks like it's tilted at an angle. He shakes his head and tries to focus his mind. He has something important to do. What is it? Oh yes.

When they hit the beach Lee takes off his flip-flops. He loves the feel of the cold sand on his feet; it's like wading through shallow water. Lee slaps the flip-flops against his thigh to the rhythm of the music – not so loud here – as they step along the beach. There's more room to move now, and Lee, feeling freer, stumbles and lurches around. It's like a kiddy's sandpit, he thinks. Playing in a sandpit. The thought makes him giggle.

About half the people here are stood about dancing, the others are sat around the chai mamas, drinking and smoking. Sol scans the crowd anxiously, and Lee looks around with a detached and interested gaze, the way he imagines Sol sees all the time.

A bare-chested man in a bandanna walks around

asking for skins. A girl in green flares with rings on her toes dances beside a man in swimming trunks. Someone talks about someone who chased a frisbee and fell of a cliff. A man with plaits in his beard squats cross-legged on the sand and hums. 'But Dad,' comes a small voice, 'I don't want any acid.' A crouching woman digs a hole in the sand, using her hands as a spade.

'Mental here, isn't it?' says Lee.

'I wonder what they think?' says Sol, pointing. Lee follows his finger and sees, high above, on the next hilltop, a line of people silhouetted against the sky, some holding hands. They are standing, watching. Locals; Lee hasn't noticed them before.

'We'll never find him,' says Lee.

'We've got to try,' says Sol.

Lee first met Paul on the steps of the post office in the village. He had just arrived, and looked a little lost. He was from Bristol, and he introduced himself as an artist, and showed Lee a sketchbook with a picture in it. They chatted and went for a Limca in a café, and Lee said he could stay with them in their hut, that it was cheap and the police never came. That was two months ago, back when Paul was normal. In retrospect Lee can see that Paul was always headed for where he is now; he gave an impression of being fuzzy round the edges. At first his behaviour was endearingly eccentric; reading the *Bhagvad Gita* on the beach, disappearing for long periods to 'commune' as he put it, filling his

93

sketchbook with twisted mazes, two-headed aliens, texts in a hieroglyphic language of his own invention. When he stopped sleeping and started meditating for hour after hour, started wandering around all day and spouting his religious bollocks and forgetting to eat, nobody paid much attention. It was assumed to be a phase, the drugs, the heat. It was only a week ago, when a girl in a restaurant told Lee that his mate was in a world of his own, that Lee thought, Yes, he is.

Well, it happened. It happened a lot. There was the man with the stick who ranted about his kids all day on one of the beaches, and the girl in white who flagged down motorbikes and swore at the riders. Some people can hack it here, reflects Lee, and some people can't.

Lee looks around but finds himself quickly distracted from his search. There are so many beautiful girls here, and everyone has a gimmick to mark themselves out. His attention is drawn to a set of arse-length dreads, an abstract black tattoo across a chest, some outrageously loud trousers, a dancing couple dressed in the orange robes of Saddhus, holy men.

'There he is!'

Sol points at a figure sat on the sand about thirty metres away. It's Paul; the hair, the dungarees, and the way he holds his hand up as he speaks, emphasizing his point with impassioned stabbing motions, are unmistakable. He's talking at a girl sat on the sand at the edge of a chai mama's mat. Even at this distance Lee can tell she's uncomfortable; she leans away from him and looks around.

'See?' says Lee. 'He's fine.'

They walk towards the pair. The girl begins to shift backwards, towards the rest of the group on the mat. She's blonde and wears a bikini top, leggings covered with a fractal day glo pattern and green trainers.

'Hey, Paul!' calls Lee.

Paul starts and looks up at them. There's something animal about the movement, and about the way he jerks upright and gets quickly to his feet as Sol and Lee pad closer. Paul turns and sprints down the beach towards the sea, his feet throwing up little bursts of sand which make Lee think of machine-gun strafing.

Sol takes off after him, moving with surprising speed.

'Paul!' calls Sol. 'It's all right!'

Lee trots forward, but he can't summon up the necessary sense of urgency or concentration to keep going. His body doesn't seem to want to move fast. It wants to flop about. His feet want to slosh through the sand and enjoy the tingling sensation. He slows, and arrives at the chai mat as Sol and Paul disappear into the crowd.

The girl looks up at Lee. She looks relieved.

'I'm sorry,' he says, 'was he disturbing you?'

'He is your friend?' Her accent is northern European.

'He lives with me. We were worried about him.'

'He is a strange one.'

'He's gone mad. But he was all right before.'

'He was talking about cows.'

'Yeah? What did he say?'

'He was talking at me, wa wa wa, really fast, and I did not understand much.' She shrugs and smiles nervously.

Lee thinks he might as well wait here, or Sol won't know where to find him when he returns. He sits down cross-legged, looks at the sea, picks sand out of his nails, looks at the sea again, then turns to the girl. Her small face is pretty in a bland way. Right.

'Where are you from?'

'Sweden.'

'How long have you been here?'

'Two weeks.'

'What are you on?'

'I have some ecstasy, but it does not work correctly. Only a little thrill.'

'Ah, that's not E. That's MDM something else. You can buy it at the chemists. There's a dodgy pharmacist in Anjuna, some scousers bought up his whole stock, now they're flogging it at parties. Good scam.'

The girl scoops the sand with her hands, burying

96

them up to the wrist then drawing them out, watching the fine stream trickle through her fingers. They talk about their drug experiences with detachment, the way farmers might talk about the weather. Lee finds he can maintain his concentration, and keep up his side of the conversation if he stares at the girl's face, hair, or trainers. If he looks aside, or at her tits, he starts to flow away, and the world tilts up again. After a few minutes he stops wondering what has happened to Sol and Paul.

'Have you heard of the acid pigs?' says Lee. 'You know that the pigs eat the shit here, yeah? They love it. They're on it before you've got time to wipe your arse.' Lee has told this story a few times, and he has a routine down pat.

'Ah, this is disgusting,' she says, but she's smiling.

'Well, around the tourist homes, right, there's so much acid in the shit that all the pigs are tripping. All the time. Psychedelic tripped-out pigs. It's true. And when the season ends they go cold turkey. There's all these pigs running around shivering and sweating, going oink, oink, where's my fix?'

'That's funny.' She laughs.

'Do you like it here?' asks Lee, trying to keep their chat going.

'Yes it is very beautiful, I think. But I do not know about the Indians.'

'No?'

>>holy cow

'I mean, they are really funny about some things, you know? Today I had a bad experience. I had to wash my clothes, yes? So I got a bucket of water from the well outside my house, and I put one of those sachets of washing powder in it, and I washed them by hand.'

Lee nods. The girl is looking at the sea, and her voice rises slightly.

'It felt very ethnic, you know, sitting there rubbing them to get them clean. Afterwards the family started to get really angry with me, you know? Shouting and screaming and pointing at the well. Wa, wa, wa, they shouted, Wa, wa, wa.'

'They're funny about their water.'

'Yes. And because they did not speak English I could not explain that I had not even used up any of their water. I had emptied the bucket back into the well.'

Briefly, Lee wonders whether he should tell the girl that the Indians were presumably pissed off that she'd ruined the water in their well. He quickly decides against it. He's pleased to learn that she's thick. It makes him feel relaxed and superior.

Sol and Paul are walking up the beach towards them, Sol's arm around Paul's shoulders. Paul is dripping wet. His dungarees cling to his thin frame. Lee and the girl watch them approach.

At the sight of Lee, Paul shies and turns away, but Sol shepherds him forward, talking in his ear.

There's something different about him and it takes Lee a few seconds to realize what it is; the red dot on his forehead has been washed away.

'We should take him back,' Sol says to Lee. Paul drips onto the sand, leaving a dark stain. He is shivering.

'I want to watch TV,' says Paul to Sol in a hoarse whisper. He looks randomly around him. There's something unfamiliar about his expression, his eyes, the turn of his mouth. He doesn't seem to be hearing anything that's said. Lee feels uncomfortable, and dips his head. He watches the girl draw a spiral pattern in the sand with a fingertip.

'There's a hospital not too far,' says Sol, 'we should take him there.'

'My bike's fucked, remember.'

Lee looks at Sol. Sol kisses his teeth.

The girl erases the pattern with a sweep of her arm.

'I'll take him,' says Sol. 'Come on, Paul.'

The girl starts a new doodle.

'I'm burning up,' croaks Paul. 'I'm on fire.'

Lee watches Sol escort Paul away along the beach. The girls keeps drawing. Sol and Paul are soon out of sight.

Lee makes zigzags in the sand with the side of his hand, the thumb stuck up like a fin, heading for her doodle.

'So,' says Lee, 'do you fancy coming for a dance?'

The girl looks at him side-on. It's a knowing look, frank, and it surprises him. Scandinavian girls, he remembers, have a reputation for being forward and practical.

'Sure,' she says.

eight

strays

The Swedish girl's name is Anna. She doesn't mess around; she kicks off her trainers, sits down on Lee's mattress and begins to take the stuff off the bed and put it on the floor. Lee lights a candle and places it on the window sill by his bed. The orange light makes the room almost cosy, and flatters both of them, concealing the blemishes and dirt rings in complexions suffering from the long night's exertion. It is 5 a.m.

After a couple of hours of chatting and dancing at the party Lee asked Anna if she fancied coming back to his. 'You mean for sex?' she said. 'Er, yeah,' he said. She shrugged. 'OK.' On the motorbike taxi back to the hut, the pair of them crushed up together behind the driver – Lee at the back, his arms around her trim waist – Lee flushed and panted with anticipation.

Anna lies on the bed, propped on her elbows, looking up at Lee expectantly. He slips off his flip-flops, lowers himself onto the mattress next to her and starts to kiss her. Result, lit up in neon, burns through his head, and a million football fans erupt. He sticks his tongue in her mouth and she sucks on it gently.

There's a knock on the door.

Lee disengages with a wet plop. 'What?' he calls.

'It's, it's, it's me.' Paul's voice.

Lee gets off the bed. Feeling dazed, he steps over to the door. Fuck, Paul will come in, and start juggling, or spouting shit, and then, thinks Lee, he'll be fucked. Or rather he won't be. Bollocks.

The door is made of thick, uneven wooden planks, held together with two cross pieces. Lee whispers through a gap between two planks.

'Paul. Hi. How are you?'

'I'm, I'm sort of, I don't know. How are you?'

'I'm OK. I'm kind of busy, actually. But you're all right, yeah?'

'Yeah. I've made some important decisions.' Paul's voice is calm and slow.

'Good, good.' Lee strokes an earlobe. 'You can't come in.'

'I can't come in?'

'No. I've got company.'

'Oh.'

'Did you want to come in?'

'I want my tikka paste.'

'Your what?'

'My tikka paste. Red paint.'

'The stuff you put on your head?'

'It's in the shrine.'

'Paul, listen. If I give you your tikka paste, will you go away?'

'Yes.'

'Wait there.'

Lee crosses the room, aware of Anna lying watching him, and reaches into Paul's shrine. The paste is in a little green plastic pot. He returns to the door.

'Listen,' Lee enunciates clearly, talking slowly, the way he addresses small children and Indian waiters. 'I'm going to give you your paste. I'm going to open the door a little bit and then I'm going to pass it through the gap, all right? But you're not to come in. You're not allowed in. Is that clear?'

'Yes.' Lee slides the bolt back and opens the door an inch. He catches a glimpse of Paul standing by the drooping hammock. He passes the pot through the gap with two fingers, then slams the door shut. He slides the bolt home and turns to Anna, who lies still, facing him, the top of her head and raised shoulder a mellow yellow in the candle-light.

'One of my room-mates,' says Lee cheerily. 'It's all right, he's decided to stay out a bit longer.'

The bed creaks as Lee climbs back onto it. 'Where were we?' he murmurs, sliding back into position next to her. He throws his left leg over hers, puts his arms around her and draws her to him, kissing her with his mouth open. His right arm is squashed underneath her, so there's little the hand can do but wander over her back. His free left hand moves with slow deliberation up her waist and around her bikini top, and then slips inside it. He kisses her harder, probing with his tongue, as if to draw her attention away. He half opens his eyes to check that hers are closed. She makes appreciative noises and Lee, encouraged, tweaks a nipple. She catches her breath and it hardens. Fucking brilliant. What a good time he's having. Their sighs, the rustling of their clothes, the squeaking of the bedstead, feel, to Lee, like the only sounds for miles. Anna pulls her bikini top down, rolls over onto her back and Lee lies on top of her, his legs on either side of hers. Her hands stroke his shoulders and back. Lee feels like the Buddha, his consciousness evaporating as he becomes lost in the succession of instants. Licking a breast, he slides his right hand down to the edge of her leggings, where it halts and moves restlessly back and forth before slipping inside. At the edge of her pants it halts again, then one finger slides inside, then another.

There's a knock on the door.

'Bollocks,' says Lee, and freezes, as if not moving would make the visitor go away. Their laboured breath begins to slow.

'Open up.' It's Paul. He bangs hard on the door. 'Open.'

Lee is suddenly furious. He pulls his hand out – the elasticated waistband of Anna's leggings snapping back with a twang – gets up and goes to the door, dizzy and blinking.

'What do you want now?' he calls.

'Ganesh.'

'What?'

'My statue.'

'Which one is he?'

'The one with the elephant head.'

'Right,' says Lee, 'I'll get it for you. But that's it, understand?'

Lee's trousers are light and baggy, and as he crosses the room his erection swings about unsuppressed. Self-conscious, he bends over slightly to minimize the tent effect. The figurine is palm sized and made of green stone. The elephant head sits atop a podgy, four-armed human body, the trunk falling down to rest curled flat on a paunchy stomach. A mouse sits at its feet.

'Ready, Paul?'

'Ready.'

'You're not coming back, yeah?'

'I'm going to the beach.'

'Good. You do that. OK, here it comes.'

Lee pulls the door open a few inches and slips the figurine through the gap. It is taken from the other side. Lee slams the door closed, bolts it quickly, turns and smiles at Anna.

'That was the last time.' He sits down on the edge of the bed, leans over and plants a kiss on the end of her nose.

'That's him dealt with. I promise.'

'Maybe I will smoke a cigarette now.'

Lee doesn't want her to smoke a cigarette now. He starts to kiss her neck. She purrs and mumbles her assent. He slips onto the bed beside her. They lie side by side and Lee slips his hands into her leggings and cups her arse. She rolls over onto her back. He pulls her leggings down.

There's a knock on the door.

'Oh, for fuck's sake.' Lee looks at Anna. 'Sorry.'

The knock comes again, louder.

'I'm really sorry about this. I'll get rid of him, now, for sure. I promise.'

Lee clambers off and strides over to the door. This time, Lee determines, he will go outside, confront Paul on the porch, out of Anna's gaze, and do whatever it takes, whatever, to dissuade Paul from returning to the hut in the near future. Possible courses of action run through his mind. Maybe he could convince him to go and meditate somewhere, or tell him the hut has been taken over by bad energies.

Lee slides the bolt back, throws open the door, and steps outside.

Two Indian men in green uniforms, carrying bamboo canes, are standing side by side on the porch. One has a hat like a Stetson on. His companion speaks, revealing red-stained teeth.

'You are Mr Lee?'

'No,' says Lee.

'Yes you are. You are being arrested.'

'What?'

'If you resist, you will be in very serious trouble.'

Stetson pushes past Lee and into the room, and Lee turns and follows him in. 'Hey,' says Lee, 'hey, what are you doing? You can't come in. Go away.'

Red Tooth spits a stream of paan onto the porch. The dark red liquid spatters on the concrete. He steps inside. Anna squeals and scrambles up on the bed, covering herself with her arms.

'Very sorry, madam,' says Red Tooth, and he and Stetson turn their backs on her as she pulls her pants and leggings back up.

Lee is surprised at how calm he feels as he quickly and soberly considers the situation. He has never had to deal with the Goan police before, but he has heard plenty of stories. How they pay more in back-handers for a Goa posting than their annual salaries, so lucrative is the practice of taking bribes off tourists. Sometimes they don't even bother trying to find any drugs, or even planting them; they just take your money. They hire out their uniforms when they're not on duty. Treat them like dogs, the local Indians advised; act tough, and wave sticks at them if necessary. Never, ever, let them into your home.

Lee, standing close to the door, looks at the two men facing him. They are both shorter and skinnier than he is. Briefly, he considers trying to fight them. He reckons he could maybe have them both, without the canes.

'Go away,' says Lee. 'I haven't done anything.'

'You have killed a cow. This is very serious,' says Red Tooth. Behind them, he can see Anna pulling up her bikini top.

'I don't know what you're talking about.'

'We have evidence,' says Red Tooth.

Stetson steps over to the light switch by the door and flicks it on. The room looks dirty and untidy in the sudden glare. Dust swirls in the air. The uniforms of the policemen look worn and shabby. They wear green plimsolls. Anna sits upright on the bed, leaning against the window sill, her arms wrapped tight around her raised legs.

Stetson taps his leg with his cane, letting his gaze wander around the room.

'I know what this is about,' says Lee. 'I'll pay you baksheesh. Twenty American dollars each. Twenty dollars. Think what you could do with twenty dollars.'

'You will come with us.' Stetson takes Lee's arms in a firm grip. 'Outside.'

'Thirty dollars.'

Red Tooth takes his other arm.

Anna is dressed. She stands up.

'You live here?' Red Tooth asks her.

'No. I just met him. I don't know anything about this. I don't know him.'

'Out.'

Anna steps to the door.

'I'm sorry,' she says to Lee. 'I'm sorry. The village isn't far, is it?'

'No,' says Lee.

'Thanks for . . .' her voice tails off. 'Thanks.'

'We'll do it again some time.'

'Yes. For sure.'

Anna walks quickly out of the hut and towards the road. Lee takes the padlock off the shelf above the door and clicks it over the catch. He spots a green jeep parked by the jetty.

Red Tooth and Stetson begin walking him towards it. He could maybe break away, but without a good start he can't outrun them. At least he should show them he's not scared. He affects nonchalance as he follows Stetson into the back of the jeep.

Stetson motions him to sit beside him on the wooden bench inside. Red Tooth gets in and sits next to Lee. They are huddled up close, like friends.

The driver, a man dressed in a white coat, starts the engine.

'Where are we going?'

'You will find out,' says Red Tooth. The jeep begins to accelerate. A dog woken by it barks as it passes.

The jeep looks like it has been built from a kit. Every metal surface is marked with nuts and bolts. In the sudden glare of a passing strip light Lee sees a plastic tree hanging from the rear-view mirror and swaying as the jeep bumps over the road.

'What's going to happen?' says Lee.

'You will go to prison,' says Red Tooth. 'Indian prison not like prison in your country. No TV like in your country. Twenty people in one room.'

Lee doesn't need to be told about Indian prisons. He once met a German girl whose boyfriend was in Delhi gaol. He had been there a year and not gone to trial. His mother had remortgaged her house to pay the necessary bribes. In a flat, almost toneless voice the girl had described how the visiting room was partitioned by two parallel wire fences, a metre or so apart. The prisoners and their visitors leapt up against the fences, poked their fingers through the wire, and shouted to one another.

'Come on, it was just a cow. I'll give you fifty dollars each,' says Lee, and in the style of the local traders, 'last price.'

'No.'

They drive in silence for ten minutes.

'Where are we going?' says Lee again.

'First,' says Red Tooth, 'we are going to the village near where the cow was killed.'

'What? Why?'

'The people there are very angry. They want to see justice.'

Lee becomes queasy with fear. He looks out of the corner of his eye at the lip of the back. It is high and the handle to open it is on the other side. Getting out would involve a sudden lunge, then a foot on the lip, then a leap into the road and a faceful of tarmac. It will have to be unexpected.

He pulls out his Gold Flake, takes one and offers them to the policemen.

'American cigarettes?' says Red Tooth.

'No, Indian.'

'Indian cigarettes no good,' says Red Tooth. They take one anyway.

'You have fire?' It's a construction Lee has learnt from hanging around with Europeans; at first he said it in parody, now it's become automatic.

Red Tooth gives Lee a box of matches. The two policemen lean over and cup their hands to make a sheltered cave in which Lee strikes a match. Lee lights his cigarette first and leans back, holding the match steady. They light theirs.

'Do you enjoy your job?' asks Lee.

The question seems to take Red Tooth by surprise. Not the fact that he has asked it, but the question itself.

'I hear that in your country people do not need to work,' says Red Tooth, 'the government gives people money.'

'Yes,' says Lee, 'this is how I live. But not much money. Very little.' He adopts Red Tooth's grammatical style as part of an attempt to ingratiate himself.

'How much?'

'About thirty-five pounds,' he says. 'That's seventeen thousand rupees.'

'A year?' says Red Tooth.

'A week,' says Lee, provoking short, sharp gasps. Red Tooth leans over and addresses Stetson and the driver, presumably relaying the information.

'But in my country,' says Lee, 'things are more expensive.' His attempt to portray himself as poverty-stricken seems to have backfired badly. 'A cup of tea, for example, is thirty, forty rupees. A packet of cigarettes is one hundred and fifty rupees. In my country this is not much money.'

Red Tooth smiles. 'I would like to go to your country and sell tea. Twenty rupees a glass. Ten times Indian price. Everyone would buy and I would make much money.'

'In my country I am poor,' says Lee. The two policemen talk to each other a moment. Lee drags hard on his cigarette.

'What is your religion?' says Red Tooth.

'I am not religious.'

'You are not religious?'

'Nobody in my country is religious. Well, some people are. Old people.'

'You have no religion.' Red Tooth drags on his cigarette. Stetson says something to him in a language Lee doesn't know a word of, doesn't even recognize.

'My friend wants to ask you,' says Red Tooth, 'in your country, does everyone have this thing called group sex?'

'What?' says Lee. Stetson talks to Red Tooth

go>>> simon lewis

for a few moments, illustrating his speech with a vigorous hand gesture; he makes a loose fist with his right hand, and pistons the index finger of his left hand into the hole between his thumb and first finger. His cigarette is upright in the corner of his mouth.

'Because he has seen on the television the programme *The Bold and the Beautiful*, and in this programme everyone is having sex with everyone else. I think people are very sexy in your country, yes?'

'That's an American thing,' says Lee, 'I'm not American. I'm English.'

'Ah,' says Red Tooth, as if at the solution to a problem.

'England is not like this,' adds Lee.

Suddenly Stetson lashes out with his leg, striking at the air in front of him. Lee's body tenses with shock. Is this the signal to begin a beating? Stetson does it again.

'Football,' says Stetson.

'Football,' says Red Tooth. 'But no good at cricket now. Very bad now for cricket.'

The driver says something and the three Indians talk among themselves for a minute, then fall silent. Lee looks out of the back and recognizes where they are – on the main coast road, a few minutes away from the spot where he killed the cow.

'The people from the village near here, they are waiting for you,' says Red Tooth. 'When they have finished we will go to the station. It won't take long. Do not worry. They have no weapons.'

'Are you married?' Lee asks Red Tooth.

'Oh yes.'

'Do you have any children?'

'Yes, three.'

The jeep slows as they go round a bend.

'How old?'

'I have a boy of seven, and a girl of nine. And another girl of two.'

'Do you have a picture you can show me?'

Red Tooth turns and reaches for his back pocket with his right hand. In his left he holds the cigarette. Lee rises and lunges head first for the open back. He puts his arms out to cover his face. Between his fingers he sees the tarmac coming close. Then he feels a jerk on his waist and he's swung round and his head slams against the inside of the jeep.

Stetson has a hold on the waistband of his trousers. He is pulled backwards and along the floor, face down. And then he feels their weight come down on him and he can smell someone's breath. They are lying on top of him.

'Don't beat me,' he shouts. 'Please don't let them beat me. Come on. We can sort it out. I've got money. Take it all.'

The two policemen climb off him and sit back down on the bench. Lee rolls over and looks up at them.

'Take my money and let me go.'

'How much?'

'Loads. Lots of money. Thousands of dollars.'

'All right,' says Stetson. He speaks to the driver and the jeep stops. Lee closes his eyes.

'We will take you back to your home.'

They sit in silence. Lee feels a rush of shame and relief. He had no option, he tells himself, none at all. He is calm and thinking rationally, but he wishes he could stop shivering.

They pass a hand-painted advert on the wall of a restaurant, a picture of a man holding a gun and smoking a cigarette. 'Four Square,' says the slogan, 'For Real Men.' Lee recognizes it; they are in the village.

The jeep parks on the jetty; the driver leaves the engine running as they climb out and head for Lee's tourist home. Red Tooth holds Lee's arm as if he is his date. Lee's earlier sense of relief has entirely dissipated. He feels angry and ashamed, and very tired.

He unlocks the padlock and goes inside. Stetson and Red Tooth stand in the doorway.

Lee's stash of money, about two thousand pounds, is hidden deep within the pile of bottles on the floor. He imagines they will take all of it. He thinks about getting it out and handing it over, and seeing their faces light up, and then he realizes he can't, he just can't.

He pulls the black-and-white bag out from under Sol's mattress. It contains Sol's entire stash.

He holds the bag a second, then hands it to Red Tooth.

Lee watches him draw out the thick wad of cash inside, a mixture of dollars, sterling and rupees, and flick through it. Lee has no idea how much money Sol has. It looks like a lot. Red Tooth seems impressed. Lee assures himself that he will make it up to Sol; he will replace it all. Of course he will. He watches the money disappear back into the bag.

'You are a very lucky man,' says Red Tooth. 'We have decided not to put you in prison. Goodbye.'

Red Tooth slips the bag onto his shoulder and the two policemen turn and stroll back to the jeep, tapping their canes on the ground.

Lee realizes he is breathing hard. He slams the door closed, shoots the bolt home, and stands beside it with his head rested against the wood. He slaps the palm of his hand against it.

'Fuckers,' he shouts, 'cunts.'

He steps backwards and jabs his neck forward, his mouth twisted into a snarl.

He hears the jeep accelerate away.

His eyes are hurting. He closes them and sees an expanse of red. He opens them and he knows what to do. He doesn't have to replace the money. Not really. No-one will know.

Lee grabs his wallet and shuffles outside. The sun is just beginning to rise, and the deep-blue sky is touched with a spreading yellow stain. He locks the door with the padlock then walks across the compound to the small wooden shed behind the restaurant. The hut is small, dusty and dilapidated. The door hangs off its hinges. He poked around in there once; it's full of fishermen's tools, mostly broken. He picks up a crowbar from the corner. The steel is surprisingly cold.

The catch on the outside of the tourist-home door is sturdy, but the screws are rusty. He inserts the wedged end of the crowbar under the catch and pulls. One hard tug and the screws pop out from the door with a crack and the catch hangs loose, the padlock swinging.

He pulls the door open then closes it again. He picks the screws up off the porch and inserts them back into the holes in the catch's base and into the splintered wood. He takes a few steps backwards. The busted catch can only be seen from up close. He wouldn't want to be broken into for real. He puts the crowbar back, lights a cigarette and watches the sea, speckled with little black fishing boats, turn blue in the growing light.

At low tide it's possible to take a short cut to the beach over the rocks at the base of the headland. It's about a kilometre away, five times that if you go by the road. Lee scrambles onto the rocks and heads away from the hut. Red crabs scuttle away as he approaches and the sea lurches against the rocks, showering him with spray. He figures he'll go and drink lemon sodas in a beach café and go back after

117

sunset. He wants Sol to get to the hut first. He rehearses the lines of shock, anger and condolence he will deliver when he returns and Sol gives him the news that they've been robbed. Maybe, Lee thinks, he will soften the blow by pointing out that at least Sol still has his camera.

The beach is surprisingly busy. Lee hits the sand and pads closer and sees that the bodies lying on the sand are fully dressed, with slitty red eyes and dirty faces; people came here to crash out after the parties. In their bright clothes they look like exotic, washed-up sea creatures. More people sit in the string of brown shacks – cafés – at the back of the beach, in front of the abrupt green line of palms. It is an oddly still scene, the motionless figures conveying an atmosphere of complete torpor. The only other moving things are three skinny yellow dogs walking in front of him and a fishing boat heading for the shore.

'Lee!' One of the figures on the beach, lying alone, sits up. Sol. He raises his hand. Lee walks over slowly, considering how he should play this.

'Sol!' Lee calls out as he approaches, willing his voice to sound cheery, 'how's it going, mate?'

'All right,' croaks Sol. He looks as tired as Lee feels. Lee sits down beside him on the sand.

'Happy christmas, mate,' says Lee.

'Happy christmas.' Sol's voice is a dull mono-tone. His elbows are rested on his knees. His camera and his shoes are sat between his bare feet. In his hands he twists his camera's shoulder strap.

'How's it going then, mate?' asks Lee. 'What have you been up to?' He tries to keep up a chirpy tone, but the phrase comes out sounding forced and stilted.

'I'm tired. I'm tired and I'm pissed off.'

'Oh. Oh dear. Why's that then?'

'Just everything. This fucked-up place. Paul.' Sol's eyes are red, his forehead wrinkled, his mouth turned down sourly, his shoulders hunched. Lee has never seen him so moody before.

'What happened with him?'

'I took him to the hospital. They said they couldn't do anything for him. And he got really wild, started ranting at everyone. So I sat with him in this room for a few hours. Then they said I could leave him there, and these two security men said they'd give him a lift back to the hut when he'd calmed down a bit. So I drove back to the party.' Sol turns to look at Lee. 'I checked on your bike, on the way back from the hospital. It was where we left it. And you're not going to believe it. The cow was there.'

'What?'

'Yeah. It was stood up eating grass.'

'What? What?'

'Yeah, seriously. It was standing at the side of the road looking stupid.'

'You're joking.'

'No. Straight up.'

119

'For fuck's sake,' says Lee, with sudden venom. He realizes that the policemen have conned him. He thrusts a hand into the sand, pulls it out and holds it palm upwards, watching the grains trickle through his fingers. In that case, how did they know about the incident at all? A thought strikes him.

'You said Paul was going to be given a lift back?'

'Yeah.'

'By hospital guards?'

'Yeah.'

'What did they look like?'

'One had red teeth, one had a hat on. Why?'

'No reason,' says Lee, lightly, thrusting both hands deep into the sand. 'I just wondered.' Lee turns to look at the sea so that Sol won't see his furious expression. He pauses for a couple of heartbeats, until he's sure he can control his voice and make it sound normal. 'So you went back to the party after that?'

'Yeah. Didn't see you there.'

'Well, I was there,' says Lee, quickly.

'Did you score?'

'No. I'm just not having any luck at the moment.'

'Did you have a good time?'

'Oh yeah, great. Brilliant. Danced like a nutter. All night long. You?' In his mind Lee goes over the terrifying drive in the jeep. He imagines taking

Red Tooth's cane and smashing it into his mouth. That's what he should have done. He wishes the fake policemen were here, now; he'd go ballistic. He hardly hears what Sol is saying.

'I couldn't stop thinking about Paul. The way he looked. The crap he was talking. I couldn't do anything for him, Lee. He hasn't got any better. Someone said he was here a while back, wandering round naked, covered in that red paint, carrying one of his statues.'

One of the dogs barks, and Lee looks to see what has attracted its attention. It points its sharp muzzle towards the fishing boat, now in the shallow water about five metres from the beach. The three men inside jump out and wade towards the shore, dragging the thin black boat along with them. They don't normally land here, and Lee reckons the café owners will complain; who wants to sit on a beach and watch people sift through a pile of dead fish? The dogs trot towards them.

'I reckon if I stayed much longer I'd go mad, too,' says Sol. 'I hate it here.'

'Why?'

'I don't know, Lee. Do you ever get . . . do you ever think, Shit, I'm a thousand miles from anyone who cares for me?'

'Don't be like that. Come on. I'm your mate, mate. Why don't you just go home if that's what you want?'

'I can't. Not yet. Not for a while.'

'Why not?'

Sol opens his mouth, then pauses. His toes, Lee notices, are wiggling furiously up and down.

'I can't. I just can't. I'm sort of hiding. Keeping my head down.'

'What?' Lee turns sharply to face Sol, who is looking out to sea. 'You mean you're on the run? You never told me. From what? From who?'

Sol looks out to sea as he speaks. His voice is quiet, and Lee leans close to hear him.

'I did something, Lee. Something really bad. I got married to this girl, right . . .'

Sol's voice tails off. He stands up, and suddenly he's tense and alert, and staring down the beach. Lee stands and follows his gaze. He sees the three fishermen bending down over their boat. With some difficulty they haul out a pale, naked man.

'Jesus,' says Sol.

'Oh fuck,' says Lee.

One fisherman holds his arms wrapped around the body's chest from behind. Another, facing away from the beach, holds his legs. The third holds the boat and starts shouting up towards the cafés. The body is slim and pink, with unmistakable short, red hair flattened down over its head. Paul. The fishermen bear his body through the frothing surf. His arms hang down, hands dragging in the shallow water, and his head lolls from side to side. The people on the beach begin to stir; a few climb to their feet.

The three dogs break into a lolloping run towards the men, their paws hardly seeming to touch the sand, moving silently and very fast.

part three

fake

nine

wedding snaps

I was getting married to this girl. She wasn't bad looking. Chocolate colouring, quite small and curvy, and she had a wide, friendly face, like the face of a sun. The kind of face that would maybe light up when she was happy. On this point, of course, I was only speculating – she looked pretty serious at that moment, you'd have thought she was at a funeral. I was glad she was attractive. I wouldn't have wanted to marry just any old muffin. That was a fucked-up way to think, I know, but that was what I was thinking as I stood and sweated in a borrowed suit.

She had this long brown-and-green wraparound dress on, a headscarf in the same stuff and a bunch of wooden jewellery like you see white college girls wearing. She was Nigerian, she was called Femi. I didn't know much else. I reckoned she must have been about my age: twenty-five.

The registrar, a short, bald white guy, spoke in solemn tones, 'Solomon Thomas, do you take this woman to be your lawful wedded wife?'

It didn't feel like he was talking about me. For a start, no-one called me Solomon. It was Sol. The surname never really felt like me, either. It was all I ever got off my father. Not a bad man, my mother said, but very unreliable; he cleared off back to the yard soon as I was born. My mum went back five years ago. She saw him once, on the other side of the street. She didn't cross it.

Why, suddenly, had my parents come to mind?

'I do,' I said.

She said she did, too, and we did the thing with the rings. They were also borrowed.

The registry office looked like a classroom. Orange carpet, a big desk at the front, plus two smaller desks, and at the back two rows of empty chairs. Music was playing, nothing I'd have chosen to listen to.

Pug did my tie for me and I thought he'd got it way too tight. They were stupid things anyway, ties, just a big arrow pointing at your dick. It was worse than I thought it was going to be. I wanted it to be over so I could go home. I kept getting paranoid flashes, like I imagined the registrar was going to halt the proceedings at any moment.

I lowered my face towards hers. Maybe nobody had told her about this bit, 'cause she flinched before understanding and turning her face up to mine. I looked into her big brown eyes and kissed her quickly on the lips. Our first touch. Soft lips.

A big open book sat on one of the side desks. We were supposed to sign it, apparently. We walked over, unsure of ourselves, where to stand, where to look. We signed our names. She had big round writing.

That was it. Now we – me and the woman stood next to me – were man and wife. It was just words and pieces of paper. I was doing her a favour. She was doing me a favour. I told myself it was no big deal.

'Photos,' said the registrar, and for a second I thought he'd sussed me. But he was only on about recording the happy event. That was Pug's cue. The only other person in the room, he was standing at the back, holding my camera, the Nikon with the busted side.

We were directed to the other side desk, where another identical book lay, and the registrar told me to sit down and hold the pen. He explained that it wasn't for real, it was for photos; it was just for show.

Sitting there with the pen poised over the blank page, I thought, Yeah, this is the photo you want to sum up this scene: a fake book and an empty pen and a little bit of acting.

'Look at me, star,' said Pug, fiddling with the camera. He was messing with the aperture setting, trying to look like he knew what he was doing. Flash. 'That's right. Lovely. And again.' Flash, flash.

Pug and me, we went way back; we grew up on

>>fake

the same block, and we went to the same school. Our mothers were friends; they worked for the same cleaning company. As kids, we looked out for each other. We were like brothers who'd grown in different directions; there was a bond that went beyond our different views on everything. He needed a bit of sanding round the edges, but he was made of gold. I always thought of gold when I thought of him.

Despite being pale pink, with blond hair and blue eyes – generally a fine example of the Aryan race – Pug dressed for full-on rude boy effect, and he wore a lot of seriously chunky jewellery. The worst of it was a gold razor blade hanging on a gold chain round his neck. Normally he wore baggy gear that flashed the name of the bloke who made it in your face, but now he looked pretty restrained in his green suit. Still looked snazzier than me, though.

He snapped me head-on. Me, I would have gone for a side shot and got high up, the pen at the centre and the big back of my shaved head black against the white page.

I stood up, Femi sat down, and Pug fired another salvo. What did he think I was going to do with the photos? Stick them on top of the telly? This was hardly an event I wanted recorded for posterity. But he was getting right into his role, like he always did.

I'd have shot her from below, and caught the uncertain smile that didn't reach her eyes, cut off the faces of the men standing around her. I thought like that, in pictures. I put borders around things. Reality was messy and confusing, but if you gave it an edge you could get it neat. If you cut things out and framed them maybe they'd start making sense.

I wondered what Femi was thinking, whether she even understood much of this. She was shy, and didn't speak much. We'd only met an hour beforehand.

That was it. Over. Big exhalations and smiles all round. I shook the registrar's hand, and he congratulated me. Yes. Reckoned I deserved an Oscar.

We went to the pub across the road and got to the point.

Pug got the drinks in, pints and a water for the lady, and we joined Terence at a table in the corner. Femi sat prim, straight and silent, next to me.

'And how's the happy couple?' said Terence. He had a surprisingly camp voice, for such a big, ugly guy. He had a pale complexion, run through with red veins and blotches, like marble, and very pink earlobes. He was smoking a cigar and had a couple of fingers left on his pint.

'We're fine,' I said. 'It went OK, no problem.'

'You should have seen it,' said Pug, slapping his hand on the table, 'the brother is a master of deception.'

'Good,' said Terence. 'That's the worst part over with. This is the nice bit.'

Terence took a little wooden box out of his

pocket and slid it over to me. I opened it up. There were two cigars in there, and a fat roll of money tied up with a plastic band.

'Three grand,' said Terence, 'as agreed. The other half to follow in a year or so, when the divorce comes through. Take a cigar as well.'

I slipped out the money. I looked across at Femi, but she wasn't even watching; her eyes were darting around like she'd never been in a pub before, which maybe she hadn't. I took out a cigar and Terence lit it for me from a clipper. It tasted rough, and the raw smoke was like claws raking my lungs. I coughed hard and Terence chuckled, rasping from the back of his throat.

'You roll it around. Don't inhale.'

I toked a second time, doing as he suggested, and managed to keep it down. I wouldn't list it as one of the best first experiences I've ever had.

A faint, patronizing smile hung round Terence's mouth. He nodded at the money. 'You can have a lot of fun with that. I imagine it'll buy a lot of drugs and loose women.'

'You don't know this man,' said Pug, clapping me round the shoulder. 'Boy's a good citizen. He keeps his head down. Ain't that right?'

'I'm going to buy a Leica', I said, 'and darkroom stuff.'

'The boy wants to be a photographer,' explained Pug, 'you could never stop him when he was a kid. Always snapping away.'

'But I've never had any money for equipment,' I said. I felt the need to justify myself, prove it was all in a good cause. 'That's why I'm doing this.'

Terence raised his eyebrows and cocked his chin. 'Have you studied?'

'No. But I know I'm good.'

'He learned it himself,' said Pug, 'from a bunch of magazines. His mum got vexed when she saw them, and wanted to take them away 'cause they were full of pictures of naked women. He kicked up a fuss, so they made an agreement; he got to keep the mags and she cut out all the nudey pictures.'

'Amusing.'

'What about you, Femi?' I asked. 'What are you going to do now?'

She looked at me, smiled and didn't say anything.

'It's all taken care of,' said Terence. He winked at me and smiled at her. 'She's going to stay with friends.'

'Why is she here?' I asked.

'I don't know, do I?' He waved a hand in the air. 'Problems at home probably. Maybe there's some music she'll face if she gets sent back.'

'Political problems?'

'Most of the people I help, it's economic; they're just fed up with being poor.'

'Couldn't she just have applied for asylum?'

Terence threw his head back and let out a heavy-duty laugh. He slapped his hand on the table. 'Asylum!' he spluttered. 'Good one. You don't

>>fake

know much about how the system works then.' He jerked forward as the laugh turned into a raking cough. He sounded like something out of *Jurassic Park*. We watched and waited. He had tears in his eyes when he finished.

'Excuse me,' he said, and drained his pint. 'Right. I have a meeting. Femi?' He stood up, and she followed.

'What happens now?' I asked. I didn't want it all to end so abruptly.

'Nothing,' said Terence, 'get in touch in a year. If you need to contact her, go through me. Happy snapping.'

I said goodbye to Femi. She nodded and smiled at me. Terence put a hand on her elbow and steered her away. He left behind a whiff of cigar smoke and aftershave.

'Weird,' I said, crushing the cigar into the ashtray. 'I'm married now.'

'Yeah,' said Pug. 'How about my cut, star?'

I counted ten tenners off the wad and passed them over. Commission for sorting out the whole deal; he'd heard about Terence from a mate of a mate, and put me in touch with him. It struck me now as a lot of wong for a couple of phone calls, but I didn't mind; me and Pug shared our stuff anyway, and as I was flush I wanted him to be in on my good fortune.

'What are you going to get?' I asked him, putting the rest of the wad in my pocket.

Pug leaned closer and lowered his voice. 'I know this ex-squaddie. Put away a bit of stuff on the side, you understand?' He crinkled the notes in his hand. 'Now he wants to ditch it, and he's having a garage sale. Bargain-basement bufties going cheap cheap cheap. I got my eye on a Mauser. Lovely action.'

'You're going to buy a gun? What the fuck for?'

'Keep your voice down, man.'

'Pug, you don't need a gun.'

'It's for my protection, *seen*.'

'Who've you got to be protected from? Everybody likes you.'

'Maybe someone wants to rip me off. You can't be too careful. Everyone's got one now.'

'What are you saying, man? It's a fashion state-ment? That's twisted. That's fucking shit, man, come on. Spend it on drugs, clothes and records, like usual. Maybe you could buy some paint and we could decorate the flat.'

'Yeah yeah yeah. Hey, don't reckon it's my round, do you?'

>>>fake

135

customer relations

Three days after the wedding a brown envelope dropped through the letterbox. A piece of headed paper. The Home Office. In reference to recent marriage application, blah, blah, blah, inquiries blah, official will be calling at your home. Signed with some quick doodle. Shit.

Pug called Terence. 'Don't panic,' he said. 'I'll come round.'

He turned up with Femi. She was wearing the same outfit she wore to our wedding, and carrying a bulging plastic shopping bag. Terence had a big hand on her shoulder.

'Relax,' he said, looking at my tense face. 'Nice view.'

That's what everyone said when they came to our drum. We were so high up you could see the Houses of Parliament from the walkway outside the front door. Strange how close they were; they didn't feel close.

We lived on the top floor of a tower block, one

of a methodical row of standard-issue stacks on standard-issue streets, in one of those parts of Brixton that hadn't yet got a Futon Express or a dance bar. The nearest off-licence had a cashier behind a grille, like in some olde-worlde bank. The post-office queue on a Monday morning stretched out along the pavement. The drum itself – three up, two down – might not have been classy, but the place was a touch; the tenant who'd bought the place, then sublet it to us, had done a runner a couple of years previously – to South America, I'd heard – and no-one had hassled us for any rent since.

'Listen,' said Terence, 'I won't come in. This visit, it's nothing. It's just something they do every now and then. Doesn't mean anything. They just check you live together, then go.'

'You mean she's got to stay? Till they come?'

'It'll only be a day or two, I expect. Just make it look like you sleep together, in case they have a look in the bedroom. Tell them how much you love each other. It won't be a problem.'

He gave Femi's elbow a push and she stepped into the hallway. She stood next to me, smiling nervously, big eyes taking in the narrow space, made narrower by the tangle of bike bits and half a hat stand. I felt self-conscious of the unpainted walls and the dirty brown carpet.

'Right,' said Terence. 'Give me a bell soon as they've gone, and I'll come and take her off your hands.' He winked at me, stepped back, then wagged a stern finger. 'Soon as, all right? Bye.'

I closed the door. Femi stood with her feet very close together. I asked her how she was. She smiled at me, and lowered her eyes to the floor.

'Well,' I said, 'I'd better show you around, yeah?' I beckoned her to follow me, and stepped through the nearest door.

'Sorry the place is a bit of a state. I keep meaning to buy a hoover. This is the kitchen.' I pointed at things, uncertain how much she understood. 'Oven. Microwave. Umm, you can put food in here. No, I'll cook for you. I haven't got much in, though. Pasta. Tuna. Mayonnaise. Is that good for tonight? Never mind the tap; it always does that.'

We went into the big room, and Pug looked up briefly from the TV screen. He was playing some racing game on the Playstation.

'Hello,' he said.

Femi looked at the screen curiously. 'Hello.'

'She's staying a couple of days,' I said.

'Yeah, I heard. Be good to have a woman around. You all right, Femi?'

'Hello,' she repeated.

'Great.'

'I'm a bit worried about the interview,' I said.

'It'll be all right. They can't prove anything.'

'She doesn't speak English.'

'Tell them you communicate on other levels.' Pug's car took a corner too fast, and it spun onto the grass and into a hoarding. 'Bollocks.'

I beckoned Femi to follow me upstairs.

'How do you like England?' I asked. 'Listen, don't worry, OK? It's going to be all right. I promise.' I thought she didn't understand the words, so I filled my voice with honey to make sure she got the tone.

We did the bathroom and the toilet, then I showed her the room next to mine. 'You sleep here. Understand? It's just for tonight, I expect. Look, I've put a mattress on the floor for you. Ignore all the other stuff. That's chemicals and shit. This is going to be my darkroom. Pictures? Photographs? You know? I make photographs. I'll get you some sheets. I know it's not very comfortable, but it's not for long. OK?'

She nodded. It seemed to be her standard response.

I took her next door. 'And this, this is my room. We have to make it look like you sleep here. So you should put all your clothes somewhere. Here, give me your bag.'

I tried to take the bag off her. She stepped back, and opened it herself. It was full of clothes. She took out a brown dress and hung it on one of the hooks on the wall, where most of my clothes were. Then she pulled a tangle of underwear out of the bag. I pointed at the floor. Well, that was where all my pants and socks were. She scattered them around, and we grinned at each other.

I sat down on the mattress. She sat next to me and we grinned at each other a bit more.

'I speak little,' she said.

'I know.'

'One two three four five.' She paused.

'Six.'

'Six seven eight nine ten.'

'Good. That's not bad. Eleven.'

'Eleven?'

'That's what comes next.'

She pointed at the bed. 'Bed.'

I pointed at a pillow. 'What's that?'

'No.' She shook her head.

'Pillow.'

'Pillow.'

'Good.'

She pointed at the cupboard.

'Cupboard,' I said.

'Cupboard,' she said.

'Good.'

She smiled. 'Very good,' she said.

Jesus was this fucked. How were we going to get through an interview? I was really worried. What could they do to me? Could I go to prison for this? Could she?

'I'm going to teach you to say some phrases, OK? For when the immigration people come. I like it here. Say it. I like it here.'

'I like it here.'

'What else?' I cleared my throat. 'I love my husband.'

'I love my husband.'

'We are very much in love.'

'We are very much in love. Husband.'

'Good. You learn fast.'

The English lesson continued for another ten minutes. Book, pen, hand, eye, clock, cigarette, ashtray. I talked her round the posters. Singer, football, photographer. I got to hear her laugh.

Boredom overtook panic. I realized that my task was futile. How much could she learn in a day? I was just going to have to see what happened.

'Good. Now I'm going to leave you here, yeah? Make yourself at home. Do whatever. Come down whenever you want.'

I left her lying on the bed, looking at the pictures in a book of photographs. She seemed pretty unconcerned, anyway. I settled into the other armchair in the big room. As Pug grunted and swore his way through his game, I toyed with my new Leica. I loved the weight of it, the sense of balance, its sturdiness and precision, the smooth noises it made: click, whirr, buzz. It felt like a detachable part of me. But playing with it made me remember how I got the money to buy it, which made me think about the Home Office visit. Maybe work would take my mind off it. I picked a bundle of white forms and a pen off the floor and stared blankly at the instructions printed on the first page – probe to negative, always thank the interviewee, blah, blah.

Pug's car expired in a ball of flame. He frowned, then sat back and lit up a zoot, one of three sitting in a row on the armrest.

'What you been doing up there?' he said. 'Showing her her wifely duties?'

'Teaching English. I hope she'll be all right. She seems a bit lost.'

'You'd think they'd learn the language before they came.'

'Maybe she had to run away. Maybe she was desperate or something.'

'Yeah. Look, she's not your problem. You look at her, you think, Cash. Just like she looks at you, and she thinks, UK citizenship. Ask us one of your questions.'

I turned the page and read out the first question on the form.

'Would you say you were happy or unhappy with the level of customer care you receive? Very satisfied, satisfied, unsatisfied, very unsatisfied.'

Pug took a long toke before replying.

'Put satisfied.'

'Not, very satisfied?'

'Satisfied.'

I ticked the box.

'How do you think customer service could be improved?' I asked.

'Who's it for?'

'A bank.'

'Right. Well I think all the female bank people should get their tits out. And give you blow jobs when you make a deposit of over ten pounds.'

'Man, that would be disgusting,' I retorted. 'Most bank clerks are wrinkled old grannies.'

'Fair point, star. First of all you'd have to rate them all from one to ten on how fit they are. Then anyone who scored over six, say—'

'Seven.'

'OK, seven, anyone over seven gets their tits out.'

I wrote, 'I would like staff to act in a friendly and sociable manner.'

Pug stretched out his hand, a zoot cocked between two fingers, and I reached out, arm straight and pincered it. We did this every day, maybe twenty times, and every time it made me think of the poster for ET the Extra Terrestrial – two hands reaching across space and just touching.

'How many more questions have you got?' asked Pug.

'Thirty-nine.'

'And they're all that boring? Man, I don't know why you bother with that shitty job.'

'I'd be a fool to give it up.'

I was a market researcher. I should have been pounding the pavement, pen cocked, eyebrows slightly raised, clipboard at the ready, but me and my supervisor had an understanding. He let me fill in most of the questionnaires myself, creating fictional A2s, C1s et cetera, and their opinions, from the comfort of my own home, and in return he got to buy top-whack green off Pug at very competitive prices.

'You got all that money,' said Pug. 'Why don't you just jack it in and take photos all day? Juggle a bit of green if you want more wong.'

'I don't want to sign on.'

'But you'd get about as much money.'

'Yeah, but . . .'

'But what? You'd rather be gainfully employed, making your contribution to society? Your thinking on this is all fucked up. As doley scum, I'm much more useful and valuable than you.' Pug flipped rapidly through the options menu of the game and chose his weapons. 'The system needs unemployed people, it keeps wages down and means the economy stays competitive. That's a fact. On the other hand, civilization doesn't need loads of made-up market research.'

'I'm not dependent on anyone.'

'You mean you think I'm a parasite? Is that it?'

I passed the zoot back in a gesture of reconciliation. Pug had a smile on his face, to show me he wasn't serious, but there was an edge to his voice. He put the controller down.

'Man, I don't believe I'm hearing this. Are you calling me a flea? Is that what you just said?' Pug's voice rose to a high tone of angry indignation.

'I'm just talking about me.'

'Well, fuck you, man,' said Pug, reaching into the space between his thigh and the armrest. He straightened and swivelled, his arm swinging round. His voice was suddenly calm and cold. 'I'm going to blow you away.'

Suddenly the barrel of a gun was staring me down, ten inches from my shocked face.

'Jesus. Fuck.'

'Nice, isn't it?'

'Is it loaded?'

''Course it's loaded. What's the point of it otherwise?'

'You think that's pretty cool, do you? You think you're the man, now, do you?' I picked up my camera. 'You shoot me and I'll shoot you.'

'I'm going to blast your head off. I'm deadly serious. It's something I've always wanted to do.'

I fixed him square in the centre of the viewfinder, brought his face up sharp.

'Yeah? Well I'm going to shoot you, man, and splash your face over my Ilford. I got you square in my sights.'

'I want to see your brains splatter over the wallpaper.'

I clicked and lowered the camera. The gun barrel didn't waver. It was starting to freak me out.

'Look, you've made your point. Pug? Hey, come on.'

The door opened. Femi stopped dead in the doorway and screamed. She quickly backed out of the room. I hurried after her. She stood in the hallway, her hands on her cheeks, fingers spread under wide eyes. I stepped towards her and she flattened herself against the wall.

'It's OK, hey, it's OK.' I touched her shoulder. She let her hands drop. 'Relax. It's OK. It's OK.'

'Gun,' she said.

'Yeah,' I said, 'good.' I patted her shoulder and let my hand drop. 'It's all right. It's all right. Relax. He's your friend. He's my friend. We were just messing about. Not serious.'

There was a knock at the door.

I called to Pug. 'You expecting anyone?'

'No.'

'Fuck.'

I opened up. It was a woman I didn't recognize. Early thirties. She had don't-treat-me-like-a-sex-object written all over her face and in the cut of her short hair. Not like you'd want to. In a long blue skirt, matching jacket and white blouse, she had the smart, high-street casual look of an off-duty rad. I felt myself heating up, adrenal glands jumping into action.

She flashed a plastic card at me and told me she was from the Immigration Office and she wanted to talk to Solomon and Femi.

'It's Sol,' I said.

'I'm Jilly.' She smiled. 'This is just routine, you

146

know,' she said, 'nothing to be scared of.'

Calm, I thought, calm. Butch it out. No problem. Act normal. I had this buzzing behind my eyes, a sudden awareness of my nervous system, and I realized I was pretty stoned. Shit. Concentrate.

I stepped back to let her in. She took a step forward and stopped. Femi was still against the wall, watching intently with a level gaze, as if trying to judge what kind of threat she presented, and I was standing by Femi, so she couldn't get any further.

'And you must be Femi,' said the woman. 'How are you both?'

'We're fine,' I said. I took Femi's hand, in case she decided to retreat. 'Still in the honeymoon period.' I looked at Femi in a way designed to signal affection.

'You're getting on all right?'

'Oh yes.'

'No problems?'

'Oh no.' I was smiling at the woman now, and so was Femi; we must have looked like a dream couple. An advert. The thought almost made me giggle. Shit. Steady.

'Where did you meet?'

'It was on holiday.'

'Do you have your passport?'

'My passport?'

'Perhaps you can show me your visa stamp.'

'I don't have it. I've lost it.'

'Do you have your passport, Femi?'

147

'Passport,' said Femi.

'She doesn't have it handy,' I said, 'I don't think.'

Femi let go of my hand, turned and walked up the stairs.

'Oh. Maybe she does.'

We stood in awkward silence. Nothing I could think of – How did you get here? Have you always been that ugly? Where did you hear about us? What did you say your name was again? – passed the internal censor.

'I get the impression that your wife is a little frightened,' said the woman eventually.

'Yes. She had a scare. Just now. My mate was messing about, well . . .' I tailed off.

What was I saying? I could hardly talk about the gun. I felt my cheeks get hotter and hotter. I licked my lips, and straight after I knew that was the wrong thing to do. I had to appear relaxed, at ease. The more nervous I got, the more nervous I knew I appeared, and the more I knew I was screwing this up, so the more nervous I got.

'As long as she's not frightened of me,' said the woman. 'I wouldn't want people to be frightened of me.'

'No.'

I heard Femi's quick, quiet tread coming down the stairs. She was carrying a little green book. She handed it to the woman and took my hand again. The woman began to study the passport, turning the crisp new pages slowly.

go>> simon lewis

'Quite a nice picture. Only a tourist visa. You realize that now you're married Femi will need to make an application to us so that she can stay here?'

'Yes, that's all being taken care of.'

'Good.' The woman snapped the passport shut and handed it back.

'Does Femi speak any English, Sol?'

'I'm teaching her. She won't talk to you because she's shy.'

'Would you like to say something to me, Femi?' I squeezed Femi's hand. 'Say something,' I told her. She looked momentarily panicked. She looked at me, then at the woman, then at me again.

'I do,' she said.

Another pause, but this one felt heavier.

'Why did you marry your wife, Sol?' asked the woman.

'We are very much in love.' I squeezed Femi's hand again.

'I see,' said the woman. 'Well, I wish you every happiness for the future.' She nodded her head and turned.

'Is that it?' I asked. 'What happens now?'

'Nothing.'

'Nothing?' I put a hand on the thin edge of the open door, as if to block her way back in should she change her mind. Realizing that was what it looked like, I let the hand drop again.

'Of course, the visa application is another hurdle.' She stepped out. 'Nice view. Goodbye.'

149

I closed the door and remembered how to breathe properly. Did I get away with it? I thought I'd got away with it. Relief rushed through me. I wanted to laugh. I realized I was still holding Femi's hand.

'Good,' I told her. 'That was good. I think.'

I led her into the big room. Pug's body was taut with concentration, still as the furniture except for his twitching thumbs. The gun was nowhere in sight.

'See?' he said. 'No problem.'

Femi eyed him warily. I sat her down in my chair, and stood in front of him, blocking his view of the screen.

'What the fuck did you think you were doing?' I felt my face flush and all the tension came out in a rush. 'You can't go round pointing guns at people. What if it had gone off accidentally? You could have fucking killed me, man.'

Pug leaned hard to the side to look round me.

'Relax. Cool your little self, all right? The guy didn't have any real ones. It's just a replica, all right? It's a fake. It was a joke. Just let me cane these fuckers, then I'll give Terence a ring.'

eleven

development

I rocked the tray of developer gently, up and down, and the single sheet of white paper moved back and forth in the sloshing liquid. Slowly, the image grew. Something out of nothing. The dark tones came first, as grey smudges; the black hole of the gun muzzle appeared, then Pug's face above it – first the line of the mouth, the nostrils, then the eyes. He was a soft, smudged thing in the crisp shadows around him. Then the shadows deepened as the mid tones blossomed out of the blankness, and Pug's face lost that ghostly quality, became hard and real.

I picked the paper up with the tongs, put it in the tray of fix, next to the developer on the wet bench, and stepped back. The ritual was nearly over, and I could relax a little now.

I blinked and rubbed my raw eyes. I felt fuzzy and blurred with lack of sleep. I checked my watch. Ten thirty-three in the morning. I'd been awake for about twenty hours. Soon as Terence had collected

Femi, I'd got on with sorting out the darkroom. I'd worked all night to get it together, spurred on by the thought of a single moment. This moment.

My first picture developed, in my first darkroom.

I started taking pictures when I was small, with an Instant my Mum gave me for Christmas. I carried it round all the time and snapped everything. Action shots of mates playing football outside the lock-ups. Glamour shots of girls in my class. I had a go at nature photography – taking the pigeons who perched on the balcony, getting up at dawn to try to catch the foxes that lived in the waste ground, snapping the guard dogs running round the car wrecks in the scrapyard. I even had a go at special effects; a mate threw a luminous sock in the air and I snapped it against the clouds. The idea was to fake a UFO sighting and get some money off a magazine.

I could nick film from the chemists – I think now they let me take it – but I couldn't get anything developed. So I took all these photos and kept the canisters in a big old pickling jar in my room. I still had it, and it was full now, maybe two hundred rolls. The canisters on the bottom were ten years old. It felt like my youth was sitting there, waiting to be developed. I was waiting to be developed.

When I was little my Mum used to take me to her church. I was impressed by the rites and the fervour and the deep seriousness; I saw it as a place where ordinary rules didn't apply, a place of baffling and irrational events. I was too small to understand what it was all about, and when I could understand, the magic died and I stopped going. Now, in the red glow of the safe light, in the silence, I remembered that feeling.

I took the paper out of the fix with the tongs and held it up to admire it. The gun pointed straight out; it was out of focus, but the hole of its barrel was a stark black circle right in the middle of the paper. Underneath it Pug's fingers clenched around the handle. His foreshortened head above was the same size and shape as the sovereign ring on his finger. He was grinning. The background – the armchair he sat in, the shelves of CDs, the posters on the wall, the corner of a window – was dark and difficult to make out.

It was a good picture. The smile on the face, the shabby ordinariness of the room and the gun at the centre. It didn't tell a story. You would look at it and it would make you wonder.

I heard a loud banging on the front door. I paused and listened. Fix dribbled back into the tray. The front door was opened; Pug said something I didn't catch, then something else, a little louder. I heard quick, light footsteps on the stairs. Pug called out, 'Hey!' I heard someone move along the top corridor and open my door, then shut it again. I heard Pug coming up the stairs. He called out, 'You can't just . . . What's wrong?' I heard my door open, then Pug's door. Pug in the corridor. 'What do you want? Calm down. He's in there.'

I looked around swiftly. Photographic paper was splayed half out of its bag on the dry bench and I'd forgotten to bolt the door.

'Don't come in!' I shouted, letting the wet print slip back into the fix. The top half missed the tray and the print flopped, dribbling fix over the bench. I reached for the paper. 'Give me a second, all right? I'm developing—'

The door opened and light streamed into the room.

Femi stood in the doorway. Her face seemed bigger, and it was twisted up tight, her lips parted and trembling, her eyes narrow. Pug stood behind her.

'Femi? What's wrong?'

She came in, her head down and hugged me. I dropped the tongs.

'Femi? Hey, it's OK. It's OK.' I put a hand on the back of her head.

Pug looked round the door. 'I couldn't stop her. She looks a bit upset. No offence, but she's your wife, yeah? I'll leave you to it, then, yeah? I've got to sign on in a sec. Got to go and fill my fucking form in.' Every time Pug signed on he had to show them a form showing what steps he had taken to find work. Every time he wrote the same thing, a list of real newspapers and fictional companies, written with a variety of pens so it looked less like he wrote it in one sitting. It didn't strike me as much of a chore, but the way he talked about it you'd think it was as much hassle as a job.

He closed the door and plunged us back into red light.

'Femi? What's happened? Hey, come on, it's OK. Here. Sit down. Sit down.'

We sat side by side on the mattress on the floor. I wanted her to say something. She was shaking a little. I put an arm around her shoulder.

'Hey, it's OK.'

She wiped her face with her hand, snuffled and swallowed. 'I fear.'

'What? What are you frightened of?'

She said nothing.

'Don't worry. Don't worry. It will be OK.'

'No go home.'

'What? Why don't you want to go home?'

Silence. Fix dripped steadily onto the floor. 'Nobody's going to send you home.'

I started to stroke her back, murmuring re-assuring sounds. I felt her breathing slow. She stroked my back. I don't know how long we sat there. She raised her face to mine. I kissed her. In the heavy red light she looked ablaze. We lay down on the mattress and kissed some more.

She curled her dress away from her. Her skin was smooth and soft, her body full of curves, her breasts heavy. I fell on her, greedy. I slipped down my trousers, entered her.

While we fucked – there was nothing else. There

>>>fake

155

was nothing in me but blood, and I felt my body winding up and up, tighter and tighter, and then snap, I was thrown back into the room with our slowing breath and the drip of fix.

I held her in silence. Oh shit. My head was all over the place as thoughts resumed their chatter. I didn't know what I felt. I wanted there to be nothing else again. I lay there with my face in her neck, limbs loose around her, and thought it would be OK and the world would stay away if I just didn't move at all.

She shifted first. I didn't know how long after. She rolled on her side and faced the wall. I looked and listened, and she just lay there, breathing, soft and deep. I looked at her back, the curve of her waist, the hard flat plains of her shoulders, the bobbles of her spine protruding beneath her skin. I traced the lines of her body, its landscape, with a finger, from her neck to her waist to her thigh. The skin yielded slightly to the touch. I felt ignorant. She was a land I knew nothing about.

I heard a knock on the front door. I raised my head. The door was opened. Voices. Someone was speaking; I didn't hear the words, just a mumble. Then footsteps on the stairs, someone coming up. The tread was heavy. Not Pug; he called up from the hallway. 'They're in the darkroom. First door on the left. I'm off now, but I'll be back in half an hour. There's beer in the fridge if you want one.' The voice on the stairs said, 'Cheers.'

Terence. I heard the front door slam shut.

Femi scrambled upright and held onto me tightly.

'No go home,' said Femi. 'No go home.'

I pulled on my trousers and stood up. I stepped outside into the corridor, shutting the door behind me. Terence stood there. He looked a little out of breath, and his complexion was even redder than usual.

'She in there, is she?' said Terence. I held my head level and stared him down, clenching my jaw.

'What's going on?'

'Don't believe anything she tells you. I'm completely in the right here. She's become unreasonable. You know what these people can be like.'

'You're not taking her back.'

'You don't understand.'

'I understand that she doesn't want to see you.'

'Son, let's be reasonable here. The woman is irrational. I want to take her back to her friends. They want to help her. Femi! Femi, come on. Come out, Femi.'

'Go away.'

'Not without her. You'd better get out of the way, son. Or I'm going to lose my temper.'

'No fucking,' shouted Femi.

'Fuck off out of my house.'

'You fuck off, son.'

He hit me in the face and I slammed into the

wall. Jesus. I was dizzy and vague as I leaned and rocked. I could feel something warm dribbling out of my nose.

'That was just a warning, all right, son? There's more of that. Now stop messing me about. I'm serious.'

I licked my lips. A sharp tang of blood. I was too stunned to move, to think. I looked up, caught his eye, and the fight glands kicked in.

'So am I.'

'You want to be a hero?'

He hit me in the stomach, and I doubled up, winded. Fuck. Pain. He hit me again, and again. I could feel there was no malice in it. I was just an object, in his way; he was doing what he thought was necessary. His face was grim and level, it was giving nothing away. The sort of face you might see on someone out for a jog, it said exertion, nothing more. I hit the deck and I was on the defensive as he took me out. I was in a bad way when he stopped. I lay, breathing hard, against the wall. I wasn't going to cry. It hurt, that was all.

'Femi?' called Terence. 'I'm coming for you.' He slammed his shoulder against the door. She must have shot the bolt; it bent but didn't open.

Fuck him. No way was that going to happen. I crawled into Pug's room, hauled myself upright and looked around.

twelve

fixed

I yanked open the top drawer with one hand. The other was across my stomach. Underwear and socks. I shoved my hand inside and scrambled around. Not there. I tried the next drawer down. Old bills, letters. Not there. Bottom drawer. More letters, keys, fags. Not there.

I stood back. I was breathing in great, gulping gasps. My heart was banging in my chest. Fuck it hurt. Where was it? Where would he hide it? I looked around the room. Posters of topless girls, football players, Bob Marley toking a zoot. A mattress sitting on bread crates. Stereo. A cupboard.

I opened the cupboard door. His clothes hung neatly inside. A pile of trainers on the floor. Not there.

Outside, I could hear Femi sobbing from behind the darkroom door.

I scanned the room, thinking, Where would I put it, if I was him? I put shaking hands to my head, fingers on my temples.

>>>fake

In the corridor outside I heard Terence shout, 'Open the door, you stupid bitch.' A dull thud; he was throwing himself at the door. He'd have it open in a second.

Pug's baseball caps, about eight of them, sat in a line across the top of the cupboard. The one on the end was black, with a white X on the front. By any means necessary. I picked it up. There. The gun sat squat and silver on the wood underneath.

I picked it up. It was cold and heavy.

Right.

I stepped outside the room into the corridor, holding the gun against my thigh, the other arm still around my stomach, fingers pushed in hard. What did I think I was doing? I felt like an idiot.

I watched Terence slam himself against the door again. He didn't even see me.

Christ. I was going to wave it around and make him go away. That was what I was going to do. I was going to make him go away.

I took three steps forward, the gun cold in my hand, the blood pounding hard in my ears. I was just a giant pair of eyes, all I could see was Terence in front of me; I was a camera. As I watched, he smashed the door again, and it opened with a crack, and he tumbled inside. Femi screamed again, louder, then her voice was a low sobbing and I heard a couple of dull thwacks; Terence was hitting her.

He dragged Femi by the elbow out of the dark-room. I raised my arm out straight and pointed the gun muzzle at his face.

'Leave her alone.'

Terence stopped dead in the corridor and looked at me.

'Jesus fuck,' said Terence. Femi looked at me, wide-eyed.

'Leave her alone,' I repeated. The gun was shaking a little. Now what?

'You fucking idiot,' said Terence. He tightened his grip on Femi's arm and she winced with pain.

'Leave her alone,' I repeated, 'and get out of my house.'

'No,' said Terence.

'If she doesn't want to go,' I said, 'she doesn't go.' The gun was wobbling. It seemed so heavy. I concentrated on keeping it pointed at Terence's big, sweating head.

'She hasn't got a choice, boy,' said Terence. 'She owes me. She works for me,' said Terence, 'or she's going to. She's got a lot of debts to pay off. The three grand I gave you, for a start. She just doesn't want to pay her debts, does she? Do you, love?' He jiggled her arm. 'Now, get out the way, son. Me and your wife have business to discuss. Get out of the way. Stop pointing that fucking thing at me.'

'Get out,' I said. I was sweating, too. I was

speaking through clenched teeth. 'Get out of here.'

'Don't be a fool, boy,' said Terence. 'You know the irony of this situation? The irony is, I'm on your side here. How do you think you're going to get your money, eh? Femi's going to earn it for you. You want your money, you move, son. Come on, now. Don't be a fool.'

'Get out,' I said.

'We've got an agreement,' said Terence. 'How do you think she's going to pay for the marriage? How do you think she's going to pay you? The deal is, I sort her out, she works for me. You get it? Get out the way, son. There's nothing you can do. And I'm grassing you to the Home Office if you don't move aside.'

'Let her go.'

'Oh, for fuck's sake,' said Terence.

'Let her go.'

'And then what?' said Terence. 'Then what?'

'You leave.'

Terence let go of Femi's arm.

'All right, see? I let go. Now what? Listen, you put that down, you let me out, with her, and I'll do you a favour. We'll forget all about it. I understand that you're a little upset, and not thinking rationally. I'll be nice. I won't report you. You'll even get the rest of the money, as promised, in a year. Put it down nice and slow. Put it down please, for fuck's sakes!'

My hand was steady now. I aimed down the barrel.

'She's not your problem,' said Terence. 'She's my problem. Let me take her away and everyone will be happy. Can't you see? Everybody's happy. You understand that, don't you? I get what I want: a worker. She gets what she wants: a passport. You get what you want: a fat wad. And my clients get what they want: relief.'

Now I understood. 'You're a pimp.'

'Sexual facilitator, if you don't mind.'

'You didn't tell her, did you? Did you?'

'Don't tell me you didn't know the score. Don't you fucking play the innocent.'

'And now you think she's yours.'

'She is mine. I own her.'

I shot him. Not deliberately. I was just going to depress the trigger a little, frighten him. I thought you had to press those things really hard. I thought it was a fucking replica, didn't I?

There was hardly a transition. One moment Terence was standing there, then he was a bloody mess on the floor. I hit him in the head. My ears rang with the sound of the shot; it echoed round and round inside my head.

Femi stood looking at me and I stood looking at her. It was like the game me and Pug used to play as kids; first person to move loses.

I was in a dream, I was underwater, I was going to be sick. I fell back against the wall, shut my eyes and let the gun slip to the floor. I opened my eyes and saw that nothing had changed. He was still

>>fake

there, laid out on the floor, blood and gunk soaking into the carpet, spattered on the wall. The smell of shit.

'He said it was fake. You heard him, didn't you? He said it was fake.' But I wasn't sorry. Not yet.

part four

ghost money

thirteen

hotels on mayfair

Sol sits in the sink behind the counter at Colosseo
Coffee, playing Tetris on a Gameboy. There's
nowhere to sit down in the shop, not even for the
customers. Like the aproned and baseball-capped
workers, or coffee consultants, they must stand; it
makes for a faster throughput.

'Sol. My turn for the seat,' says Black.

'I've only had ten minutes.'

Black bends down, takes hold of Sol's ankles and
tries to pull him down.

'Tchisin,' says Sol, kicking out. 'Nutter.' Black
lets go.

Like the shopping centre it stands in, like the city
itself, the shop is cramped, full of metal and plastic,
and gleaming clean. The bright fluorescent light
makes the display bags of coffee, the machines and
the metal instruments look immaculate, and Sol and
Black, the coffee consultants, look ill.

'Tchisin gwailo,' says Black. 'You're more tchisin
than me. You're tchisin to the max.'

Like many Hong Kong Chinese, Black uses an English name for dealing with gwailos. His choice is an obvious one; the long-haired teenager always dresses in black jeans, T-shirt and boots, his shining silver belt buckle and earring providing the only contrast. The music coming out of the shop's speakers – Cantonese heavy metal – is his idea.

The blocky shapes flowing down the screen remind Sol of the architecture in the city outside. The tower block he's building is full of holes and growing upwards, giving him less and less time to make the necessary manoeuvres to the shapes coming down fast from the top of the screen. The machine makes an electronic farting noise: Game Over. Sol gives Black the Gameboy and gets down, allowing Black to take his place.

Sol leans on the counter and closes his eyes. The back of his legs ache from standing all day and all he wants to do is go home and sleep and not be here. It's four in the afternoon, and he's passing into the delirium that hits him after working for five hours. The next two will be the worst; the final hour, when he achieves a state of numb acceptance, too tired to be pissed off or angry, is not so bad.

He prefers it when it's busy. A few customers would at least take his mind off how slow time is. This is like Chinese water torture; you go mad waiting for the next one to happen. He looks out at the shopping centre beyond the window, at the façades of a Belgian chocolate shop, Segaworld, a record store, a French-style bakery and seven clothing boutiques; but the view, so familiar it's begun to appear in his dreams, provides nothing to keep his mind occupied.

'My Cantonese is pretty good, huh?' he says. '*Yap* dollar, *yee* dollar, *san* dollar, *si* dollar. *Sai tai kafei?*'

'What?' Black glances up from the Gameboy.

'Do you want a large or a regular coffee?'

'Your tones are all wrong. You just said you like to bark like a dog.'

'*Tchisin.*'

Sol steals a muffin from the counter display and eats with his hand under his mouth to catch crumbs. He's not hungry, and it tastes of nothing, but he feels obliged to take as much advantage as he can of the absence of the shop's owner, the Uncle. Recently he has taken a childish pleasure from such tiny acts of rebellion. On his way to or from work he stands outside the designated standing zone, demarcated with yellow lines, on the platform of the MTR, the tube. He has started shoplifting for the first time in years, stealing pointless little things: a pen that writes in gold ink, a novel, a torch keyring, socks, a lighter with a picture of chairman Mao on the side which plays a tune when you open it. He knows that such dumb actions are merely expressions of protest at the sense of alienation he feels.

'Hey, lover.'

Sol looks up and breaks into a crumb-flecked

grin. A girl is striding into the shop, moving with bouncy enthusiasm, swinging a large, glossy shopping bag. Vix. She's tall and slim and wearing jeans and a crop top. Her brown hair is cut short and run through with blond highlights. Her features are large, her tanned face is lined and she looks older than her years; she's only twenty-one. She's wearing red lipstick. It's the first time Sol has seen her wear make-up in daylight.

They kiss over the counter. Vix places her hands on Sol's cheeks and waggles her tongue playfully in his mouth, then steps backwards, breaking into a grin.

'How are you doing?' Vix's Welsh accent is irresistibly exotic to Sol.

'I'm tired and pissed off and I hate my job.'

'I know. I thought I'd come and cheer you up. Hi, Black.'

'Hello,' Black mumbles. Although she has been coming into the shop most days for the last few months, he's still shy around her; he ducks his head and retreats back to his game, kicking his heels on the cupboard underneath.

'Where were you this morning?' Sol asks Vix.

'I got up at nine.'

'What for?' Vix works nights as a hostess at Sophie Chow's, a club in Central. She gets back to their room around four or five in the morning. Sol awoke at ten this morning to find her gone. A heavy sleeper, he didn't hear her come in and he didn't hear her leave; the only evidence that she'd spent the night with him was the faint smell of sandalwood perfume and shampoo in the bed, and an indentation on the pillow.

'I've been shopping.' Vix places heavy emphasis on the last word, and underlines it by simultaneously dumping the shopping bags down on the counter. The bag is big and classy; whatever is making it bulge is likely to be expensive, and immediately Sol feels anxious.

'Ah, Vix, have you Hong Konged again?'

In their private language, Hong Konging means succumbing to the desire that is constantly stimulated by streets bristling with shops and choked with ads, the desire to buy shit you don't need. Vix suffers more than Sol; she gets periodically broody, and unless Sol can talk her down, she blows half her wages on clothes. When Sol criticizes her for it, she mentions the amount he spends on film and photodeveloping. They are supposed to be saving their money, but neither have proved very good at it.

Vix lays a hand on Sol's arm. Unusually, she has red nail varnish on her short, bitten nails; she usually wears silver or blue.

'No, no, listen, you won't believe what's happened. But I'll only tell you if you make me a drink. Mocha with a chocolate shot, please.'

Sol begins to make Vix's drink. She steps back; she likes to have room when she tells a story.

'Last night, right, I was at work.'

>>>ghost money

'Yeah.'

'And I was sitting there, pissed and knackered, and I was thinking, Six quid an hour plus booze, six quid an hour plus booze. Which is one way to get through it. And these blokes come in. They're giving it the large, and they're all pretty drunk. They're regulars. Triads. Their boss is this tall, thin guy who speaks good English. And there was this other boss type there, a new guy, from the mainland. He had these bodyguards with tattoos. And he picked me to sit with him. Well, you know what it's like when you sit with triads. They get pissed off their faces and try to feel you up, and start hitting each other with ashtrays to see who's hardest. So I'm like, can I even be bothered? But I went through the motions, you know, and we did all the usual, drinking and playing dice and singing karaoke and that. I just sat there most of the time.'

'Isn't that what happens every night?'

Sol puts two squirts of chocolate sauce into her drink, the way she likes it. She has a sweet tooth.

'Listen, listen.' Vix slaps the counter, and rushes to the end of her story. 'The point is the tip this guy left me when they went.'

'A thousand dollars?' suggests Sol, stirring the drink.

'Exactly.'

Sol stops and the liquid swirls around the rigid spoon.

'Fuck. A hundred quid? For getting pissed and

172

singing?' To earn that he'd have to sweat over an espresso machine for, what, four days.

'No, no, a thousand US dollars.'

'What?'

'It's the biggest tip anyone's ever got. All the other girls were really jealous.'

Sol puts the drink down on the counter. 'Jesus. Vix, that's brilliant. What have you bought?'

'No, it gets better. This guy said he'd like to take me out shopping. So I met him this morning, and we've just been trawling the stores all day.'

Sol begins to make himself a cappuccino, his fifth of the shift. In the five months he's worked here Sol has become a raging caffeine addict. He allows himself a coffee every hour and a half, on top of the two he drinks when he begins work. Unless, as now, the Uncle goes walkabout, he has to pay for them – employees are permitted only one free drink (regular sized) per day – and they take a considerable slice out of his wages. On his one day off a week, the first thing he does, before heading off to wander the city and take photos, is go into the shop, lean against the other side of the counter, and get Black to fix him a drink.

Sol has to turn aside to work the espresso machine. He's glad he has something to do, and that Vix doesn't see his expression. He knows she would find his jealousy absurd. Ever since Vix started working as a hostess he has feared that a customer will charm her away from him. They offer glamour

>>>ghost money

and wealth; good restaurants, stylish bars, hotel rooms with double beds and air-conditioning. All he can give her is the stale sandwiches and muffins he takes home after his shift.

'Look what I've got.'

Sol looks over his shoulder as Vix reaches into the bag and draws out a cuddly toy, a fluffy green rabbit with giant eyes.

'We went to an arcade and I won this on the hoopla.' Its ears flop up and down as she waves it around. 'I'm going to call him Vomit.'

'Are you sure that's appropriate?'

She strokes the toy's spiky fur.

'He's a punk bunny.' She puts the toy down on the counter, reaches into the bag again and pulls out a black rubber shoulder bag, bristling with pointy spikes.

'And I got this. Funky, huh? And this.'

She drops the shoulder bag back into the shopping bag and reaches inside again. She pulls out a silvery blue dress that ripples in the light. She holds the dress against her with one crossed arm.

'This is amazing. I tried it on in the shop and it's like wearing warm water. It clings in all the right places and it only comes down to here.'

Vix puts her free hand level with her upper thigh. Sol puts his drink down on the counter and leans close to Vix.

'What's he like?'

Vix puts her hand on his arm.

'He's old, ugly and rich. He's from Shanghai, and he's going back there in two days.'

'You said you weren't going to go out with customers.'

'He's just this bloke who wants to spend loads of money on me. Look what else I've got.' She takes her hand away, drops the dress back in the bag and pulls out a blue case the size of a paperback.

'Has he asked you to shag him?'

'He's harmless. He wants to hold my hand, that's all.'

'You held his hand? Did you take his hand or did he take yours?'

'Sol, I'm a status symbol. He just wants to impress his friends. He wants a nice white girl hanging off his arm. I'm decoration.'

'You hang off his arm?' Sol picks a sachet of sugar out of the dispenser on the counter, holds it between his fingers and swings it back and forth.

'Check this out.' Vix flicks the catch on the case and opens it up. Inside, a slim, silver watch sparkles on a bed of red velvet. Sol peers at the oval face, hardly larger than his fingernail. There are diamonds where the numbers should be.

Vix nods at her own watch, a cheap digital from Temple market. It says 'Happy Birthday' on the strap and speaks the time in Chinese when you press a button on the face.

'He said this wasn't beautiful enough.'

'Fuck. Vix, this guy must really like you. Are you going to wear this?'

'No, it's crass.'

'Why did you choose it then?'

'It was the most expensive one in the shop. And look what else I've got.' Vix picks out a scrap of paper tucked beneath the velvet, and waves it in Sol's face.

'A receipt.'

'Correct. You win tonight's star prize. Get the picture now, muppet features?'

'He's going after the handover?'

'This guy is our ticket off this fucking island. Fuck slogging our guts out for months and scrimping and saving. I let him buy me stuff, he goes, we take it all back to the shop, and we're out of here before you can say jammy dodgers.'

Vix takes the watch out and dangles it in front of Sol.

'Hotels on Mayfair.'

Vix and Sol met on the plane from Calcutta to Hong Kong. They were sitting next to each other. Both were broke, and were heading to the colony to look for work. They toasted the happy coincidence and got drunk together. As the plane began its descent, dipping towards the clutch of skyscrapers, Vix told Sol to imagine they were beginning a game of Monopoly. The metaphor stuck.

Sol sips his drink.

'He wants to take me out again tomorrow. He's

going to take me to lunch, and then more shopping.'

'What if he asks to shag you?'

'I'll say no.'

'Have you told him you've got a boyfriend?'

'If he asks, I'll tell him. And if he asks if I love the guy, I'll say yes.'

'What if I said you can't see him?'

'I'm not seeing him. He just buys me things. But if that makes you unhappy, you can try telling me not to go tomorrow. I'll ignore you, but you can tell me anyway. Come on Sol, think about it. I'll give you some money. We can get out of here. I'm so excited.'

Vix puts her hands on Sol's cheeks and plants a kiss on his nose.

'Uncle coming!' hisses Black. In one fluid movement, like a t'ai chi step, Black launches himself out of the sink and into position beside the espresso machine, while secreting the Gameboy in the pouch of his apron.

Sol steps back quickly. In the shopping centre he sees a thin, suited figure walking swiftly towards them. He pushes his drink towards Vix.

'Take this.' He opens a cupboard behind him. 'The music.' He stretches for the controls of the CD player inside and ejects the disc. 'Shit, shit.' He takes another CD from the top of the player and puts it on. Too late.

'What is this rubbish?' The Uncle is in the shop and in Sol's face without having seemed to have crossed the intervening space, as if he's in command of a limited teleportation device.

The Uncle has a clipped public-school accent, manner and haircut. He's English and wants everyone to know it; his tie has a repeated design of tiny cricket bats. Like most of the other expats Sol has met, or rather served, he's arrogant, talentless and rich, the three qualities Sol most despises.

Madame Butterfly wafts from the speakers.

'It's Pavarotti,' says Sol.

'What was on before it?'

'It wasn't Pavarotti.'

'And what are the rules?'

'We only play Pavarotti.'

'And why is that?'

'Because coffee's Italian, and so is he.'

Sol has developed a profound hatred of opera.

'Right.' The Uncle stretches the syllable into a patronizing drawl. 'Give me an iced tea.'

Vix slips the case and the bunny back in the bag and thoughtfully considers her two drinks. Black begins to prepare the tea, leaving Sol on corporate hospitality.

The Uncle makes a big thing of splaying his leather wallet and paying for his drink – an attempt, Sol guesses, to set an example to his staff.

Sol rings up the sale.

'I leave you two unsupervised for an afternoon and you completely take the Michael. I thought I could trust you. You have a sloppy attitude, Sol.'

Black hands the Uncle his tea in a transparent plastic cup. He takes a straw from the dispenser, inserts it in the lid with a pop and sucks.

I hate you, thinks Sol. For you I've busted a gut and been treated like a machine. And I've had to wear a fucking apron. You posh ponce.

The Uncle sucks heavily on his cup and Sol notes the way his eyes bulge. Bug-eyed posh ponce.

He tips the cup towards Sol. The straw points like an accusing finger. 'You shouldn't be kissing people,' he glances at Vix, 'or playing computer games or eating the food – oh yes, I saw you – or not playing Pavarotti. You can both consider yourselves severely reprimanded. You're both on a warning. And it's not your first, is it, Sol?'

Sol looks at Vix. Being told off in front of her has made him angry. An image of her new watch rises unbidden in his mind. He can't buy her shit but at least he's got some pride.

'Ah, fuck off,' says Sol. He takes off his baseball cap and slaps it down on the counter. He pulls the apron's top loop over his head, unties the string around his waist and lets the apron fall to the floor.

'Well, well,' says the Uncle.

Sol raises the hinged section of the counter. He concentrates on keeping his composure as he steps out into the shop. The Uncle takes a step away from him. Vix picks up the shopping bag. Sol focuses hard on the door as he steps towards it.

He hardly hears the Uncle.

'Don't you think this is rather rash?'

Vix joins Sol at the exit and they stroll into the shopping centre. Sol, feeling about eight feet tall, suppresses the urge to look back.

'I'd buy you an expensive watch', he says, 'if I had any money.'

'I wouldn't like you any more for it,' says Vix. 'You realize you're going to be cut off from your coffee supply?' She squeezes his arm. 'Maybe that's just as well.'

fourteen

promenading

Sol steps out of the mall on the bottom floor of
Chungking Mansions, the tower block in which he
lives, and onto Nathan Road. He takes a drag on
his cigarette, a Double Happiness, and steps up to
the pedestrian crossing. A cluster of people waiting
for the green light watch him as he dashes through
a gap in the traffic and crosses the road.

He moves slowly along Peking Road, with no
particular destination in mind, out of step with all
the clean, modern people going up and down the
clean, modern street.

He passes the Bottoms Up club, a dark doorway
framed by glossy photos of half-naked women with
stars over their nipples.

The first time Sol saw this place – as he walked
the streets with Vix on the night of their arrival –
he was struck with a powerful sense of déjà vu. Vix
suggested, in a sardonic tone, that he had been here
in a previous life. Then he remembered. James
Bond nearly got shot outside here, in *The Man*

With The Golden Gun. He ran through what he remembered of the scene. Scaramanga put his clever gun together and leaned out of an upper-storey window. The dashing spy walked along the alley below – this alley here. The shot. A man walking behind Bond dropped, dead. Sol felt a sense of reflected glamour, and drew half-serious parallels with his own situation and that of the British secret agent. He, too, was embarking on a dangerous mission in an exotic foreign location. He even had a glamorous and mysterious woman to flirt with. The thought consoled him as they looked for the cheapest hostel.

It's a muggy afternoon. The pavement is busier than usual. The street is choked with upmarket cars and red taxis. The majority of pedestrians are neat, well-dressed Chinese. Most of the rest are Western, and easily divisible into expats – in suits or casual clothes – and tourists – less fashionably dressed and slower moving. Wearing plimsolls, faded jeans, a ragged T-shirt and multi-pocketed waistcoat, with a camera around his neck, Sol looks like a tourist down on his luck. The occasional brown face moves among the crowd and no other black ones.

Sol passes the stairs that lead down to the underground McDonalds and smiles as another memory rises. In their second week here, he and Vix spent a couple of afternoons down there. Their money had run out and they had yet to receive their first pay. They would buy shakes and sit down, keeping an eye out for diners who left without finishing. On spotting one, they moved over to the vacated table and discreetly ate the leftovers. Vix, being vegetarian, would eat the buns and fries or the discs of egg from inside discarded McMuffins, leaving him with the burgers and the gherkins. Not having enough to eat was a disturbing experience; an obsession with food precluded almost all other thought. But Sol's memory of the hours spent there is a good one. It was there that they became more than just friends sharing adversity. There, over the remains of someone else's Happy Meal, they kissed for the first time.

Sol walks on. He's in a good mood, and a chirpy tune rattles around his head; 'Super Job! Super Job! Super, Super Jo-ob!' He watches so much ad-saturated TV here that sometimes he feels colonized by jingles.

He passes a beggar prostrated on the edge of the pavement, his face wrapped up in cloth, kowtowing before his begging bowl. His shoes are the same make as Sol's. Two suited men walk past, side by side, one Chinese, one Western, both talking into mobile phones. Sol fires off a photo, shooting secretly, without looking through the viewfinder. He doubts if it will be a good one; the image will be too easy because the contrast is too obvious, like the postcard pictures of junks in the harbour with skyscrapers in the background.

He avoids the temptation to look into the

window of a camera shop and turns to look at the Welcome Supermarket on the other side of the road. He considers going inside just for a blast of the air-conditioning.

Sol speeds up and moves to the outside of the pavement as he passes a branch of Colosseo Coffee. He hopes he'll be screened from the staff by other pedestrians and the three pilots in Alitalia uniforms, downing espressos at the counter. He knows the workers in there slightly, but doesn't want to say hello. No doubt the supervisor there will have heard of his resignation the day before, and might ask if he has another job, and smirk when he says no. The thought awakens a worry. Sol doesn't know what he will do now. He has a little money saved, enough to tide him over for a couple of weeks, but he will have to find a new job soon. He has a vague idea that he'll go to Wanchai and ask for work in the bars. But now is not a good time; some are closing down, which means more competition. The thought of going through the whole job search process again – cold calling, dressing up, lying – depresses him. He feels that after six months he's right back where he started.

Tomorrow, Sol decides, tomorrow I'll worry about it; today I'm on holiday. To prove it to himself, he decides to go to the art gallery overlooking the harbour. It's only five dollars to get in if you say you're a student, and the sofas are the most comfortable he has ever sat in. He turns left onto Kowloon Park Drive and walks the fifty or so metres south to Salisbury Road, beyond which lies the seafront zone, a long plaza surrounded by ostentatiously modern buildings.

There are more tourists here than usual; sitting on the steps of the Cultural Centre, milling around, walking along the promenade or stood at the railings looking at the harbour and the skyscrapers beyond it on Hong Kong Island. He realizes they are here for the changeover at midnight tonight. It will be a big party. Sol hasn't paid it much attention. It's not his England leaving the place. The only way the event has impinged on his life is the way the now almost continuous coverage messes up the TV schedules.

His destination momentarily forgotten, Sol strolls down the wide, paved promenade. It's lined on one side with benches and the other with a railing. All around, people have their cameras out and are taking pictures of each other with the view as a backdrop. Photographing your spouse, Sol believes, is the most popular hobby in this city. He snaps people snapping.

Sol looks through his camera's viewfinder, down the line of people along the railing, composing a shot of a receding row of backs. He's careful to cut the skyscrapers, the subject of their gazes, out of the frame. The striking similarity of most of the poses – weight on one leg, the other bent back, front part of the shoe on the ground, arms on the rail, head

forward – is thrown into relief by the few excep-
tions – a Chinese child stood on the bottom rail,
hands on the top, leaning back, a Western girl in a
short blue dress at the edge of the shot, stood
upright with her arms folded. Sol lowers the
camera. He looks again, takes in the girl's hair, the
curve at the back of her knees, her trainers and the
friendship band around one of her sockless ankles.
Vix. Only the dress is unfamiliar – this morning, she
again left the room before he woke up – and it's a
second before he realizes it is the dress she showed
him yesterday.

Sol approaches. 'Hey, gorgeous,' he calls.

Vix turns. Her expression on seeing him is not
the impish grin of delight he hopes for; she looks
taken aback, then uncomfortable. She's wearing an
unfamiliar perfume. Her face is subtly, but artfully,
made up. On her wrist is a thin slither of silver.
The watch.

'Sol,' says Vix, 'what a surprise. How are you?'
Her tone is unusual; she sounds like a bad actress.

The Chinese man leaning on the rail next to her
turns around and watches them.

'I'm well,' says Sol, in a similar tone of strained
naturalism; her reaction has confused him.

'Good. I'd like you to meet my friend, Mr Li.'

'Hello,' says the Chinese man, with a heavy
accent.

Mr Li is short, shorter than Vix, stocky and fairly
light-skinned. Rolled-up shirtsleeves expose broad

arms. His face is fleshy and topped with an efficient crew-cut. Late forties, Sol reckons.

'Friend, Victoria?'

Sol can hardly understand him.

'Yes,' says Sol. He looks at Vix, who has fixed a smile on her face.

'African?'

'What?' says Sol.

'No, he's English,' Vix says to Li.

'English gentleman.' Li smiles, revealing crooked teeth. Sol wonders why he hasn't had them fixed.

Li nods curtly. 'Good.'

A pause. Sol stares out at the distant skyscrapers and their wobbling reflections in the water. Though now familiar, it's a view that inspires mixed feelings in him. It's spectacular but clinical; he finds something oppressive in the myriad of angles. In a way it reminds him of the estate at home.

'Job?' says Li suddenly.

'What's your job?' says Vix to Sol.

Sol holds up the camera.

'I'm a photographer.'

Li claps thick-fingered hands together

'Very good. Very good. You take picture?'

'Yes.' Sol holds up the camera.

'Picture me, Victoria.'

'What?'

'I no camera. You picture me Victoria.'

Sol shakes his head.

'What?'

'He wants you to take a picture of me and him,' says Vix.

'What?' says Sol.

'Pay money,' says Li.

'How much?' asks Sol, unconsciously twisting the rings of his lens.

'Fifteen dollar.'

'US dollar?'

'Hong Kong dollar.'

'Twenty-five.'

'Fifteen.'

Sol can't think of a reason to refuse.

'OK,' he says slowly.

'Here.' Li strikes a casual pose, one hand on the rail, one on his hip, head high. Sol retreats a few steps and holds the camera up. Vix shuffles closer to Li, her hands on her thighs.

Sol decides to take a terrible picture. Peering through the viewfinder, he moves sideways so that Vix is slightly closer than Li, thus exaggerating the difference in height. He takes one step further so that a particularly large skyscraper in the background will appear to be emerging from the top of Li's head.

'Smile,' he says. Vix looks straight at him, her face blank. Li arranges his mouth into a grin. Sol pauses a moment, until Li's face is a study in insincerity, then snaps.

'Good,' says Li. 'Again.'

Li takes Vix by the elbow and arranges her in

front of him on the promenade. Mentally, Sol shrugs. It's easy money, and someone is treating him like a proper photographer.

Passing pedestrians speed up to move out of shot, or stand and wait. Sol takes a picture and they move on.

Vix sits on a bench and Li stands behind it. Li sits on the bench and Vix stands in front of him. Vix and Li sit on the bench.

Sol peers through the viewfinder and feels like he's far away. Li fusses over details of background, dress and pose. He seems to be enjoying himself.

Vix leans with her back against the rail, and Li stands facing her, in profile. Vix stands in front of a big blobby abstract sculpture that sits on a plinth at the back of the wide promenade, and Li peers through one of its holes.

Li holds up his hand; enough. Sol and Vix face each other. Instantly Vix is the person he knows. She pulls down on the hem of her dress, blows a stream of air through pursed lips. He can read her; she's bored, pissed off. She raises her thick eyebrows. Sol shrugs. Then Li pockets the comb and turns around, and Vix smiles cheerily, putting on a face as easily as a pair of sunglasses. Sol is alarmed at how accomplished she is. He has never witnessed her professional side before, and the reality of what she does for a living hits him. At the same time he wonders if she ever does this with him.

'Last,' says Li. He stands on the promenade, back to the view, in front of Vix. Sol crouches down for a low shot and peers. He pulls them into focus and is shocked to see a demonic grimace on Vix's face. Her mouth is stretched as wide as it can go, her top lip is pulled back, her nose wrinkled.

'Lovely,' says Sol, and shoots.

'No more I,' says Li, 'take picture Victoria.'

'What?' says Sol.

'More picture Victoria.'

'He wants you to take some pictures of me,' says Vix.

Li sits down on a bench and mops his brow with the back of his hand. Sol is aware of him watching as he takes a head shot of Vix.

'More,' says Li.

To take another, Sol lowers himself with spread legs, so that Vix's jaw is more prominent, her cheeks fuller, her broad forehead lowered. Out of loyalty to the subject, he wants to make these pictures good.

'More,' says Li, and claps.

Half-profile, profile, full figure, portrait. Sol shoots quickly, moving around her, making her move. He forgets the situation and concentrates on getting the shots right. She's a good model; natural-looking, not quite catching the camera's eye. He has taken her picture often, but never, he realizes, in this way – without context, just to make her look attractive. Then it's over and the film rewinds, buzzing like an insect.

Sol crouches down to keep the camera in shadow as he guts it. Vix stands and taps her fingers on the rail, looking at the view. Li, on the bench, watches Vix while getting a slim metal container, not much bigger than a credit card, out of his pocket. It occurs to Sol that this composition, the three figures equally spaced apart at different levels on the bright paving, each involved in their own small, private actions, might make a more interesting photograph. A more truthful one, anyway. It's a joke, he thinks, to say that cameras never lie. They always lie.

Sol moves to hand the canister to Li, who waves him away. 'Hotel,' he says, 'tonight.' He slides a business card out of the container, and takes a bright metal pen out of his shirt pocket. 'Eight, five, seven,' he says, and writes the numbers on the back of the card, and then the name of a hotel. Sol recognizes it; one of the most expensive in the city, he has heard.

'His room number,' says Vix. 'I assume.'

Li hands over the card, holding it with both hands in the formal way.

'Ten. Pay money.'

'Ten o'clock. Right,' says Sol.

'Very good to meet you,' says Li.

'Yeah. Yeah,' says Sol.

'Good.' Li turns to Vix. 'Tired?'

191

'No.'

'Shopping?' says Li.

'That would be nice.'

Li stands up. 'Mr Sol,' he says. 'Goodbye.'

'Yeah,' says Sol.

'Goodbye,' says Li.

'Yeah. Goodbye.'

'Goodbye Sol,' says Vix. 'Nice to see you again.'

'Yeah,' says Sol, 'and you. Goodbye.'

fifteen

telefishion

Sol lies on his bed, his hands behind his neck, looking up at the circular blur made by the spinning blades of the ceiling fan. He has just discovered that if you stare at it for long enough you see a spiral rotating inside a circle. From the TV set mounted on the wall in the corner comes a stream of Cantonese, sounding, to him, like birdsong or animal impressions. The blades whir, the language bubbles. He doesn't want to be doing this, but he can't think of anything better to do. Even watching TV has no appeal. He looks forward to feeling like having a cigarette.

The problem, he concludes, is that his mind is thinking too hard to stop and decide what his body should do. At least before, he thinks, he was busy, and he didn't have to think.

He looks aside at Vix's Happy Birthday watch on the shelf by the bed, next to a glossy paper wallet of photographs. Eight thirty. Normally, he would have got home from work about fifteen minutes

193

ago. He would be sitting here with Vix and they would be eating a takeaway meal with disposable chopsticks: Rice and vegetable with an egg and brown gunk, perhaps, with muffins for after. Then they'd maybe have sex, Vix would go to work and he would watch TV: Cantonese soap operas, the racing highlights, American films, anything. At closedown, instead of a blank screen one channel showed *Telefishion*, a steady shot of an aquarium. Sometimes he watched that too. He thinks about his favourite character, the angelfish, who acts like a true professional, teasing the viewer with glimpses of his fins before making a grand entrance from behind a lump of coral, doing a circuit of the tank, then gliding stylishly back into hiding.

Caffeine withdrawal is making him twitchy. He thinks about how good a double shot cappuccino would be now. At least before . . . No. He reminds himself that his life was crap before. He was a machine. A machine which didn't have to do any thinking, though, or make any decisions; whose future, although uncomfortable, was assured.

A cockroach, looking like a tiny toy sports car, begins walking up the wall. Sol wonders if he should get up and squash it. But Vix always asks him not to; apparently, they keep their eggs under their wings, and when you squash them the eggs fly everywhere and the end result is more cockroaches. God knows how many there are in the room already. Sometimes at night he imagines them all, holding raves and rallies in the darkness under the bed. The cockroach looks insolently at ease, like it owns the place, which Sol reflects, it pretty much does. It was here before he arrived, and it will be here after he has left.

The door opens and the cockroach scuttles back down to its HQ. Vix stands in the doorway, still wearing the blue dress and carrying a shopping bag.

'Hi,' she says.

Sol sits up. Behind her he can see the narrow tiled corridor and the door of the room opposite theirs, open as usual, and through it a pair of pale hairless legs stretched on a bed, lit up blue in the glow from a TV.

'Hello,' says Sol, trying to sound nonchalant. 'It's late.'

'I've been dragged around the shops.'

'Did you have a good time?'

'No.'

Vix takes one step inside, pushes the door to, takes another step forward to the bed, sits down on it and kicks off her trainers. Sol shifts up for her.

The room is barely big enough to swing one of its cockroaches in. The bed, the TV and the shelf are the only furniture. The single bed is almost, but not quite, long enough for Sol to stretch out on. Vix and Sol's stuff is under it or on the floor next to it, about the only place it can be.

'I'm knackered,' says Vix.

'You haven't done anything.'

'Nodding and smiling and shopping. It's all work. What have you been up to?'

'Watching TV.'

Sol glances at the TV. It's showing a historical drama set in China. It's subtitled in Mandarin. He put it on for the weird hairstyles. The men have a long pigtail on the back half of their heads and the front half is shaved smooth, and the women have mutant beehives.

Vomit the bunny grins down at him from the top of the set.

'How was it after,' says Sol, 'with Li?'

'OK. Boring. He got me this.'

Vix pulls a box out of the shopping bag. Chinese characters are printed around a picture of a camera on the side. She begins to open it. 'I'm going to keep it,' she says, and pulls a camera – an ergonomic Nikon – out by the shoulder strap.

'You want me to show you how to use it?'

'Oh no, it's all electronic.' She hands it over. 'It does all the complicated stuff for you. You just point the thing.'

Sol examines it. It looks expensive. 'Nice, Vix; it's really nice.' On the top, there's an LCD display and a lot of little buttons. Sol presses a few and watches the display change. It reminds him of Black's Gameboy. He has only the vaguest idea how it works.

Vix picks up the wallet of photos on the bedside cabinet.

'These the pictures?' she says.

'Yeah. They're terrible.'

The first few are images of Vix and Li on the promenade. Vix studies each for a second, then puts it down beside her on the bed.

Sol puts the camera on the cabinet. Unwilling to join Vix in scrutinizing the pictures, he looks at the collage of photos tacked above the bed, an attempt to make the room, with its windowless white walls, look more homely. Most are black-and-white pictures he took in India. One of the images, a picture of a group of fishermen beating a man with palm leaves, is scarred with a furious biro scribble. Sol blames the fishermen for the fact that he is here, convinced that it must have been one of them who stole his money. Last week, getting back after his shift in the coffee shop, Sol defaced the image in a sudden fit of anger, while imagining what he would like to do to the man who robbed him. The print next to it is a full-figure portrait of Lee, dressed only in striped cotton trousers, stood on the left side of the porch outside their tourist home in Goa. If it wasn't for Lee, who lent him three hundred pounds – just more than the price of a train ticket to Calcutta and a flight to Hong Kong – Sol would, he feels, have been completely fucked.

'They look all right,' says Vix; 'they're all in focus.'

'But they're boring.'

'They look OK. That one's good.' She points to

a picture on the bed of her and Li standing by the railing, skyscrapers jagged behind them.

'The composition's crap.'

'What's wrong with it?'

'You're too far apart.'

'It's nice.'

'You know, this will be the first time I've ever been paid for taking pictures?'

'There you go,' says Vix, 'you're on your way. You're a professional photographer now.' She returns to flicking through the images, and Sol watches her as if the contours of her face will reveal what she's thinking.

Vix holds up a portrait photo of herself. 'Can I have this one? It's the nicest picture anyone's taken of me. Ever.'

'You mean it's flattering.'

Vix smiles. 'Yeah.'

Sol strokes her hair and kisses her on the neck. Vix takes off the silver watch and lays it on the shelf.

'I don't want anything else off him,' she says. 'I'm glad he's going tomorrow.' She puts her arms around Sol and they lie on the bed with their faces a few inches apart.

Sol strokes her back. 'I thought you said he was a gangster. He looked ordinary to me.'

'Didn't you see the bodyguards?'

'No.' Sol pulls back an inch; he's interested now.

'They were standing by the railing.'

'No way.' Sol casts his mind back, but can't think

go>> simon lewis

of any likely candidates. The thought that he was being watched by silent men – he imagines them wearing sunglasses and sharp black suits – makes him retrospectively self-conscious.

'Maybe he's the head of gangs of bank robbers and drug smugglers.'

'Maybe he runs a construction firm and gets workers beaten up for joining a union.'

'He must be making a deal with the other guy, the one who speaks English. Now the border's opening they've decided to get together. Or—'

'Or he runs a factory making computer components,' says Sol. Vix looks into Sol's face.

'You've got such a squishy nose, you know.' Sol moves closer, hauls himself up so his face is over hers and begins to kiss her.

'Mind,' she says, 'you're lying on the photos.' She disengages and sweeps the pictures onto the floor. Grinning, she wraps herself around him. Sol squeezes her closer, and they kiss deeply. The fan whirs and the TV bubbles. Sol draws her dress up her thighs. The material is soft and feels almost weightless. She slips off the shoulder straps, making a soft grumbling noise at the back of her throat which he loves. They change position; he pulls the dress off, kisses her belly and thighs, and pulls down her pants. He goes down on her till his tongue is numb. The TV programme finishes and the news comes on, in English. Changeover stuff, who's arriving and what they're saying. Now they can understand the speech, it's a distraction; Sol gets up and turns off the set. He strips, and they make love.

Afterwards, they lie face-to-face.

'I went to a travel agents today,' murmurs Vix, stroking Sol's back. He is still inside her, enjoying the cosiness of the contact.

'What for?'

'Thailand's really cheap from here. And Indonesia. And it's nothing to go to China. I quite fancy China. I haven't been there. Temples. Kung Fu. Communists.'

'What will you do when you've been every-where?'

'I'll go to Area fifty-one and find a spaceship to beam me up.'

'I don't know, Vix. I haven't got much money.'

'I said I'll pay for you.'

'I don't want charity.'

'Well, you shouldn't have given up your job then, should you? I'll give you a few thousand dollars.'

'I won't live off a woman.'

'Well, it's either that or make some money fast, then.' Vix pulls back and Sol slips out of her. 'I don't understand you. I hate it here as much as you, you know.' Vix glances at the silver watch. Nine thirty. 'I've got to get ready for work.' She gets off the bed and pulls jeans and a T-shirt out from under it. Sol lights a Double Happiness and watches her dress.

'Do you ever think about going home?' he asks.

Vix, rooting around in her make-up bag, looks momentarily alarmed. 'What for? There's nothing there. It's boring.' She looks down into the bag, and her groping fingers move faster. 'I'd rather be here, even, than there. What's there? People only stay there 'cause it's convenient. Like it's handy for the shops. Fuck, where's my fucking eyeshadow? You'd better get up, you've got to go and see Li soon.'

'Yeah, yeah.'

Sol reflects that Vix often talks about the places she's been in the last two years, about Vietnam and Cambodia and India and Thailand, but rarely mentions her home beyond the occasional wish that her friends could see her now. He has the impression she's always been like this: living in the present, wandering. He can't even imagine what she was like before she left Wales.

'I'll come with you,' says Sol.

Vix looks up sharply.

'To China?'

'Out.'

Vix leaves the room, carrying her make-up. Sol changes into the shirt he keeps for interviews and his only clean trousers, a pair of green jeans. He picks the photos off the floor, slips them back in the wallet and puts it in his back pocket. He joins Vix, who's touching up her lipstick in the cracked full-length mirror in the corridor. Standing behind her and to the side, he checks himself out. The jeans are the only luxury he has bought himself in weeks, and now they feel like a fashion error.

Fred, the owner of the guest house, an elderly Chinese man in slippers, a vest and baggy boxer shorts – his habitual outfit – squeezes past them, saying hello.

The lift takes ages; there are only two for the whole block, so they use the stairs. They live on the fifteenth floor, and these days Sol has thighs to be proud of. On their way down, they nod greetings to an Indian couple heading up to the twelfth floor, the Nigerian hairdresser standing by his chair on the stairwell of the tenth, the six-foot Chinese transvestite talking to a customer on the seventh.

The mall at the bottom of Chungking Mansions is full of poky stores, jammed with clothes, plastic toys, pornography, watches and electronics. They eat a plate of dahl and rice in a cramped café and watch the owner arguing with two customers in what Vix identifies as Bengali. She has a flair for languages and is always picking up phrases; she can say 'fuck off' and 'I love you' in nine different tongues.

The transition onto Nathan Road is like stepping from Brixton into Oxford Street. It's dark and raining hard. The blocky buildings are dressed up in tarty neon. Streets that feel like Basildon in the daytime now look like the Blade Runner set. Vix hails a taxi and Sol stands on the pavement under the shelter of an awning and waves her out of sight.

go>>> simon lewis

He considers going back to the room for his coat, but balks at the effort. He hunches his shoulders, dips his head and walks down the road towards the harbour.

Shop windows bristling with electronics spill light onto the pavement. Girls, Girls, Girls. Instant Credit. Seems like every other building is a strip joint or a bank. The traders that hustle the passers-by don't give him a second glance; he hasn't got a money glow. Sol feels less at home in the streets than he does in the giant stack of inner city that is the mansions; here, he feels more of an alien, an impostor even, too poor and too badly dressed to be legitimately walking around.

He spots a damp banknote in the gutter and dives to pick it up. He smooths it out and smiles at his mistake. 'Currency of the Otherworld', it says on the face, '$1,000,000,000' next to the head of a stern Chinese deity. Ghost money, the stuff burnt at funerals so the deceased will be rich in heaven. He puts it in his wallet anyway, and hurries along.

Mr Li's hotel is only a few minutes' walk away, but Sol is drenched by the time he arrives. The doormen don't let him in until he shows them Li's card. Inside, it is cool and spacious, the nearest thing to a palace he has ever been in. The lobby reminds him of an art gallery; the same wanton stretches of empty space, the same hush. The uniformed staff stand stiffly behind the reception desk, like dummies in a window display. Guests sit in

>>>ghost money

armchairs or stroll about, all looking like they own the place. The marble floor tut tuts as he crosses it in his plimsolls. Sol feels himself coming under heavy scrutiny and becomes more aggressively defensive with every step. Who do these people think they are anyway?

The lift is bigger than his room and more comfortable to be in. There's a man in there whose job is to press the button he is told to press. It can't be much of a job, thinks Sol, who would rather press his own buttons. Soft music plays and there's a pot plant in the corner. It feels wrong somehow, keeping a plant in a lift. He gets off at the eighth floor, the top, into a corridor which is as silent as a temple. His feet make no sound on the carpet.

The door to Li's suite is answered by a broad, muscular Chinese man in shirtsleeves, who holds the door open and steps aside for Sol to enter. He takes a step inside, and pauses as he takes in the room. It is the kind of place he has only ever seen on TV, in costume dramas; it could be a drawing room in an English country house but for the ceiling fan and the view from the window of Hong Kong Island's skyscrapers – a series of black blocks now, peppered with neon squiggles. Sol wonders where the bed is, and spots a couple of doors. Jesus. So this is how the other 0.1 per cent live.

The door is closed behind him and the man freezes, blank-faced, beside it, like he's trying to win a who-can-look-most-like-a-statue competition. An opponent, pretty much identical, stands in the corner of the room by the window. The bodyguards, Sol assumes.

In the centre of the room sits a glass table with two large, black, inviting chairs on one side, a sofa on the other. Li is on the sofa, his legs apart, head bent low over the table in front of him, exposing a thick, square neck. Next to him sits a tall, thin Chinese man with a pinched pale face, dressed in a sharp black suit and a gold tie. His hair is mid-length and carefully arranged. He holds a cigarette, primed elegantly in his right hand. His legs are crossed and his upraised right foot wags slowly up and down.

Li looks up and nods at Sol. 'Ah, hello.' He waves him forward encouragingly, and Sol feels a little less uneasy.

It takes seven steps to reach the table. The carpet feels more comfortable than Sol's mattress. He pulls the wallet of photos out of his back pocket.

'I've got the pictures.' He holds them out. Li takes them from him, then gestures at the man next to him.

'Friend. Good English.'

'Good evening,' says the man, his voice crisp and unaccented. He nods curtly. 'Nice to meet you. My English name is Jeremy.'

'Sol,' says Sol. He feels awkward and exposed standing on this carpet in this room, with all these men looking at him.

'Drink whisky?' asks Li.

'Yeah. Yes.'

'Sit. Sit.' Sol perches on the end of a chair opposite Li. Li says something to Statue Two, who raises his head attentively. You lose, thinks Sol. Statue Two fixes Sol a drink from a cabinet by the wall with hands that make the bottle look cute, like a toy.

Li begins to rifle through the pictures, a smile breaking out on his face.

'You are a photographer,' says Jeremy, looking at Sol with an appraising gaze that makes him conscious of his damp and rumpled clothes.

'Yes.'

'Are you here to cover the handover?'

'No,' says Sol. 'There's a million photographers here doing that. I'm just travelling around, taking pictures. I'm here to make some money.'

'Of course,' says Jeremy.

'Are you from China as well?'

'No. I am, how do you say, indigent.'

Statue Two gives Sol a glass and Sol notices a tattoo of a sinewy Chinese dragon curling round his upper arm and down towards his wrist. The boggle-eyed, wide-jawed head sits just below his elbow.

Li has found a picture he seems to like. He holds it close to his face, then leans back to look at it from further away, cocking his head a little to the side.

'Very good,' he tells Sol, then leans across and fires a stream of Mandarin at Jeremy. Jeremy translates while Li grins at Sol.

'Mr Li would like you to know that the pictures are wonderful. He says you have the eye.'

'Yeah. Yes.'

Li says something in Mandarin to Sol, and Jeremy translates.

'He says she is a pretty one.'

'Yes.'

Sol sips. It goes down smoothly. He puts the glass on the table. Chink. Jeremy leans forward and taps ash into a crystal ashtray. Sol had taken it for an ornament. Jeremy leans back.

'Mr Li would like me to ask you something. Victoria – are you very close to her?'

Sol picks up the glass again and turns it in his hand. 'She's . . . she's my friend. I like her.' Sol looks at the statues, aware that they are watching him. He sips. Smoother.

Li gently taps the stack of photos on the table, to get them neat, and puts them down carefully, like they're the most valuable thing in the room. He stands up abruptly, crosses to the window and looks out at the view, his hands clasped behind his back.

'Mr Li likes her. He likes her a lot, he tells me.'

'Oh.' Sol puts down the glass again. Chink.

'You look surprised.' For a moment Sol can think of nothing at all to say. He looks around the room, then blurts out the first thing that pops into his head.

'Doesn't he meet pretty women everywhere?' Jeremy turns and says something to Li. On hearing

Sol's remark translated, Li waves a hand dismissively. He shoots out three short, blunt phrases.

Jeremy inhales, then speaks, punctuating with the cigarette. 'Mr Li says they are all the same. They bore him. He says Victoria is unique.'

'I see. Yeah.' Unique in what way exactly? Sol likes her a lot, too, but he wouldn't describe her as unique, no more than anyone else. She's normal. But then, maybe normal is pretty unique to this man. Mr Li talks, seeming to address the stack of offices beyond the window, and Jeremy translates.

'Mr Li says she has a certain quality. She is strong, she is proud, she has . . .' He waves his cigarette in the air. 'Balls? Is that the word?'

'It could be.'

'Mr Li wants her.'

Sol takes another sip. He can hardly taste it now. 'He wants her,' he repeats slowly.

'Yes. He wants to sleep with her. He wants to know, how much money do you think he will have to offer her?'

Sol turns the glass around and around in his hand. 'I don't know,' he says.

'Ten thousand dollars, he thinks, will be sufficient.'

'I don't know. I don't think . . .'

Jeremy taps his ash again. 'It is a generous offer.'

'What if she doesn't want to?'

'He is, I believe, open to negotiation.' Sol swigs

at his drink. It could be water now. 'You look shocked. You think that is too much money, perhaps?'

'Oh no,' says Sol.

'Mr Li wants to ask you a favour. Tonight, now, he and I are going out. It is Mr Li's last night, and we want to celebrate the business links we have established. We will go to Sophie Chow's. Mr Li wants you to come with us, to ask this Victoria if she will sleep with him for the ten thousand dollars I have already mentioned. Tonight.'

'What?' Sol puts his glass down heavily. 'No. No way. You can both . . .' He glances at the statues. 'You can both . . .'

'You will be handsomely paid for this service.'

'Paid? I don't understand. Why doesn't he just ask her himself if he's so keen?'

'Have you ever cut a deal, Sol? It works like this. You meet the person you want to deal with. You talk about it. You drink together. You become friends. You play some golf. Then your lawyers meet his lawyers, and they battle it out. You have made a friend, you see? You do not want to fight with the friend. You have lawyers to do the throat-cutting. Do you understand what I am saying?'

'So you want, like, a lawyer, here?'

'Precisely. You are the best qualified. You are her friend. She has your respect.'

'What will happen if I say I won't?'

'Then he will find someone who will. You will

be handsomely paid for this service. Two thousand dollars.'

'What if she says no?'

'You will be paid, be certain.' Sol looks at Li's wide back, at the statues, at Jeremy's cultivated face. He looks at his feet, then his fingernails. He looks up.

He needs money. Vix won't sleep with the guy. They can put another one over on the old cunt. And his slimy friend. Get some more money for nothing.

'Three thousand. Plus nine hundred dollars for the photographs.'

Jeremy turns to the side, lays his arm along the back of the sofa and addresses Li. Li turns round, and the two men have a short conversation.

'He will write a cheque,' says Jeremy, 'now, for three thousand nine hundred dollars.'

Sol coughs, swallows. 'Deal.'

sixteen

the handover

Sol is in another lift. It goes up fast; he feels like his ears are about to pop. For a moment he entertains the idea that all the lifts in the city are connected, a giant system of pistons, full of citizens, driving some infernal engine. The walls are mirrored all around. He looks at them obliquely and is surrounded by a myriad of Lis, Jeremys and statues, receding into the distance. He turns and catches his own eye. He looks very serious.

He looks at the bodyguards beside him. It's a novel experience, to be bodyguarded. He doesn't know quite how to treat them; whether to minimally acknowledge their presence or whether to ignore them completely. He's ignoring them, copying Li's attitude, but he feels awkward doing it.

The light on the lift's control panel tells them they are at the tenth floor. The doors slide open and they step out into a lobby like a brothel that's just been converted to a florists. Gold figurines of naked women are tucked between sprays of flowers gushing out of giant vases placed all around the edges of the bright-red carpet. A blue neon sign over a set of double doors says 'Sophie Chow's' and something else underneath in Chinese characters. A woman in a red dress, slit right up to her thigh, stands behind a plinth as if she's going to deliver a lecture. She smiles at them, bows and holds the doors open. They file through, shuffling to get into a pecking order; Li goes through first, then Jeremy, then Sol, with the statues bringing up the rear.

The girl looks twice at Sol. 'Sorry,' she says, 'you cannot come in here.'

'Why?'

She looks him over and fixes on his feet. 'You do not have appropriate shoes.'

Jeremy addresses her harshly in Cantonese. She blushes. Whatever he says works, because she bows deeply to Sol.

'Very sorry, sir,' she says to him, 'very sorry.'

Li and Jeremy argue about who's going to pay at the booth in the corridor beyond. Li wins; he is faster at drawing his credit cards. Beyond the corridor another set of doors leads into the club proper. They head in, and curiosity overtakes Sol's uneasiness. He has never seen where Vix works before.

When he first enters the room he can make out only bright spots of neon and disco lights, and shapely female silhouettes – and the less shapely ones of the customers. Some light Chinese techno

212

is playing, but not too loud. There is a bar along the wall next to the door. Before it is a sitting area, a lot of chairs and tables, and beyond that is a busy dancefloor.

There are roughly a hundred and fifty people in the room. The girls – around thirty of them – are all dressed in see-through white blouses with baggy black cotton trousers – what Vix calls the Ali Baba outfit. Apparently, it is less revealing and more comfortable than the tight leather of their other costume, Mad Max. Looking for Vix, Sol checks out the girls and recognizes a few: friends of Vix who have popped into the coffee shop on occasion. There's Mikiko laughing, Wang Li sipping a cocktail, Arabella leaning forward to have something whispered in her ear. The customers, mostly men in shirtsleeves and slacks, seem hardly less uniform than the girls. Sol remembers how Vix has described them to him; few are pretty and fewer still are ugly, their faces are as expressive as their credit cards.

No Vix. Automatically, Sol scans the room for black faces, and as usual there are none. He thinks about the girl on the door. He has been the subject of more blatant prejudice here than he ever was in England.

Another woman in a red dress, who appears older than the hostesses, approaches the group. She's a mamosan, one of the women who act as brokers between the customers and the girls, who know which girls sleep with customers and which don't, and how much they charge.

The mamosan gives them the most blatant example of the Hong Kong look that Sol has yet seen: a sweeping once-over from shoes to watch to face, taking in all the labels on the way. Jeremy emerges with the highest status; it is he she addresses. Sol catches some of the numbers they are talking.

A group of men drift away from the near end of the bar, and Vix is revealed sat beyond their vacated stools. He should have known she'd be there; it's the only place in the club where the girls are allowed to smoke. In her heavy make-up and costume she looks glamorous, but less like the Vix he knows.

She is talking to a Chinese girl, Mary Anne, her best friend here, who Sol has met a couple of times. She wears blue contact lenses, and works in a bank during the day, doing this at night for shopping money. Her surname is Ng, a noise like a grunt made at the back of the throat. Vix says she always hangs out with the local girls; the other Westerners, she complains, are boring, always going on about clothes and their Thai boyfriends.

As he watches, Mary Anne gives Vix a half-smoked cigarette. He remembers Vix telling him that they're sharing as part of a plan to cut down. She drags on it, and as she does so she casts her gaze around the room. She sees him, does a cartoon double-take, and her mouth opens. She drops the cigarette in an ashtray, slips off the stool and hurries over in her regulation heels.

'Sol? What are you doing here?'

Li cuts in before he can reply.

'Ah, Victoria. Good.'

'Mr Li, hello.' Vix smiles sweetly. Jeremy smiles at her and leans over to address her, smoothing his gold tie down to his chest.

'Mr Li has invited your friend to accompany us,' he says. 'You are free at the moment?'

'Yes.'

'Drink?' asks Li.

'Of course,' says Vix.

Jeremy turns to Sol. 'Beer?'

'OK.'

Jeremy addresses the mamosan.

'Come,' Li says to Vix, 'come sit.'

Seeing Jeremy's courteous manner and Li's wide grin, Sol feels suddenly furious. These drooling old fucks, who do they think they are? He begins to feel ashamed of himself. He feels compromised and obscurely humiliated, and reminds himself that, really, he is putting one over on them.

The mamosan motions for the group to follow her.

'Come,' says Li. 'Come.'

Li, Jeremy and the statues follow the mamosan through the crowd towards the far wall, where a series of doors lead to the karaoke rooms. Sol and

Vix follow a few paces behind. He whispers at her.

'He's paying me to ask you to shag him.'

'What? How could you?'

'It's free money. It beats slaving over an espresso machine. I'll just tell him you don't want to and go home. Easy. Three thousand dollars, Vix! That's what he's paying me.'

The mamosan opens a door and ushers the group inside with the upright wave of a traffic policeman. In silence, Sol and Vix stand outside and watch them go in. The mamosan swishes back across the room.

'There's no harm in it, is there?' says Sol. 'You say no, I tell him, and in a couple of days we both go wherever. China. Thailand. Wherever you want.' Sol's voice is cheery and upbeat, disguising his uneasiness. He feels defensive. He wants Vix to smile and congratulate him on his blag, to say, yeah, clever, nice one, the reaction he imagined.

'Tell him straight away, no. No. No.' Vix crosses her arms. She looks distressed.

'Let's get it over with, yeah?' says Sol. 'I'll tell him now. Come on, you know I love you.' He darts forward and plants a quick kiss on her cheek.

Sol goes inside, followed by Vix, who closes the thick door behind her. Abruptly, the noise of the club is shut out.

Seven men and two hostess girls, all Chinese, stand in front of the black leather sofas that line the back and side walls of the large, softly lit room. The girls are stunning. All the men are casually but expensively dressed and have close-cropped hair. One is wearing sunglasses. A lot of bowing, hand-shaking and shoulder-slapping is going on as they greet Li and Jeremy.

On a black stand by the door sit a computer and a widescreen TV. The walls and carpet are the same colour as the TV screen, a uniform blue. Glasses and ashtrays sit on a table in the middle of the room. Sleek black speakers are set high into each wall. On the back wall hangs a scroll, an ink painting of a clump of bamboo; a skilled flurry of brushstrokes and a lot of empty space. This is standard, Sol knows from Vix's descriptions. There are ten rooms at the club all identical to this except for the picture.

The greetings over, the group shuffles around to let Li and Jeremy sit on the back-wall sofa, at their centre.

The statues, Sol notices, are standing in the corners of the room, on either side of the door, hands clasped in front of them. They seem to have an ability, he reflects, to go unnoticed.

Vix steps forward and sits on the left-hand sofa. Sol moves to sit beside her. There's not much space left and she has to wriggle up to let him perch on the end.

Sol feels the heat of curious glances. Feeling awkward, he looks at the table to avoid catching anyone's eye. There's a remote control and a micro-phone among the glasses. A long lead stretches off

217

the mike; it coils on the floor and disappears into the wall. He glances at one of the menus; a list of Chinese characters.

A cloudy veil of smoke is suspended in the air. The voices around him are loud and boisterous. He realizes that most of the group are drunk.

Vix crosses her arms.

'Tell him, then,' she hisses.

'I can't just blurt it out, can I?' whispers Sol. 'I've got to be a bit, you know, discreet about it.'

Three waiters in white shirts and red bow ties, bearing large trays, come in. The first bears beers and cocktails, the second four champagne bottles, the third another bottle and a cluster of champagne glasses. The waiters transfer the contents of the trays to the table, replace them with used glasses and drift out.

People choose fresh drinks and toast each other.

'Cheers!' says Li, looking at Sol and Vix. It's the first English anyone has spoken. After the acknowledgement, Sol feels the attention shifting away from him; he is accepted into the group.

Sol picks up a beer and slurps it. It's the first beer he has had in months, almost since he's been here, and he finds the taste slightly alien.

Vix takes the umbrella out of a cocktail and drops it on the table, then slugs on the drink. Sol remembers that she gets twenty-five dollars for every drink that is bought her.

'What's that for?' asks Sol, pointing at the

computer. He has guessed its function, but he's anxious to start a conversation with her.

'It's a karaoke machine,' says Vix.

'Karaoke!' shouts Mr Li. 'Victoria karaoke. Very good.' Everyone looks at Vix. Jeremy smiles at her. 'Please, sing us a song.'

'Sing a song! Sing a song!' chant the two Chinese hostesses.

'OK.'

Vix punches three numbers on the remote control. She stands and picks up the microphone. 'California Dreaming' by the Mamas and the Papas appears on the TV screen, 'Number 435' with a couple of lines above it in Chinese. Vix moves to the end of the sofa, beside the wall. Her weight is on one foot, one arm is crossed over her chest, the elbow of the arm bearing the microphone rests on her hand. She looks at the TV as the song's intro-duction swells out of the speakers. A video begins, of a Chinese couple mooning about in Hong Kong's scenic spots. The lyrics scroll along the bottom of the screen. A green ball bounces on the letters to show the timing. Sol knows she doesn't need it; she has told him she always sings this song, mainly because there's a long instrumental break in the middle and it's over with pretty quickly. Vix begins to sing.

Sol realizes he has never heard her sing before. She has a good voice, clear and low. The audience is respectfully silent. Both Li and Jeremy look rapt.

219

Towards the end of the song, Li gets up and sits next to Sol. He raises his eyebrows at him.

'She says she won't,' whispers Sol. Li looks away and watches Vix. 'No possible. No. No want to. Sorry. She's positive on that.' Sol pauses. 'It doesn't mean she doesn't like you.'

Li turns his head away, leans across the table and speaks to Jeremy in Mandarin then whips his eyes back to Vix. Jeremy leans forward, addressing Sol across the table.

'Tell her twenty thousand dollars.' He picks a pink menu off the table and opens it.

'She says she won't,' Sol says, having to raise his voice a little louder to be heard. 'She doesn't want to. She has a boyfriend.'

Li runs a finger down the list of songs, then turns the page.

'Twenty thousand dollars. You ask her.'

Vix finishes and bows her head. The people on the sofas applaud, Li the loudest of all. Sol begins a little late and is one of the first to stop.

Vix stays standing with the microphone and Sol leans up to her. 'He's gone up in price so I have to talk to you again. Sorry.'

'I thought you told him.'

'I did. He just upped the amount and I'm supposed to tell you.'

'Tell me, then.'

'What?'

'How much does the fucker think I'm worth?'

'Twenty thousand.'

'Twenty thousand dollars? Jesus.'

'What? What do you mean, Jesus? Why did you say Jesus?'

'It's a lot more than the going rate.'

'What, so you're impressed?'

'Tell him to fuck off. Why did you even need to ask?'

'I didn't need to ask, all right?' Sol works to keep a note of irritation out of his voice. 'I just have to talk to you, to make it look like we're talking about it.' He feels a wave of hostility from Vix. Suddenly he realizes how stuffy it is in here.

Jeremy stands up and steps around the table. The others make encouraging noises at him. He takes the microphone off Vix and moves to the centre of the room. Vix sits down on the edge of the sofa.

'So I'll talk to you for a bit,' says Sol, 'and then go and tell him, yeah?'

'Yeah.'

Jeremy punches numbers on the remote control, and a set of titles, Chinese characters and the number 235 appear on the TV screen.

'Your drink any good?' asks Sol.

'I'm sick of the things,' says Vix.

Jeremy begins to sing a slow ballad in Cantonese. His voice is off key, but he sings with unexpected relish.

'So, are these those dodgy blokes?' asks Sol.

'Yeah. Most of them look familiar.'

>>>ghost money

'I wouldn't like to meet them on a dark night.'

Vix deems his inane comment unworthy of a reply.

Sol turns to Li.

'She won't,' he says. 'No. No. Understand?'

Li sips his drink.

'More,' he says.

'What?'

Li plucks the silver pen out of his shirt pocket, picks up a napkin from the tray on the table and rests it on his knee. He writes, '50,000', then underlines it twice.

Jeremy finishes his song. The group cheers and claps. Sol gets the impression that they are careful to make more noise than they did for Vix. Applauding, Sol turns to her.

'I'm supposed to talk to you again.'

'What do you mean?'

'I mean I'm supposed to be negotiating. Again.'

'I thought I said to say no?'

'I said no. He just raised the price. Fifty thousand. I guess he really likes you.'

'I'm going to tell him to fuck off.'

'Wait,' says Sol, 'let me do it.'

Li stands up and goes over to Jeremy. They have a brief conversation as the microphone and remote control are handed over. Li punches up a tune, number 593.

Li looks at Vix as he sings. His voice is terrible, warbling from a throaty grumble to a squeaky wail and back again. Sol doesn't need to speak Cantonese to tell that the song is a slushy declaration of love. Behind him, the TV screen shows a girl in a one-piece bikini splashing about in a pool; a fully dressed man sings to her from the poolside, while throwing his arms out or clutching his chest.

'He looks like he's having a heart attack,' says Sol.

Vix is scratching at the design on her drinks mat. 'Who?'

'The man on the TV.'

Jeremy leans across to address Sol. 'Two hundred thousand,' he whispers.

Sol doesn't see Vix leaning close towards them, straining to hear.

'Two hundred thousand?' repeats Sol, incredulous.

'Oh, fuck this,' says Vix. She stands up abruptly and strides swiftly to the door, wrenching it open and letting in the din of the club. Sol gets up and moves to follow her out. Li stops singing. His expression is of baffled concern.

'Victoria!' he says as Sol passes. He is still clutching the microphone, and his words are amplified in the little room. 'One million!'

Sol closes the door behind him. The dance floor is packed now, and Sol senses a buzz of excitement in the crowd. He looks around for Vix, can't see her and imagines she has left. He steps forward to head for the exit, then spots her standing in the shadows against the back wall, about ten metres away. Her arms are crossed. As he approaches, Sol sees that she's breathing hard.

'Vix, come on.'

'The cunt. The sleazy prick. What fucking right has he? He's a cheeky fucker, that's what he is. He's a fucking . . . He thinks you can just . . .'

'Fuck them,' says Sol. 'Fuck them all. Fuck this fucking place, they think they can just buy anyone, anything. Well, fuck their money. Fuck their million fucking dollars.'

Vix looks across sharply.

'How much?'

'The dirty old man.'

'He said a million? He said that?'

'Yeah. The old cunt.'

'But that's a hundred thousand quid,' says Vix. She pauses, biting her bottom lip. 'What would you do with a hundred grand? I could travel for ever. I'd never have to work again. We could go away together for . . . for years.'

'What?'

'A hundred grand? And it's just straight, bog standard, down the line, boring only sex? It's just a shag.' Vix laughs. 'He doesn't look like he's got it in him. Imagine that. Imagine if he couldn't even get it up. I hope he wouldn't ask for a refund. He's really little as well. Maybe he's got such a tiny nob you wouldn't even know it.'

'You want me to tell him yes, then, do you?'

'I'm just saying we should think about it.'

'What do you mean? No we shouldn't.'

'No, think about it. I mean think about it. We're allowed to think about it.' Vix looks at the spotlights doodling over the flushed faces on the dance floor. 'I'll give you some.'

'What? Vix, Vix. Fuck it, Vix. Fuck it.'

Suddenly the whole crowd erupts with a cheer. Couples hug, on the dance floor people start shouting and cheering.

'What's that?' says Sol.

'It's midnight. The changeover. That's it, the British are out.'

Sol's attention is drawn by a loud pop. A man at the bar has opened a bottle of champagne; it's foaming over the lip and spraying around. Girls are laughing and giggling. Another cork is popped by another man; his spray is bigger. Suddenly the atmosphere is noisy and unrestrained. The music kicks faster and the sound is louder.

'If you want to do it,' says Sol, 'you do it. But you fucking tell him. 'Cause I'm fucking not. All right? I'm, I'm . . . I'm fucking out of here. I'm out of it. Forget about it. Forget about us.'

'I'll give you a quarter, Sol. Come on. Don't be like that. I'll give you twenty-five grand. Twenty-five grand. Twenty-five grand. But you stay with me. You stick by me. You come with me. Twenty-five grand.'

Jeremy and the two hostesses come out of the karaoke room. Sol watches Jeremy close the door and the three move towards the dance floor. Jeremy peels away from the girls and quickly walks towards the exit.

'What do you want to leave for?' says Vix. 'I'm not doing it because I want to. I won't like you any less. I'm just going to hire myself out. Think about it. Come on. I'll give you loads of money. All right, thirty. Thirty grand. Just because I like you. You can take pictures wherever you want. You'll be free.'

For a moment, Sol grimaces, squeezing up the muscles in his face, pressing his eyes shut. He puts his hand over his mouth. Then his face clears, he drops his hand and exhales.

'OK.'

'OK?'

'Sure, OK. I'll tell him then.'

'All right.'

More champagne bottles are opened around the room. Five popping sounds come from inside the karaoke room.

'I'm going to go and tell him then,' says Sol, but doesn't move.

'Yes. Do.'

'You're sure?'

'This is it. I'll be set up. For life. We'll be set up for life.'

Sol sees the door to the karaoke room open again. One by one, the men begin to walk out. They are silent and don't look at one another. Their faces are flushed. They move quickly towards the exit. The man with sunglasses brushes something off his shirt. They don't notice Sol and Vix.

'I'll go and tell him then,' says Sol.

The seventh man out closes the door behind him.

'What's going on?' says Vix.

Vix and Sol move towards the room. Sol opens the door. He is struck by the overpowering smell of shit. There are red spatters all over the walls and the picture. Statue One leans against the wall in the corner, his legs splayed out straight in front of him. Half his head is missing. Statue Two lies on his back, parallel with the other wall. His foot twitches. Li is face down on the floor, his arms out, microphone clutched in his hand. His head is at the centre of a dark pool of liquid. Most of the glasses on the table have fallen over and beer foams over its edge onto the carpet. The two pools, beer and blood, spread out towards each other.

Song number 593 continues. On the TV, the man jumps into the swimming pool. The green ball bounces over the scrolling lyrics.

part five

teenage riot

top night

I threw myself against the door. He was leaning on it from the other side; it didn't shift. I felt like a cloth being wrung, and words and tears were squeezed out of me as I twisted up tighter and tighter.

'Fucker! Let me out! Let me out!'

The key turned in the lock. Schneck. I heard him take it out and walk, dum dum dum, away down the corridor.

In my mind I could see him, his big, broad back passing the photos on the wall of me and Mike as little babies. But I couldn't see his expression; I didn't know that. I beat against the door with my fists. It hurt, but it was a good pain, a pain that I could cope with, that smothered all the other pain, and I continued hitting harder and harder till long after I couldn't hear him. I gave one last shout, a screech that rose scorching from my lungs and left me feeling scraped out inside.

'Dad! Let me out!'

I slid down the door and lay in a heap, and I cried big, ugly tears and great choking sobs. My eyes ran out of juice and retched, it felt like blood would come out next.

I was naked and spattered with mud. My thighs were cross-hatched with scratches. I could feel a burning patch of red skin on my back. My tits hurt, and all my toes and fingers. The sides of my hands were red. My face felt puffy and sore. I could feel bruises rising on my wrist, my waist, my neck, all over. I was turning blue. Like I was rotting.

Good. I wanted to die, right now, like this. I wanted my ghost to see them find my body – how delicious to observe their remorse. I wanted them to come and see what they'd done to me and to be so sorry it ripped their lives apart.

I sniffled up the gobs of goo in my nose and rubbed my raw eyes. I knew that feeling was wrong and I willed it away. It didn't get me anywhere. Crying started out good and pure, and then, like with a lot of stuff, you did it too long and you weren't doing it for the right reasons any more. Tears got self-indulgent and mean; you only kept on because you wanted other people to see what a state you were in, or because you enjoyed feeling like shit. That was no good to me now. I pulled myself together, literally; in my mind I was picturing repair work going on all around my body, welding and stitching, all my insides shifting and untwisting and sliding back into place. It was a rough job, a shabby refit, a cut and shut, but it'd have to do.

I was locked in my bedroom. The curtains were open and the room was lit up blue in the light of the moon, just gone full. 2:27, said the red digits of my radio alarm. Kurt Cobain and James Dean looked down at me from the walls. They were saying nothing. I was on my own.

The flue for the wood burner in the living room went right up through the corner of my room. It was a big, ugly tube, and I kept meaning to hang drapes round it. The thing was, though, all the noise from the living room got sucked into it and up to my room, even hushed conversations if I stood up close. I'd heard lots of stuff I wasn't meant to, like Mum telling Dad she thought I was schizo, or Mike's mates taking the piss out of him for his weird sister.

Now I could hear an argument raging in the living room, coming up at me loud and proud.

'You vandal. You fucking . . . I can't believe it. I can't. Not you, not you, son.' Dad's voice, tones of anger and reproach.

'I'm sorry, Dad, I'm so sorry. I know it was wrong, but if it wasn't for them . . .' Mike, pleading. He'd got no imagination, my big brother, but he could talk his way out of a donkey. He knew how to brown-nose and suck, the little fucker.

Mike had won a gold star for staff excellence at the electrical shop where he was assistant manager.

Mike was making a success of his life. Mike owned an expensive open-topped sports car with go-faster everything. Mike played hard and worked hard. Mike was engaged to a lovely girl with child-bearing hips. Mike was a good boy. Of a Saturday afternoon Mike liked a drink with the lads. Mike never took the blame. Ever. Because he was Mike, and Mike didn't do wrong. He'd get out of this one, even.

'You could go to prison, ruin your whole life. Why, son?'

'I did it for Mum. You know what they did. Someone had to do something. And if it wasn't for her . . .' He meant me. He was trying to blame me. The fucker. Good job they'd locked me in. If I could have got out I'd have gone down there and killed him, I'd have wrung his pus-filled neck.

Underneath the dialogue was a constant refrain, a small sound like a bird being tortured. My Mum, my poor Mum.

'Nobody saw you, did they?'

'No. Nobody knows.'

I knew. I knew, and I'd never forgive him. Mr Normal. What the spawn of my parents ought to be like. The liar, the spineless turd. Christ, he could have killed me.

'What a fucking family,' said my Dad. 'What's happened? It's fallen apart.'

And it was my fault. It was. It always was.

All my banging had achieved was to knock off

234

some of the pictures and flyers that were tacked to the door. I picked up a strip of passport photos. The whole crew crammed into a photo booth, gurning for the camera. I held it with two hands, blinked my eyes clear and said hello to them, raised a pale smile. There was Shell's chin jutting up at me from the middle of each picture. She was the only one on the stool. Just like her to bag centre stage. Cian, her off and on boyfriend, was leaning over her; you could see the top of his shaved head and, in one picture, a single eye. He'd tried it on with me once, a few years back, and he'd never told her. There was Cosmic John's hand, doing a peace sign. I went out with him for a bit. There was Frog, who worked in the office and called himself a jungle DJ. Shagged him once, no, twice. Loo's big nose. On the back, 'To Vix, happy 18th birthday, love yer mates, big sloppy kisses.'

I leant back against the door. They'd given me that six weeks ago. Now that, that was a good night. A top night. And this was where it got me.

We'd been in the Nag's Arse, which was a hole, but less of a hole than the other pubs in this dump. It was poky, and the pool table was broken, and Big Fat Bastard, the landlord, was a big fat bastard, but at least it had padded seats and a couple of decent tunes on the jukebox.

It was near closing time, and we were all trashed to fuck, me especially: I'd been bought a lot of birthday pints. The pub was full of all the same people. Mike, the ugly twenty-two-year-old who happened to be my older brother, was sat in the furthest corner from me with his mates, bog-standard casuals all out of the same plastic mould.

Cian said what do you call a three legged donkey? And Shell said a wonkey. Frog set fire to the ashtrays trying to show us this trick with matches and Big Fat Bastard gave him a look and said he'd not serve us again and how old were we anyway? Me and Shell were the only ones technically old enough to drink, but we were all eighteen as far as he was concerned. Frog shut up and went red, like he used to at school, and Loo pretended to warm her hands on his face. Shell started trying to tell a joke about this kid who takes his mate home to meet his parents and his Dad is examining a matchstick with a magnifying glass and his Mum is on the sofa, naked, putting a beer bottle up her cunt. Before she could finish, not that she'd have remembered the punchline anyway, these two blokes walked in, and we turned to clock them.

They were inspiring interest all round, 'cause they were new. They looked like those people you see on the news sometimes being dragged out of trees by security guards. One bloke had dreads and a hooded top, the other had a skinhead and a bunch of earrings, and they both had muddy army boots on. They had a big, skinny dog in tow. They lined up at the bar and stared at the spirit bottles. Big Fat

Bastard strolled up to the other end of the bar and Linda, the beautiful gay barmaid, served them a half of bitter and a Coke.

Cian said they were travellers who'd parked up by the old railway line the week before.

'Maybe they've got some decent drugs,' said Shell, looking pointedly at Frog, who punts shit hash. 'Let's ask them.'

There was only an inch left on mine and Shell's drinks so we had an excuse to get up and aim for the bar, where they stood sipping. We sidled up to them, clutching change. They looked sound enough on close inspection. Some loud comments about soap from Mike's table gave me an opening.

'Sorry about that,' I said, 'we're not all wankers round here.' I gave Mike a deathstare, and he and his mates hunkered down over their pints. One thing about people thinking you're mad; nobody fucks with you. Shell did some flirty work on Linda and we got the lagers in without too much hassle. We invited the new arrivals back to our table and they ambled over.

The guy with dreads was called Renaldo, the other Dean, and the dog, a beautiful big whippety thing, curvy and sleek and long-legged like a doggy superwaif, was called Stimpy. They all had this woody smell about them. The blokes sat, and the dog crawled under the table and folded itself cleverly up like one of those bikes that collapse into a briefcase.

They said they came from London.

'I know a couple of people in London,' said Cosmic John.

'So what do people do around here?' asked Dean.

'We get pissed,' said Shell.

'There's a good night at the youth club every Friday,' said Frog. 'Actually, I do a set there. I'm a DJ.'

Dean crashed a round of fags. His hands were webbed with fine wrinkles, and he had dirt under his fingernails. Big knuckles, but slim fingers. I love hands. They're my favourite part of the body. You can tell someone by their hands better than their face. You can lie with your face no problem, but it's hard to tell fibs with your flippers.

'Course, it hadn't escaped Shell and me that there were two single men at our table, not bad-looking, not yokels and quite possibly possessing brains bigger than their egos.

Cian, Shell reminded him, had work in the morning. Frog felt inspired to get some sounds together. Cosmic John said he had to focus his energies, a novel term for the things blokes get up to in their bedrooms at night. One by one they peeled off to their separate comfy beds, leaving me and Shell with the new boys. We got to work.

Renaldo was the looker, and he knew it. He flicked and twisted a dangling dread about the way I play with the phone cable. Dean was a talker. His narrow eyes bored into me and held my attention hostage while he went on. He was old, thirty-two he said, but quite well preserved; his number-one cut minimized the effect of a receding hairline, which I thought made him look quite distinguished.

Renaldo said something about sheep-shaggers, certainly the funniest thing you can say to a Welsh person.

'So, if we were black,' I said, 'would you call us golliwogs?'

'Can you speak Welsh?' asked Dean, smoothing it over.

'Groesco y Cymru,' said Shell.

'What's that?'

'Welcome to Wales,' I said. 'You see it on the road signs. Newyddion Saith.'

'News at Seven,' explained Shell.

'All being Welsh means here', I said, 'is you don't get Channel 4. You get that crappy S4C instead.'

'It's a beautiful country,' said Dean.

'But Wales is crap,' I pointed out.

An explanation was demanded.

'The only thing we're famous for is rugby and singing and now we're shit at both. And we've got the naffest culture in the whole world. All chintz and dollies and doilies.'

I always found myself disagreeing with men I found attractive. As a tactic, it didn't work very well; Shell played it to the opposite extreme, and she did a lot better than me.

Now, for example, Shell was blonding it up to a shocking degree. Renaldo was having a great time showing her the different ways to light a Zippo, on your jeans, or in one thumb-flick, or whatever, and then she would have a go, and couldn't do it, and she'd giggle, and so he'd show her again. Honestly.

Dean talked to me about his kids from his first marriage. He showed me a photo. They weren't very pretty, but I didn't like to say anything, obviously.

Shell asked if they had any hash. They said they did, and a plan was voiced, by Shell I think, to go back to theirs for a smoke. Right.

The sudden quiet of the summer night outside had a sobering effect. They were staying about a mile out of town. We turned off the road and climbed over a gate, Shell valiantly assisted by Renaldo, and saw two trailers parked up at the bottom of a steep railway embankment, between a wood and a barbed-wire fence. Dean opened the door of the smaller trailer.

'Welcome to my humble abode,' he said.

We took off our shoes, following his example, and ducked through the door. Inside it was well snug, once he got the oil lamp lit. It was like camping. There was about as much space as in the downstairs bathroom at home. There was a little cooker, a burner, a mattress covered with quilts and books everywhere.

Dean put some weird music on a stereo linked to a car battery — ethnic stuff, lots of drums — and got the burner going. Renaldo plonked himself down on the bed and started skinning up. Dean talked about how great it was to have so much dead oak around. There was nothing like oak, he said. Shell hopped on the bed and curled up by Renaldo, so no prizes what was in store on that front. I wasn't so at ease with Dean; we were both still checking each other out.

Shell asked if they'd got some cards and three spoons. Cards was no problem, but Dean only had two spoons, so Renaldo went off to his trailer and fetched one more. We sat them down next to us on the bed with the spoons in a pile in the middle, and explained that we were going to play a game. A simple card game, in which, when someone won, you had to pick up a spoon from the pile and put it on your nose. When you saw someone else putting a spoon on their nose, you had to do the same, and the last person, the one left without a spoon on their nose, had to tell a truth. Me and Shell, we played to lose. We knew everything about each other anyway.

Renaldo asked us standard questions, like what was the kinkiest thing we'd ever done and did we spit or swallow, but Dean got weird, asking stuff like, when were you last truly happy? And what geometric shape would you like to be? Mind, he was toking like a trooper. I discovered that he'd slept with fourteen women, had once had sex in a disabled toilet, had been married twice, hated watching operations on telly, once pissed himself in a school geography lesson, liked having his feet massaged, had a tattoo of the Tasmanian Devil out of *Bugs Bunny* on his bum, and had once slept with a bloke.

Then, obviously, we played for forfeits instead of truths. Shell took off her socks and Renaldo wore them on his ears, I picked Dean's nose, Renaldo did a moony, Dean sucked my big toe. Then Shell lost and I told her to snog Renaldo. They went outside to do it and I knew they weren't coming back.

The air got heavy between me and Dean. A log cracked in the burner, and we both started, then smiled at each other. One of us has to do something, I thought, so I stroked his hair, which felt like the fluffy side of velcro. I love hair, I told him, and heads, the shape of heads. When I was a kid I told my parents I wanted to be a hairdresser and they threw an eppy; I was supposed to be a nuclear physicist or something.

The fire was warm, and it gave off a cuddly orange light. I lay down and snuggled into the duvet.

'Don't you have a home to go to?' said Dean, which made me wonder if he wanted to fuck me at all. I said that I'd pretend I was staying at Shell's, and she would tell her folks she was staying with me.

242

'I don't want to get you into trouble,' he said. I told him trouble was what I was looking for. I asked him what was wrong. He said he didn't want to take advantage of me. I told him I wanted to be taken advantage of.

He kissed me softly and offered to walk me home. Well, OK. To be honest, the spliff on top of the booze was an error; by that point I was a jelly baby, living in a wibbly-wobbly world of my own.

So Dean walked me home, and I felt young again. Everything was quiet and fresh, you could almost feel the world holding its breath, and there was only the rhythm of our feet and our quiet words.

I wouldn't let Dean walk me the last hundred yards. We copped off on the road and I felt my hormones prickling. He said he'd like to take advantage of me when I was straight. I said he'd better, and promised to go and see him soon, then turned and ran, feeling squishy, which could have been the hormones or the beer.

After Dean's trailer, the house felt gigantic; it was like I had to run a marathon underwater just to get to the downstairs loo. I only just made it. A wave rose from my guts and I rode it till it broke through my mouth and crashed into the bowl. Woof. And again. And again. And then I was empty. I flushed the loo, but stayed slumped there for ages, too knackered to move, looking at my reflection in the water at the bottom of the bowl. I reckoned I was pretty good-looking. My face in the water looked like a Greek statue's face, like you'd see in a museum, pale and hard and elegant. All things considered, like I said, a top night.

redundant

It was 4 a.m. I was listening to the flue. They were just talking now. Dad had lowered his voice.

'Let's try and put this behind us, hey? Pretend it never happened. It was a nasty thing to do, and it was wrong, but I'm not saying I don't understand.'

Boring, boring. I didn't want to hear the chimney's news any more, so I sat on the bed where it was a background mumble and looked at the giant sky, picking out the constellations Dean had shown me. Underneath them there was a lot of dark, dark country, and in the distance the big, sharp hills, the horizon jagged, like a torn page.

I crawled under the duvet. It was nice under there, warm and fuggy and quiet. Maybe I would never have to come out. Just give me some food, rig up some sort of device so I could shit and piss, and it wouldn't be too bad. It would be just me under there and eventually, maybe, everybody else would forget I was there.

I love sleeping. It is my hobby. It is my

passion. And I am an expert dreamer. I can make myself dream whatever I want. Sometimes I wake up and I can go back to sleep and slot myself back into exactly the same dream. But I wasn't going to do any sleeping that night. I knew it. I had to put my head down, grit my teeth and work through the whole handful of bony night hours.

As a comfort freak I had loads of bedding. I stretched out and smelled the sheet, the duvet, the covers, snuffling like a bloodhound. I was probably imagining it – he had only romped in here with me once, that first time, and that was a month ago – but was there a faint whiff in there, a tang, of Dean?

I'd been in my room, lying back on the bed and feeling comfy and warm in the oblong of sunlight coming through the window. I was looking at the wooden ceiling, which was polka-dotted with knots, and in my head I was joining the dots, creating constellations. It was a habit I'd got into as a kid, when I couldn't sleep, and now I couldn't help it. I could hear ambient music on the stereo. One hand was absently stroking Mr Pickles the floppy monkey, the other was curled around the top of Dean's head, squeezing softly, like I was testing a melon. I was naked, so was he, and he was licking me out. He had a very creative tongue. If only he could have breathed through his ears, he'd have been perfect.

I heard a shout from downstairs. 'Yoo, hoo!'

I crashed back to earth like a wonky rocket. Hell on toast.

Dean's head rose above the horizon of my thighs, his mouth all gunky.

'Fuck, fuck, fuck!' I struggled onto my elbows. Dean sat back on his knees.

'What was that?'

'That was my fucking dad,' I hissed, sitting upright. 'Buggerfuckshitwank.'

'I thought nobody was supposed to be coming home?'

'Put some fucking clothes on. Or something.'

'Is my little girl ho-ome?' cooed Dad.

I could hear him crashing up the stairs, taking them two at a time, which meant he was drunk.

'Get under the duvet.'

'Ah, come on—'

'You don't know my Dad.'

Dean buried himself under the duvet and I bunched it up over him.

I could hear Dad pounding the corridor. I shouted through the door.

'Hang on. I'm just putting some clothes on.'

'You not up yet? It's three in the afternoon, girl.'

'I got up. Then I went back to bed. I had a headache. You can come in now.'

Dad opened the door and saw me sat on the end of the bed in my dressing gown, dishevelled and red-faced, with the duvet scrunched up behind me.

247

I spread my arms out across the end of the bed. He stood in the doorway.

'Hello, Dad. Did you have a good time in Czech?'

He was swaying a bit. 'The usual. The usual.'

Dad sold industrial machinery. He worked all over Europe, and he was away a lot of the time. Whenever he got home, he went on a bender; the longer he was away, the bigger the bender. Czech was one of the longest; he'd been gone a month. But he wasn't due back for another week.

'Did you see any good birds?'

'A few plovers. Some falcons, and a shrike.'

Dad was a keen ornithologist.

'How's things been while I've been away, eh?'

He stepped forward and pinched my cheek, quite hard, with his thick, gnarled fingers.

'They've been fine. Mike might get his promotion. You missed a good documentary about excavations of a Roman bath the other day. I videoed it for you.'

Dad was also very keen on archaeology.

'Sorry I missed your birthday. But I got you a present. Some duty-free perfume. It's in my luggage.'

'Thanks.'

I saw that Dean's foot was visible through a gap in the rucked up duvet. I smoothed it down.

'How long are you back for?'

'For good,' said Dad. 'For good. That's good

news, eh Vicky?' He sat down next to me on the end of the bed and squeezed the skin at the top of his nose. His eyes were closed as he said, 'I've been made redundant.'

He opened his eyes wide, raising his eyebrows, and put both hands heavily down on his knees, the fingers curled tightly round. Together we looked at them, at furrowed skin and cobwebbed knuckles.

'I'm sorry, Dad.' I put a hand on his shoulder. 'Never mind.'

'No, never mind. I thought that now I'm home I might clean the house. Your mother hasn't kept it as nice as it could be. I don't suppose you've helped. Going to mop the floors. Clear out the porch. Mow the lawn. Gardening. There's . . . shit all over, you know?' He stood up abruptly, and my hand dropped.

Dad looked around the room, and I realized that Dean's clothes were still on the floor. So were all mine, though, so they weren't that noticeable.

'So what about you, my girl? When are you going to get yourself sorted out, eh?'

My A-level results hadn't been good enough to get me into college. I was going to try again next year, or at least that's what I told people. Till then I was working part time as a chambermaid, an activity I hated with a passion.

'Soon, Dad.'

'Just don't go spending all that money, for Christ's sakes.'

I got a couple of grand off a trust fund on my birthday.

'No, Dad.'

He frowned at my shelves, then said, 'There isn't a bypass being built is there?'

'What? No.'

'What are all those hippies doing in the village?'

'They live here. There's a site. There was only a couple at first, then loads more turned up.'

'Well, I wouldn't mind if they were here for a reason. If there was a bypass going to be built, then fair enough. I hate roads as much as the next man.'

'They've got a right to be here.'

'I saw a bunch of them in town, right miserable they looked, and not clean. And what are the visitors going to think? I was talking to Idris in the pub, and he says they steal from the off-licence.'

'That's a small minority.'

'Trust you to defend them. They help you pick them magic mushrooms, do they?'

He paced up and down in front of the bed, and I shifted from side to side in time. He sniffed.

'Smells like a wrestler's jockstrap in here.'

'I've tried to give up smoking, you know I've tried.'

'Well, don't do it in the house any more. Is that clear?'

'Yes.'

'Right,' he said. 'I'm going to get the kettle on.'

'OK.'

'Just one more thing. Who's hiding in your bed?'

There was a pause, then Dean threw back the duvet, a guilty smile on his face.

'Good afternoon. I'm Dean.'

Dad looked him up and down.

'Christ. What are you doing in her bed?'

'Lost my contact lens?'

'Don't cheek me. Get out of my house.'

'Ah, Dad—' I said.

'I'm on my way.'

'Jesus, some fucking homecoming. I wonder why I didn't stay in fucking Czech.'

Dean got out of the bed, the duvet wrapped around him, and crouched down to root round for his clothes.

'Look at him. He's got filthy nails. Filthy. He's got tattoos. You been fucking him? Eh? While I've been gone?'

I heard Dad's breathing change. He was working himself into one of his states. He took a big puff of air.

'You fucked all of them, have you? Have you? Jesus. My own daughter. A prize. Now look at you.'

Dean was hopping about trying to get into his trousers. He'd left his pants off, which was understandable. 'Hey, come on,' he said, 'that's out of order.'

'I'm out of order?'

You didn't contradict Dad when he was in a state. You just didn't.

'You get out of my fucking house.'

'I said I was going, all right? Leave her alone.'

'Go on,' shouted Dad.

More than anything, I felt terminally embarrassed. I felt so ashamed. My eyes had got so hot, they were hurting. I buried myself under the duvet and in the blackness I pressed it hard against my head.

'Go on, you, go on, take your fucking lice and germs and go, go on . . .'

nineteen

new age

Finally, everyone had gone to bed. Except Mum, of course. I could hear her moving around downstairs. She couldn't sleep any more. She got up in the middle of the night; I heard her sometimes. She wandered around downstairs, from the lounge, past the stairs, through the dining room to the kitchen and back again. I saw her once, dressed in her white nightie, her hair all over the place, looking about five hundred years old. She looked like a ghost, she looked transparent. She was fading from view.

I could hear her putting the kettle on. More camomile tea. I hoped you couldn't overdose on the stuff. She was on pills now, but in the past she'd always put her trust in herbal remedies, and in the softcore occult of the New-Age trinkets she sold in her shop in the village.

Half the shop was Amazonian rain sticks, crystals, multi-coloured candles, joss sticks, meditation tapes, ethnic wooden stuff of mysterious use and posters of unicorns under rainbows. The other half was just as twee and unrealistic: Welsh bollocks, strictly for the tourists. Little dolls in black skirts and frilly bonnets, the Welsh national dress invented for us in the nineteenth century by an Englishman; mugs with pictures of sheep on; tea towels decorated with local beauty spots, or phrases in Welsh, plus their English translation; love spoons. What use is all that shit? People came here and they trotted up the hills and down again, and they wanted to buy a tea towel to remember it?

I'm sorry, Mum. I'm sorry.

I sparked up a fag. I couldn't be bothered to hang out the window and light a joss stick; it really didn't seem to matter any more. The fag's glowing end, and the blocky red digits on the alarm – 4:37 – were the only lights in the room. Everything else was misty and grey, background, but these glowing things – the time and the fag – seemed urgent, pressing, clear.

I got an idea. Immediately my stomach lurched at the sick joy of it, my heart shivered. I rolled up my sleeve and exposed the inside of my wrist. It was so pale, the colour of the moon, and the skin was ever so soft.

I tapped the ash off the fag. I was shaking with giddiness and fear. I held the hot little pyramid a couple of centimetres above my flesh. I thought about what it would be like when I ground it in; the flash of pain taking me to another place, where everything, including me, was white and pure and clean and cold; so cold – frozen. The shuddered gasps of breath, and then long exhalations; the unwinding. And after that, I'd be shaky and high, wired, I'd be lit up.

Sitting on the bed with the fag poised, I started to laugh at my accidental pun. Lit up. Geddit?

I started to lower the fag, slowly, slowly. I watched, fascinated; how interesting. It was like someone else was doing it, I was just an observer.

No. No. No. No. I couldn't. It wasn't fear; fear didn't frighten me. I whipped the fag away and ground it out on the bedpost. It died in a shower of tiny sparks.

I wasn't getting into that again.

I used to hurt myself; nothing major, just fags, razor blades, knives heated up on school Bunsen burners. It was quite a little hobby, for a while. I knew, if I did it again, ever, it would be as if I'd walked through a door in my mind and I'd be back in that place again, that clean white room where hurting yourself was an option, where hurting yourself was cool. Things were easy when you were in that room, nothing could get to you. But once you were in that room it was hard to get out again. You wanted to stay in that room, or go further, through doors that lead to other even cleaner, whiter rooms.

I wasn't getting into that again.

Mum has these little cards, Angel cards, she calls them. Each one had a word on it – serenity, peace, kindness, love, tenderness, giving, joy, et cetera, et cetera. They sat face-down on a plate in her bedroom, and she picked one up every morning, and that gave her a word for the day, like a prophecy.

I went through them once when I was pissed. Every card, and there were about thirty, was positive, except for three blank ones. I thought, she's just not being realistic. What was the point of playing Russian roulette and not putting any bullets in the gun? So I wrote 'anarchy', 'chaos' and 'destruction' on the three blank cards, and put them back on the plate. I shuffled them about, and picked one out – compassion. I picked another – grace. Another – chaos.

I know I never left them there. I've thought back about it a thousand times, and I know I never left them there. I know I didn't. I reckon Mike found them in my room and slipped them back. That was his style. Perhaps he'd calculated that his stock was slipping and mine was rising, and a little correction was needed.

I took the blame, of course. When Mum came downstairs wailing one fine school morning, with 'destruction' in her hand, I took the blame.

'You getting anything off that pill?' asked Shell.

'I dunno. I feel quite in control. And I'm not having any bad thoughts, for once. It's like the good thoughts part of my brain is telling the bad thoughts bit to quit moaning for a change. You know what I mean?'

'Yeah. Let's take another one.'

'OK.'

I reached into my pocket, pulled out the packet of Prozac and popped a couple more out of the foil. We swigged them down with glugs of cider from a water canteen.

'Your Mum won't notice they're gone, will she?'

'She's crap like that. She'll think she's taken them and forgotten about it.'

'How long has she been on them?'

'Ever since Dad got home, funnily enough.'

I looked across at the crowd clustered around the sound system on the other side of the field. It looked like a single creature, a giant throbbing blob of limbs. 'Maybe they'll make us feel like dancing.'

We were sat on the back seat of an old car plonked outside Dean's trailer. It was very late or very early. Around us were all the knackered traveller vans, about ten of them now, plus a few benders.

Thirty or forty cars, some quite posh, were parked in circles at the other end of the field. More kept arriving and spewing out little gangs of ravers, who got swallowed up quickly by the hungry blob. There were maybe five hundred people there.

'How is it now, with your Dad around?'

'Not good. He says things have slid while he was away, and he wants to get them back on course. But

257

he just hangs around the house reading the paper and drinking tea. Or checking the jobs pages on Ceefax.'

'But he let you out tonight?'

'No. I'm supposed to be in my room. Playing with dolls or something. Reading about horses.'

A whoop of sirens erupted from the road, and we turned to watch the arrival of a gang of pig vans. A dark figure approached. I could tell straight away it was Dean by the way he walked, the silhouette of his smooth head. Stimpy trotted beside him. He crouched down next to us. 'All right, love?'

'Yeah. You all right?'

'Yeah. How's it going?'

'Good.'

I pointed at the road. Pigs had spilled out and were lining the verge, peering over the hedge. 'They going to bust it?'

'They'll just make sure it doesn't get any bigger. They'll move in and clear it in the morning, when everyone's knackered.'

I patted Stimpy's head. He looked huge from the side, but head-on he almost disappeared. One thing I'd noticed: some of the human beings on site looked pretty sub-standard, but the dogs were princes.

'Good party,' said Shell. 'Where did all these people come from?'

Dean shrugged. 'Everybody loves getting off their head in a field.' He looked out at the ravers raving. 'In the morning this place'll look a state, and we'll have to clean it up. And we'll get the blame.'

'You lot didn't set it up then?' asked Shell.

'Nothing to do with me. It was the new arrivals. Party people.' He nodded over to one of the vans. It was orange, with 'Sticky Wicket' spray-painted on the side.

'My kind of people,' said Shell.

'Hardly. They're smackies.'

'I thought you didn't want any junkies living here?' said Shell.

'I can't say who can live here and who can't. At least now we won't get busted.'

'What do you mean?'

'E sites and hash sites get busted. But they never bust a smack site. It's legal. You coming inside?'

'I want to dance,' said Shell, and got up.

Someone was shouting. 'I'm going to fucking get me a big fucking stick. No copper cunt's taking me out.'

'I'll come,' I said.

'Sorry I'm so boring,' said Dean as he fiddled with the oil lamp. 'You sure you don't want to go and dance with your friends?' He got it alight and a gentle orange light engulfed the trailer. Stimpy curled up in his spot on the bed.

'I want to be with you.'

'OK.'

We sat down on the mattress. It felt very quiet in there; the music outside was a distant irrelevance.

He reached over and looked in a box on a shelf.

'We're nearly out of tea,' he said, 'and grass.'

'I love you,' I said.

I took hold of his head and I put it on mine, the first move of a familiar sequence. We wound up shagging.

I lay there afterwards, next to his gently snoring body, and I felt like I was glowing softly, I felt like I could do anything, and the lyrics of trashy songs I'd sneer at in public were going through my head.

There was a knock on the door. It opened. I raised my head. Shell.

'What?'

'Vix, there's a riot in the village, Vix.'

'Yeah, right,' I said. 'It'll be like the last riot. A bunch of dickheads on top of the off-licence shouting legalize drugs. And a car window will get smashed. And someone will have a nosebleed.'

Dean twitched awake.

'No, it's the real thing. There's cops all over.' It was Frog's voice. I sat up and saw that the whole crew were there as well: Cosmic John, Frog, Loo, Cian. The outside world beyond them was a cluster of shadows and grey shapes. Cian spoke up.

'We're going to go and check it out. Maybe we won't have missed it all. You want to come along? We thought you'd want to come along.'

Dean turned over. 'You go,' he mumbled into the pillow. 'I can't be bothered.'

'Close the door,' I said. 'I'm going to get dressed. Be with you in a sec.'

Outside, the party was still going on, but there were more people milling around looking lost, and more casualties crashed out in the mud. We headed into town. The road was choked with cars parked on the verge. There were a lot of pigs about, and more arriving.

'Apparently a load of pissed-up beer boys ran rampage when they couldn't get into the party,' said Frog.

'No. It was ravers, after they were beaten up by the police,' said Cian.

'It was people at the party, who saw their chance to go off and do some looting,' said Shell.

Cian slashed at the hedge with a stick. 'One guy got his head kicked in by the police.'

Shell whispered, 'I heard a policeman got taken to hospital.'

We passed three men sitting motionless in a car in a lay-by. Just sitting there, three dark shapes, looking well suspect.

There were lights on in most of the houses, downstairs lights. A woman in a dressing gown stood framed in her doorway. Some cops gave us the eye. Cian explained that we were local, just on our way home, and they waved us past.

On the main street, there was a lot of litter about, and I saw a single trainer lying in the middle of the road. But basically, nothing much seemed to have changed; we'd obviously missed the action. Disappointed, we headed on.

'It's because of the full moon,' said Cosmic John, pointing up. 'All that weird energy.'

We went over a dip in the road and started down the hill. The window of the off-licence had been smashed. A couple of fat pigs stood outside. We were walking silently now, looking around. It felt like there was something weird in the air: the ghost of something, a static charge.

The newsagent, further down, also had a smashed window. As had the café. As had Mum's shop.

I ran to check it out. The fangs of glass left in the frame were orange in the street lights. The smell of incense and shortbread wafted out of the gaping hole. I peered in. Crystals and glass shards sparkled on the floor. Scented candles, novelty mugs, postcards, biscuit tins and Amazonian rain sticks were scattered all over.

The little dolls in national dress looked so funny lying about all higgledy-piggledy like that. They reminded me of the drugged-up casualties at the party. I couldn't stop laughing for a while, then I started crying, and then someone took me home.

twenty

burning up

Five a.m., and the house was silent; it almost felt like peace. Everyone was asleep, or at least lying in bed. I put the light on, blinked and looked around. Every year my room seemed to get smaller. It was full of stuff. Stuff, everywhere. I didn't need all this shit. I didn't even like most of this shit. I got dressed, then pulled my rucksack out from under the bed and stuffed it with clothes, pretty much indiscriminately. I thought I'd be traumatized at having to decide what to leave behind, but I wasn't, I felt triumphant as I looked around and thought, Don't need that, don't need that, don't need that. Lipstick? Fuck it. Alarm clock? Bollocks. Novelty lamp? Nope. Smurf collection? Redundant.

Bank book, chewing gum, fags, tampons, passport, et cetera went in my old school bag. There wasn't much room for any non-essentials, but I allowed myself my Walkman and a bunch of tapes, and scoured my shelves for books to take. Christ, what crap. Manuals about riding. Teenage romances. When did I read those? Felt like about seven centuries ago. I grabbed my favourite Camus and a first aid manual. A little bit of room was left on top. I picked up Pickles the Floppy Monkey and stuffed him in, too. I folded the passport photos of my mates into my purse.

Now, how was I going to get out? I couldn't pick the lock with a hair grip; I'd tried that once before. I opened my window and looked down. There was a sloping slate roof beneath – the top of the extension – then a drop of about two metres onto the patio.

I bundled up the duvet and shoved it out. It hit the roof, unfurled and tumbled over the edge. Maybe it'd break my fall a bit. I dropped my bag out after it. It made a big thump as it hit the ground, and I froze, listening. Nothing; I reckoned I'd got away with it.

I shifted the bed so it was under the window. Then I stripped the sheet and tied the end to the bedpost, curled up the rest, tied a knot in the end and threw it out. I was always good at gym at school, and I coped pretty well with the perimeter wall at Glastonbury, but this wasn't going to be easy. I climbed onto the window sill, turned myself around, held onto it and lowered myself down to the roof, which took about five minutes. I hung terrified for a couple more. I grabbed the sheet with one hand. By then it was too late. I was breathing hard. I let go with the other hand and took the sheet. My weight was on it, and I almost screamed as I dangled there. Gulping air in frightened gasps, I started clambering down the sheet. I made maybe a metre. I hung there a moment, my feet over the edge, before I heard a ripping sound and the stupid sheet started to tear in two. I slid belly down along the roof, scraping the tiles, going, 'Ahhhhhh-hhhhh!' As I went over the edge I let go of the sheet and grabbed at the gutter, I missed it and fell straight down, feet first, onto the patio, and landed with a smack beside the duvet.

Fuck. My feet were sore, and my thigh, and my elbow was scraped. It was a miracle I hadn't broken anything. I picked up my bag. Above me the torn sheet flapped, but there was no sound from the house.

Only six hours earlier, I'd been lying next to Dean in his big soft bed, looking at his shoulder, which was a soft blue shape among all the other blue shapes. It was just the right side of being too hot under the heavy covers. Stimpy was lying on the other side, and I could feel his foot quivering as he dreamed some doggy dream.

'Dean. In the village, everyone is saying something should be done. They blame you for the riot last night. I think you're going to get evicted soon.'

'Yeah. It won't be long now.'

'But you'll stay as long as you can?'

''Course. 'Til the bailiffs turn up.'

'Do you love me?'

'You know I do.'

'Why not stay, then? Live here.'

'This is what I do, Vix.'

'So you want to go?'

He turned round and propped himself up on one elbow. His face was big and dark and hovering over me. I saw his eyes glinting. I felt the pressure of his hairy chest on my side. His breath was warm.

'I love it, blatting round the country. I move around and meet people. I don't do much else, you know.'

'I'd gathered that.'

'But that doesn't mean I won't miss you.'

I felt tears prickling at the corners of my eyes. Fuck. I willed them back. Maybe he hadn't seen, 'cause he continued.

'I've been in this place long enough,' said Dean. 'I've got the urge.'

I reached around and held him.

'You've got the urge?'

'Yeah. See new places. You know.'

'I know,' I whispered, 'I've got it, too.'

'Come along, if you like.'

I felt Stimpy's body go suddenly tense. He barked in my ear and bolted for the door.

'What is it, Stimps?' Dean's voice was loud and urgent. He pulled away from me and sat up in bed.

'Maybe he can smell a fox or something,' I suggested.

Stimpy barked again and kept barking, a savage sound.

'Something's burning.' Dean scrambled out of bed. He grabbed Neighbourhood Watch, that was his name for the metal bar he kept by the door, and he was out of the trailer while I was still blinking and getting the covers off. Cold night air rushed in. Stimpy leapt out, followed by Dean.

Outside, more dogs started barking.

'Get out. Vix, get out!'

I reached for my clothes.

'Get out, Vix!'

I felt my chest thump and I lurched out of bed. I stood outside in the field, standing on the scratchy grass, feeling mud slide between my toes, holding my arms around me.

'What is it? What is it?'

Dean ran to the front of the trailer. 'Jesus. Fuck. Christ.'

A flickering orange glow was growing there. I heard a crackle.

Fire tongued its way around the trailer, a big red ugly smear of it, coming from underneath. It spread along the bottom and fluttered up the sides.

'Fuck!' shouted Dean. 'Fuck!' His body flickered orange as the fire started eating up the front.

I smelled petrol.

Other people were getting out of the vehicles near by.

'Water!' yelled Dean, 'Water!'

There was a sound of coughing and swearing above the cackling of the flames. People stood around, or ran about shouting for water, or held their heads as the fire snarled and slavered. It grew and grew, and in seconds the whole trailer was just a black shape inside a yellow ball.

I realized I was shivering. A couple of people stumbled up with jerry cans. I heard a car start up in the road. I turned and saw its black soft-top roof above the hedge as it accelerated away.

I held Dean's shaking arm as we stood and watched the trailer burn down.

'I'll fucking kill them,' he ranted, over and over, with a twisted face. 'I'll kill them.'

Someone gave us blankets.

'I have to go home,' I told Dean quietly.

I let go of his arm. He didn't look at me as I walked away. I hugged the blanket around me and stumbled across the fields. It was quicker if you went along the road, but I'd always gone through the fields. I felt safer. No-one would see me. I knew the route by heart now, every tree stump and sudden dip; where the hedge was lowest; where to get through the barbed wire. I heard owls hoot and the rustles and calls of creepy night things. Leaves batted my face, thorns slashed my thighs, twigs prodded me all over.

I approached the house through the long back garden, I went past the big tree, the pond, the old rabbit hutch, the little herb garden that was now choked with weeds and towards the back door. I could see a light on in the kitchen.

The back-door key was under its usual stone, but the door was unlocked.

Mike was sitting at the kitchen table, dressed in black jeans and a black jumper, stirring a cup of tea. A paper was open in front of him. A pile of clean plates sat by the sink. The clock was calmly ticking.

He turned and stared. Dirty and naked, with a muddy old blanket around me, I must have looked like some desperate refugee.

'You could have killed me!' I shouted.

'What?'

'You fucking idiot,' I screamed. 'You fucking fucking; I fucking hate you, stupid fucking—'

'What are you on about?'

'I hate you!' I reached for his mug and knocked it flying, and tea exploded over him. The cup hit a unit and smashed on the tile floor. He stood up, knocking his chair over.

'You stupid cow!' he shouted, holding his sodden top away from his body with tweezered fingers.

Then I lost my temper.

The blanket slipped off me as I leapt across the kitchen. I was possessed. My vision came to me in bright clear flashes, like film stills, as I slapped and kicked him. Mike's bigger than me, but I got in some good hard smacks and scratches and slashes, and he bent down, arms up to protect his head.

Then he lunged up punching, our arms tangled, and the weight of him pushed me down. We fell to the floor together and squirmed in the boiling tea. He got on top of me and punched a tit and held my head and smacked it on the floor.

Dad wrenched us apart. He was dressed in pyjama bottoms, and his hair stuck up all over.

'What's going on?' he yelled, and we got up and both started screeching at once.

'He nearly fucking killed me!'

'She nearly fucking killed me!'

Mum was in the doorway, her mouth a black hole, wailing.

'I've just nearly got burnt to death!'

'She's gone mental!'

'He set Dean's trailer on fire!'

'She just attacked me. Look what she did to me!'

'He set Dean's trailer on fire!'

'She just lunged at me!'

'He set Dean's trailer on fire!'

'Have you been sneaking out?' said Dad. 'I told you—'

'What does it matter what I was doing there? He just nearly burnt me alive!'

'What?' said Dad.

'Mike did it.'

'What are you saying, girl?'

'I saw his car!' I pointed at Mike, my finger quivering. I felt as if I couldn't breathe, as if we were all under this huge and heavy pressure. The room was bright with hate.

'Is that where you've been?' said Dad to Mike. 'Is that what you've done?'

'It wasn't me!'

'I saw his fucking car! He could have killed me. And Dean.'

Dad turned on me. 'Shut up! Shut up!'

'Yeah,' said Mike, 'calm down.'

For a moment I could hear us all gasping for breath.

'Fuck you! I'm not calming down! I don't want to fucking calm down!'

I swept my hand across the kitchen work unit and sent the stack of plates crashing to the floor.

Dad grabbed my arm and slapped me round the face. It stung like crazy, but it didn't make me feel any less angry, it didn't stop me boiling over.

'Mad,' said Mike. 'She's mad.'

Dad turned and slapped Mike, and he fell to the floor. He crouched on his elbows and knees, clutching his head, crying out, trying to make it look worse than it was. Dad stood and looked down at what he'd done. Mum's wailing went higher.

Mike rolled into the space between the fridge and the pedal bin and leant against the wall. He looked up. His voice was low.

'I didn't know what they were going to do. I was

271

only driving. You saw what they did to Mum's shop.'

'You shouldn't have done it, son.'

'Someone had to do something, didn't they?'

I dived across the room and started lashing out. I wished I had shoes on, so I could do some real damage. Mike drew up his knees, held his hands over his head and jammed himself tighter into the space. 'She's mad,' he shouted, 'get her off me!'

From behind, Dad grabbed me round the waist with both arms.

'I hate you.' I discovered I was still shouting, my mouth on automatic.

Dad pulled me back and up, and now I was kicking air. He wrenched me round and ran me into the wall. It hurt.

'I hate you all!'

'Fuck you!' shouted Dad. And then a lot of other things that I didn't understand. At first I thought he was snarling like some animal, then I realized he was swearing at me in Welsh.

'I'm going to live with Dean.' The words tumbled out high and scratchy. 'I don't want anything more to do with any of you.'

'No you're not,' roared Dad. He tightened his grip and walked me to the door.

Mike was still on the floor, clutching his head. Mum ran to him dumbly and held him in her arms and rocked him back and forth.

Dad walked me out of the kitchen and into the

dining room. His grip on me got tighter and tighter, and I thought I'd pass out, he was crushing me so hard. I windmilled my arms and knocked over a vase and framed photos of my parents' wedding and Mike's graduation on the sideboard. I didn't make it easy for him; I thrashed and bawled. And I'm not a little girl, not any more. His chest hair was prickly on my back. He got me out, into the hallway, to the bottom of the stairs. He let go with one of his arms, and I almost slipped away from him there, but he grabbed me back. He stepped backwards up the stairs, hauling me with him. We were both breathing hard now, with the effort. In my head I could hear his voice, from another time, from long, long ago: 'Up the wooden hill we go, up the wooden hill we go.'

It took a lot of bawling and effort all round, but we got there. In the end I let him do it. I could delay him, but I couldn't stop him. He was too strong and too determined. He dragged me along the corridor, into my room and threw me down on my bed. I lay there naked and he stood in the doorway, rasping, his wide chest going up and down, and just for a moment I thought, Anything could happen now, the worst, the worst thing was suddenly possible.

He took the key out of the door and closed it.

'You're going nowhere,' he said.

And then I was up and crying again. I threw myself against the door.

273

Dawn. I walked over the fields towards the site. The sun was rising, the birds were singing and the ground was fresh with dew. I watched the sky go streaky. It was beautiful here. I felt quite empty as I strolled along, like gravity had stopped working on me quite so hard. I saw nobody. A fox in a hedgerow caught my eye and gave me a frank and appraising stare. Then it trotted off, with an insolent lack of concern.

I remembered something Dean had told me once. Speed is the guarantee of freedom. Get out, go places, keep moving. That was what I was going to do.

I swept the twigs and brambles out of the way and headed to the field in a straight line. It was an easy walk in the light.

They were all gone. There was nothing there. Just the burnt-out wreck of Dean's trailer, a smashed-up black mass in a black circle of burnt grass. Apart from that it was just another muddy field.

import export

twenty one

hard seat

The hole in the counter's thick glass barrier is the size of Vix's face, and arch-shaped like a cartoon mouse hole. Vix puts her elbows on the shelf just below it and leans forward and down, her head twisted sharply to the side, to speak through it. A man behind her presses into her back.

'I want two tickets to Beijing,' she says. '*Liang* tickets. Beijing.'

On the other side of the glass a woman in a dark-blue uniform, with a lovebite on her neck, stares back at her vacantly. On either side of the woman sit two racks, and on them hang hundreds of cardboard stubs – tickets. Vix looks at them with longing. She holds up two fingers in a reverse V sign, with the other hand waves two-hundred-yuan notes.

'Beijing,' shouts Vix. '*Ruan zuo.*'

The woman blinks, looking bored.

'*Mei you,*' she drawls.

277

>>>import export

Vix thinks the woman might not have understood, and reaches into the rubber bag slung over her left shoulder to pull out her brick of a guidebook. As she flicks through the creased pages, looking for the language section, the man behind reaches an arm over her right shoulder, a wad of money in his hand. It's the closest she has been to a man since the last time she slept with Sol. She can feel the pens in his shirt pocket. He leans into her, as if about to embrace her, fires off a string of loud Mandarin in her ear, directed at the woman behind the counter, and slips his hand into the mouse hole. The pressure of his heavy arm on her shoulder forces Vix to bend down further. She drops the guidebook, and stoops to pick it up from a concrete floor dirty with cigarette butts, peanut shells, husks of sunflower seeds and dried gobs of spit. The man leans over her. She raises her head and it bumps into his paunchy stomach. She has been in this queue for nearly half an hour; she is sweaty and uncomfortable and prickly with irritation. She feels her face flush.

'Fuck off!' she shouts at his shoes.

With slim, deft fingers the woman counts out the man's change, and passes it through the hole with two brown cardboard stubs. He scoops them up and slips aside. Vix stands up, launches herself forward and jams her face up against the warm glass. Another body is pressing into her back.

'Beijing! Beijing!'

The woman sighs. '*Mei you*,' she snaps.

A hand bearing money appears in the gap between Vix's elbow and her chest, and snakes towards the hole.

'Beijing! Now! Please! I have to get to Beijing!'

'*Mei you*,' repeats the woman, and bats her hand across her face as if a fly were bugging her.

Vix squeezes to the side; instantly the crush of bodies behind slaps itself forward to the counter. Stomach-high railings keep the queue segregated from the ones at the counters on either side. Vix slips along the metal bars, stepping sideways away from the counter. When she's free of the scrum she stands alone in the wide, high ticket hall and looks about her, ordering herself to be calm.

There are ten counters ranked along the length of the wall. Some have no queues, some have no staff, some have a queue and no staff. Charts of numbers and Chinese characters painted on the wall to her right, presumably list which trains go where and which destinations are served by which counters. She wishes there was something somewhere she could understand, but the only English she can see is the odd slogan on a T-shirt: 'Red Sand', 'Elton Shows His', 'Hello Terracotta Sunday'.

Most of the people in the hall are men, and most are dressed in outfits of garish artificial fabrics that make her think of Seventies made-for-TV movies. Some of the older men dress quite differently, in blue cotton shirts and trousers and Mao caps. They look like characters out of a gritty but uplifting documentary about the workers' struggle to build socialism, who have wandered into this movie by mistake. All share the preoccupied look of people in train stations everywhere, so at least here, she thinks, not that many people are staring at her.

Vix heads for the exit, a wide gap in the far wall. The other foreigner sits just inside the hall, slumped on his kit bag, one hand draped over her green army rucksack which is beside him, the other clutching the handles of a blue bag placed between his legs. It's the kind of cheap sports bags she has seen in department stores all over the country. It says, 'World People Unite', on the side, the letters curling around a picture of a globe.

He's lean and wiry, with a tangle of lank, unkempt hair topping a narrow face. He's dressed in jeans and a black hooded top. She guesses he's a little older than her. His skin is heavily weathered, lined and tanned, with dark circles around his bright, narrow eyes. His big, sharp nose and sloping forehead give him a look of aggressive energy. Vix classifies him as ugly in an interesting way. He's called Lee.

He jerks his head up and thrusts it forward as she approaches. 'Any luck?' he calls out, and an old man lying on the floor close to him, curled up on sacks tied up with string, cap pulled down over his face, grunts in his sleep.

'She said she didn't have any.'

'Fuck's sake.' Lee runs a hand over the stubble on his chin, then reaches into his pocket and pulls out a soft pack of Stone Forest. 'Fag?'

'I don't.' Vix has stopped smoking. She hasn't had a cigarette for three weeks, the whole time she has been in China. As she watches him pull out a cigarette, she reminds herself that she feels much better for it. She's proud of herself. And to do it here of all places, in a country where it seems every male over the age of eleven puffs like a steam train, makes it seem more of an achievement.

'I've got to get out of this shithole,' Lee says. 'I've got to get to Beijing and get the fuck out of this fucking awful country.'

'I'm supposed to meet my boyfriend in Beijing,' says Vix. 'We've got tickets for the trans-Siberian express, which leaves in two days. If I don't get a train today, I'm going to miss it. I'm going to miss him.' Vix bites down on a fingernail, sinking a tooth into a cuticle. 'What are we going to do?'

'Got to get matches. Look after the luggage, yeah?'

Lee flips up the hood of his top, stands and steps out. Vix watches him go. Outside, it's raining hard. Lee strides briskly down a set of steps to a concourse packed with minibuses. A line of stalls at its side sell oranges, nuts, magazines and bright, plastic children's toys. He walks towards them, dodging through the crowd with his head down and bobbing, knees turned slightly outwards, hands thrust into the front pocket of his top.

When she first saw him in the station, Vix felt a flood of relief. Realizing she was stuck in a crappy little Chinese town in the middle of nowhere was making her panic. Sharing the experience would surely help. But in the two hours they've spent trying to buy tickets out, the man has been little use. He speaks no Mandarin, complains all the time and watches his bags as if everyone in the station were plotting to snatch them. They've talked very little, and about nothing outside their situation; they're just strangers united by a common purpose.

For a moment Vix sees herself and Lee as the Chinese must see them; big-limbed strangers from another world, well fed, dishevelled, in dirty and expensive clothes.

Then her attention is drawn to the swarm of cyclists on black bikes in the street beyond. Many have plastic ponchos on, only their head and hands poking out, and they look like overgrown mechanical toys as they tick past, dodging puddles and potholes.

The buildings lining the street are constructed of streaky concrete or faced with white tiles. The area is packed with people. Vix's attention is drawn by a toddler so swaddled in clothes he looks like a teddy bear, by two men pissing against a wall, by an old woman struggling with a suitcase. Above the sound of bustle, arguments and traffic, and the industrial patter of the rain, rise the persistent refrains of minibus conductors calling out their destinations.

The quality of people's clothes, the lack of cars, the state of the road and the architecture tell Vix she's in a backwards rural town. It lags perhaps a decade behind the Chinese cities she has seen, with their atmosphere of thrusting busyness. She is right out in the sticks.

Sol would like it here, she thinks; he'd get a whole film out of it.

Vix squats down on her heels, back against the wall, and opens the guidebook. She has hardly glanced at it before, except to read about what diseases she could get. The town she's in is marked on the chapter map of Shaanxi Province, but there is no entry for the place. It's like an official confirmation; she is lost, she is far from anywhere she wants to be, there is just her.

'You know you're alive,' Vix tells herself. It's her mantra for helping her cope with difficult situations. It means, at least you're not bored, at least it's not dull, at least you're not stuck at home watching telly. But in the last few hours she has repeated it so often it's lost its power, and the tone of her mental voice has developed an hysterical or ironic edge. 'You know you're alive.' She remembers a time, a year or two ago, when she almost welcomed such situations, seeing them as challenges and believing they were good for the soul;

now she knows they're just bad for her health.

Vix becomes aware of a girl watching her from the steps. She's wearing a brown floral dress, and a white plastic sun hat with a wide brim, which quivers as raindrops hit it, and she is watching Vix with an unnerving, level gaze, like she's window shopping and Vix is a well-dressed dummy. Having grown used to such frank attention, Vix ignores her.

Beijing is three inches north-east on the same map; eight hundred kilometres away. She is supposed to meet Sol in Tiananmen Square, outside the Memorial Hall to Chairman Mao, tomorrow afternoon.

'Hello,' calls the girl, and smiles shyly. Vix looks up, nods and smiles, then looks down again. She doesn't want to have to cope with anyone now. Perhaps, as usual, the girl will smile and stand a while, or maybe, as happened with some school-girls on the train yesterday, she would repeat the only phrases she knew in English; how are you, I love you.

'You look not happy,' says the girl in a clear, bright voice. 'Can I help you?'

'Yes,' says Vix, snapping the guidebook shut. 'Shit. Yes. I want to go to Beijing.'

'You will not get tickets here.'

'No?'

'No.'

'What am I going to do?'

'I want to help you. I know a way. You will have to come with me.' The girl steps up and stands just inside the hall, out of the rain. She crouches down. Vix notices she has black high heels on, decorated with little bows on the top and spattered with mud. She is slim and short, around Vix's age perhaps, but she finds it hard to tell.

'What is your name?' asks the girl.

'Vix. Short for Victoria.'

'Like the dead queen. Very beautiful. I am Jing Wen, but you can call me Xiao Wen, which is what my friends call me.' She smiles broadly.

Lee steps up towards them, calling out to Vix and ignoring the Chinese girl.

'Guy tried to overcharge me for matches. Matches. I mean . . . matches.' He sucks hard on his cigarette.

'This girl says she can help us,' says Vix.

Xiao Wen stands and takes off her hat.

'Hello,' she says, holding it in front of her with both hands.

'Yeah, hi. You can get us tickets?'

'You have to walk with me. Not far.'

Lee points at the luggage.

'Someone has to stay and look after these.'

'I'll go then,' says Vix, as he sits down in the dip in the middle of his kit bag.

'Where are you from?' asks Xiao Wen as she leads Vix down the steps.

'England,' says Vix.

'I know England. Tesco. The parish church.'

They step around the minibuses. One leaves, revving noisily, with maybe thirty passengers crammed inside. A conductor stands in its open side doorway, holding on with one arm, her bag of tickets swinging. Xiao Wen walks quickly, dodging ably between the people squatting by their luggage. Vix has to concentrate to keep up with her.

'Country seat. Kwiksave. Coach and fours.'

Vix holds her hands over her head in a futile effort to keep the rain off. It feels harder than British rain – the impacts of the lumps of water sting her fingers.

'The Duke of Rochester. Safeways.'

'What happened to the train I was on?' asks Vix as she follows Xiao Wen around the side of the station. 'It just stopped here. I couldn't believe it. Just stopped. And they kicked everyone off. We got hassled off the train and left here. No compensation, nothing.'

'Yes. Floods very bad now. Train cannot go. But there is special train, which goes back to Xi'an, and then takes the other line. But very hard to get tickets for this train.'

Xiao Wen heads up a thin unpaved alley at the side of the station. The walls lining it are brick, and they lean inwards, as if bent with exhaustion. Rubbish is piled outside the odd door. Puddles

go>>> simon lewis

glisten in the dirt track. Vix is surprised at how quickly the environment has changed. It makes the modern buildings around the station seem, in retrospect, a little unreal, like a façade.

Xiao Wen approaches a man standing in front of a window, under a striped red-and-white awning. She addresses him and he answers her curtly. He's dressed in a green shirt and trousers; Vix stops a few paces away under the awning and wonders if he's a soldier, or a policeman, or just fashionable. Through the steamy window Vix can see a little room full of blurred figures hunched over bowls. A noodle shop.

'When do you want tickets for?' Xiao Wen asks Vix.

'Today. As soon as possible. Two tickets.'

'Hard or soft?'

'Hard sleeper, please. But anything will do.' Xiao Wen talks to the man, and he scratches his chin and takes a drag on his cigarette. The long fingernails of his little fingers are painted red. He exhales and answers her.

'He can maybe get you tickets for tonight. He says they will cost five hundred yuan.'

'Together?'

'Each.'

'That's loads. That's really expensive.'

Xiao Wen talks sharply to the man, and he raises his voice back at her. She turns back to Vix.

'He says that's the price.'

Nearly fifty quid; it seems an outrageous amount. The situation makes Vix uneasy; it reminds her of furtive drug deals, and she suspects a con.

'There is no other way to go now,' says Xiao Wen, 'unless you want to take a bus.'

'How long would a bus take?'

'Maybe three days.'

'That's not quick enough.'

'Then you will have to get this train.'

'Bollocks,' says Vix. She puts her hands on the back of her neck to stop the droplets shivering down it.

'I have to ask that other guy. Let's go and see him.' Vix feels it would be wiser to negotiate in public.

Xiao Wen and Vix turn and begin to walk back down the alley, the man with the nails following a couple of paces behind. Vix leaves her hands by her side; she'll just get wet. Xiao Wen takes Vix's elbow to stop her stepping on a dead rat sinking in the mud.

Lee bows his head and grinds his cigarette into the floor as Vix tells him what happened. His hood is still up and she cannot see his expression.

He looks up, staring at the man with the nails, posed in the entrance, one hand in his pocket. Xiao Wen, standing next to the man, smiles nervously.

'Can he give us the tickets straight away?' Lee

asks. Xiao Wen translates, and the man with the nails replies curtly.

'He says he will have the tickets tonight,' says Xiao Wen. 'He says he must go and get them. Now is not possible.'

'So we give this pair a load of money,' says Lee, 'and they go away with it?'

'Yeah,' says Vix.

'It's a blag.'

'What?' says Vix. 'You want to hang around here? There aren't any tickets. We haven't got a choice.'

Vix turns to Xiao Wen.

'We'll give him the money', Vix says, 'when he gives us the tickets.'

'But he needs the money to buy the tickets.'

'No way am I just giving a stranger a load of money,' says Lee.

'You can trust this person,' says Xiao Wen.

Lee beckons Vix away with a wave of his hand. He lowers his voice.

'Listen, I've been in this country a while. I know. You can't trust any of them.'

'She seems sound.'

Lee addresses Xiao Wen, raising his voice. 'What are you getting out of this deal?'

'Nothing.'

'No commission? No money? Nothing?'

'I very please to practise my English.'

Lee whispers to Vix again. 'I don't believe her. I don't believe him.'

Vix feels herself losing patience. She can sense that the people around them are watching and talking about them. She studies Xiao Wen. The girl has a tight smile on her face. In the weeks she has been in China, Vix has learned to interpret this expression as a sign of suppressed nervousness. If the girl was a blagger, Vix considers, she would be pushy and not look so unsure of herself.

'I think we should take it,' says Vix. She turns to Xiao Wen. 'OK,' she says, 'but he definitely won't get the money till we see the tickets. We will go with him to buy them.' The two Chinese begin to talk to each other, and Vix turns to Lee. 'You happy with that?'

Lee shrugs. 'Yeah. But don't blame me if it all goes wrong.'

Xiao Wen turns to Vix.

'He says he will see you here at eight o'clock and you will go with him.'

'Is that OK, do you think?' says Vix.

'I do not know. But I worry you. You want, I will come with you.'

'Do,' says Vix. 'That's good of you.' She turns to Lee.

'What are we going to do till eight?'

'You should get a room,' suggests Xiao Wen.

'Yeah,' says Vix.

Xiao Wen points at a building on the other side of the station concourse. It looks like a giant breeze-

go>>> simon lewis

block with windows. Gold Chinese characters stand up on the flat roof.

'There is a hotel.'

Lee stands up and hefts his kit bag onto his shoulder. 'Let's get a room then.'

last stop

The hotel lobby looks like the waiting room of a grimy hospital. A few armchairs upholstered in faded green material stand randomly around the concrete floor. On the wall behind reception is a map of the world, continents cut out of brown plastic and pasted on. Australia is peeling off. The rooms are a lot more expensive than Vix expected. Xiao Wen tells them it's the only hotel in town permitted to accept foreigners. Vix imagines they don't see many, judging by the giggles and sly glances of the yellow-uniformed girls behind the reception desk.

'Let's share,' says Vix.

'Sure.'

Xiao Wen helps them fill out white forms in Chinese asking their personal details. The work unit gets left blank. A girl rifles through their passports, another takes their money, another gives each of them a room card – a piece of plastic with a number on it.

Xiao Wen waves them goodbye and they walk up the wide, dark staircase at the back of the lobby.

'I reckon', says Lee, 'they're in league.'

'Who?'

'That girl and the guy. They're probably married.'

'They can't make a living out of fleecing tourists,' says Vix, 'there aren't any.'

At the third floor they head off into a long, dim, carpetless corridor. Two yellow-uniformed girls sit at a desk by the stairwell and play with a baby chicken. One puts it on the desk top, it runs up to the end, then the other turns it around and it runs back the way it came. They look up, see Vix and Lee, and giggle. Vix shows them her room card and one gets a set of keys out of the desk drawer. Vix and Lee follow her to a door halfway along the corridor, which she opens.

The room has two beds, a bathroom, a TV next to a plastic vase of flowers on a table and a fly swat hanging on the back of the door. On a bedside cabinet between the beds stands a thermos the size of an aqualung, two lidded teacups, a sachet of green tea and a notice that says, among a lot of Chinese, 'Do Not Smoke In The Bed', and 'Pay Attention To Civilization'.

Vix sits down on the bed by the window, next to the table. Out of unconscious habit she always picks the bed furthest from the bathroom door. She drops her shoulders and wriggles to slip off her rucksack, letting it topple behind her onto the mattress. She starts to undo her shoelaces.

Lee drops his sports bag on the other bed, drops his kitbag upright on the floor and slips a leather neck band out from inside his top. A shell, a stone and a couple of keys hang on it. He leans over the kitbag, bending almost double, and unlocks the hefty padlock securing it.

'So how long have you been here?' asks Vix, slipping off her trainers, which fall, clunk clunk, to the concrete floor.

He straightens, hoists the kitbag up, and holds it mouth-down over the bed. He starts to shake it violently.

'A couple of weeks.' Musty clothes flop out onto the sheet.

'Where've you been?'

'I came from Pakistan. Overland.'

'The Karakoram Highway?'

'Yeah.'

Lee shakes harder, and more stuff is disgorged. Vix watches and waits for him to ask her a question or make a comment, but he seems entirely engrossed in unpacking.

'That must have been cool,' she says.

'What?'

'Coming all that way.'

'If you like sitting on crap buses.'

Lee gives the bag one last shake to make sure everything's out, throws it aside and delves into the mound of creased clothes on the bed, scattering them over the sheets.

'Why are you going to Beijing?'

'I'm going to Berlin. On the train.'

'The trans-Siberian express? No way! That's what I'm doing. Well. If I get to Beijing in time. I've heard Siberia is really beautiful. And . . .'

Lee dives on a small, round object wrapped in crinkly silver foil. Vix trails off; he doesn't seem to be listening. 'What have you got there?' she asks.

'Food.' He peels back a corner of the foil and shows her; a couple of dumplings. All that effort, thinks Vix, for *bao zi*? He puts the precious packaged dumplings in the pocket of his sweatshirt and picks up the sports bag.

'I'm just going to freshen up, all right?' He steps swiftly into the bathroom, carrying the bag. The lock clicks shut.

Vix reaches over, puts the TV on and twists the dial until the static fuzz resolves into a picture. Dancers in stylized military uniforms. She looks for another channel. Pamela Anderson, in a red bikini, addresses a distressed child in rapid Mandarin. A man in swimming trunks carrying a surfboard strides along the beach in the background. Vix makes herself comfortable and begins to watch. A minute later she realizes she's seen this episode before, and her attention wanders from the screen to a brown stain, like a raincloud, on the ceiling. She hears scraping sounds coming from the bathroom.

She looks at her digital watch. 16:41. Remembering a recent resolution to try to use time more constructively, she reaches into her bag and takes out her diary and a biro. The diary is a foxed, grimy hardback. A collage of train tickets and packaging is pasted on the cover.

She opens the book to a page about three-quarters of the way through, to the end of the last entry, written the night before: 'I've decided. Yes. Yes yes yes yes. I'm lying on my bunk in this train and I can't sleep. I'm excited. I wish I'd got him a present.' She writes 'Fuck!' then stops and taps the pen against her teeth. She stares at the page for a minute, then she writes 'Fuck!' again. Then she crosses both words out.

Deciding she just doesn't feel in the mood to write, she turns back about twenty pages to where 'CHINA' is written in big, bold capitals. She turns the page and begins to scan the dense black lines of neat, curvy handwriting.

The first entry begins, 'I'm sitting on a train looking at little green rice fields. The weather here is really hot and the people are nice. The food is supposed to be good, but I can't eat most of it; it's all meat. I saw snakes and monkeys for sale in a market today. I've just realized, suddenly I don't feel numb and shivery any more. I've stopped dreaming about it. I think I've been suffering from shock. Getting the fuck out was definitely the best thing to do. We've got enough money to stay here a month and just chill out for a bit. Then Sol's going home. He says he's realized that's all he's wanted to do for ages. I persuaded him to do it overland, and then at least I can go with him as far as Moscow. I've always wanted to see dead Lenin. I've done Ho Chi Minh, and I'll do Mao next and then I'll have the set. I don't know what I'm going to do after that. I haven't decided.'

Boring, boring, boring, thinks Vix. She turns a few pages, and continues reading, skimming rapidly. Random impressions are thrown in around a catalogue of places she has been.

'China is really flat and there are cabbage fields everywhere. People wear triangular hats and go round on bicycles, but mostly it's not what you expect; it looks like a crappy industrial estate mostly. We're in Yanghou now. There are loads of travellers here. You can eat banana pancakes as good as the ones in Nepal. I've met some cool people.'

Her own style is beginning to annoy her, and the words seem to convey so little. They just sit there; they don't work properly.

Vix flips a few more pages.

'Keep having these arguments over stupid little things. Like today it was how pissed off I am that he can't get up in the morning and I'm sat around the room for an hour or more, every morning, twiddling my thumbs waiting for him to emerge.'

She stops reading; the memory's painful.

Turning over, she notices that her writing gets progressively larger and messier.

'Worked it all out. It's because I can't decide if I want to go back home with him and live with him and have a Proper Relationship, or, do I just want to say it was a good laugh, and leave it there??????? He thinks I should come back with him, but I just don't know; it's ripping me up. I'm going through all this shit in my head. Move or make a go of it. Responsibility or freedom. And 'cause it's doing my head in, I'm resenting him the whole time, and taking it out on him. We talked for ages and ages, and the restaurant owner wanted to shut, so we had to keep ordering more food to keep him happy, and we weren't eating any of it. At the end, I decided I needed a bit of space. And Sol said he needed some, too. So I'm going to go off on my own for a week and have some adventures and do some thinking, and he's going to go and take pictures of some Buddhist caves, and then we're going to meet in Beijing, and by then I'll have sorted my head out and decided.'

Struck by a sudden thought, she flicks to the book's end. On the last few pages she has written the addresses of people she has met in the time she's been travelling. She collects them fastidiously, though knowing from experience that she's unlikely to get in touch with any of them, even those who were like best mates at the time. But a ritual exchange of addresses makes the goodbyes easier. The few entries written in unfamiliar scripts – Thai, Cantonese, Japanese, Korean – stand out. She scans the list of names, reaches the last and feels sick with fear.

She closes the book, drops it and draws her knees up; she sits with her hands over her face.

The toilet flushes and the bathroom door unlocks. Vix composes herself.

Lee steps out and lets the sports bag fall from his fingers to the floor. His necklace hangs by the key from the bag's padlock, and the shell taps as it hits the concrete. Lee sways.

'Are you all right?' says Vix.

'Tired,' mumbles Lee, and he flops down limply on the bed, on top of the bedclothes, face in the pillow, feet hanging over the side.

'I've just made this terrible discovery,' says Vix.

'Yeah?' His voice is muffled; the syllable comes out as a non-committal grunt.

'See, I haven't got my boyfriend's address.'

'Yeah.'

'If I don't get out of here tonight, I'll miss the train, and I'll have no way of getting in touch with him. That's it, gone.'

'Yeah.'

'It's so stupid, but you don't think, do you? I mean, that's so crap. It's so stupid. See, I couldn't decide if I wanted to go home with him or not.' Vix feels her voice rise. 'And now I've decided I do. And maybe it doesn't even fucking matter

>>>import export

because I'm not going to see him again anyway because I haven't even got his fucking address.'

Vix's face feels hot. She feels a little stupid, and experiences a wave of anxiety rise from her stomach. Lee is a stranger, after all, and maybe he'll think she's unbalanced. But her outburst has had no effect on him at all. It's as if he didn't hear her.

'You must be really tired,' she says.

'Yeah.'

Vix notices his cigarettes and matches, flagrant and obvious on the bedside cabinet. She turns her head away and stares at the TV. *Baywatch* is finishing with a shot of a nuclear family walking along a beach together, holding hands in a row, like figures in a paper chain, while the sun sets over the water. Their perfect bodies and their confident, upright poses remind Vix of the statues she has seen here in public squares, on roundabouts – giant images of bulky, muscled workers and their angular wives and children, striding boldly forward as if into a certain future, lantern jaws held high. Abruptly, a news programme begins.

Vix decides she wants to be alone.

'Well, my turn for the bathroom, then,' she says, and gets her towel and wash bag out of her rucksack. Walking across the room, she accidentally knocks one of Lee's overhanging feet as she passes. She apologizes, but he doesn't seem to notice. Vix is used to sharing rooms with strangers, and hardly thinks twice about it. The man had seemed sound enough before, but now his behaviour is beginning to make her feel a little uneasy. She hopes he isn't mad or dangerous.

By the sink in the bathroom sit two little plastic bottles of shampoo, a plastic toothbrush, two tiny tubes of toothpaste and a wrapped oblong of soap. The toilet is noisily filling up with water. A couple of burnt matches spin in the bowl. She cleans her teeth and runs herself a bath.

Vix lies and looks up at another brown stain on the ceiling. The shower drips regularly, and the noise is loud in the steamy room. She cleans herself methodically, then pulls out the plug and squats until the gurgling water has drained out as far as her ankles. The panic she felt earlier has settled to a queasy sense of unease. Sitting on the edge of the bath to dry herself, she looks at her indistinct image in the steamed-up mirror. She imagines it as a picture of what she really looks like; her body is becoming vague, dissolving, she's going out of focus.

Back in the room, she gets a novel out of her bag – *Hard Times*, published by the Foreign Language Press. The only books in English she has seen here are Victorian novels. She finds the book exhaustingly tedious, and reading it is a triumph of will, but at least it plugs up her worries and stops her looking at her watch.

Three hours later there's a quiet knock on the door. Lee still hasn't moved. Vix gets up and opens it.

'Hello, Xiao Vix,' says Xiao Wen. She's wearing a short, white dress and purple shoes with high heels. She has put make-up on. She still wears the same sunhat, now cocked at a jaunty angle. 'We will go now, yes? And buy the tickets.'

'Yes. Now. Lee! Lee!'

Lee is awake; he sits up, shaking his head. 'Tickets,' he says. 'Tickets.'

Vix puts on her shoes while Lee drags himself off the bed. Leaving the hotel, Xiao Wen asks each of them a string of questions: are you married? How old are you? What is your job? Do you have any brother or sisters? Vix, reminded of her GCSE French oral, answers politely. Lee replies in mono-syllables. He is twenty-four, apparently, unmarried, an only child, and a DJ. Vix asks Xiao Wen what she does.

'I am a worker in a factory. Make plastic super-market bags for export. My uncle is a manager, so I do not must work hard. Instead I study English. I like to read Jane Austen.'

It's dark outside, and still raining. The unlit streets are slick. Everything looks closed, and there are few people around.

A taxi, a battered Russian car, waits for them. The man with the nails is in the front seat, his arm out of the open window, hand on the door frame, nails tip-tapping against it. He's wearing a flat, green hat, with a wide peak jutting out over his forehead.

Lee stops. 'He's a policeman.'

'Of course,' says Xiao Wen. 'Let us get in.'

'You didn't say he was a cop.'

'So you don't want to go now?' says Vix. 'Do you want to get out of here or not?'

Lee stands a moment, looking around him, then shrugs.

'OK, OK.'

Vix and Xiao Wen climb into the back of the small car, followed by Lee. There's not much room inside, and they are squashed up, leaning forward, shoulders hunched. A few raindrops come through the open front window and spatter Vix's face. She leans forward and looks closer at the door. There's no handle to wind it shut; it must be broken.

'Where are we going?' says Lee.

'I do not know,' replies Xiao Wen.

'Ask him, then.'

But the man with the nails just turns, grins and winks.

They drive very slowly, for five minutes, in silence, down straight, empty streets, past squat, dark buildings and brick walls. Both the men in front are smoking, and Vix follows the moving tips of their cigarettes.

Xiao Wen, the driver and the man with the nails chat among themselves.

'What are you talking about?' asks Lee.

'You,' says Xiao Wen.

'What about us?'

'They say you are both beautiful, but you have

big feet.' She stifles a giggle and points at him. 'And you have a big nose.'

'What?'

'You should know, this is a good thing. It means you are lucky.'

They pull up on a wide street, outside a large, low building, one of the few with lights on inside. The façade is undecorated; it looks official to Vix.

'We are here,' says Xiao Wen.

Vix pays the taxi driver and they get out. The man with the nails walks up a short flight of steps to the double doors at the front, beckoning them to follow.

Lee stops dead. 'It's the cop shop,' he says. 'I'm not going in there. No way.'

Vix moves forward, and through the glass panes in the door she sees gangs of young men and women in the entrance hall beyond, and a woman sitting at a wooden counter decorated with fairy lights.

'I don't think it is,' says Vix.

'This is the dancehall,' says Xiao Wen.

Lee gives out a short, sharp laugh.

'A disco? You buy train tickets in a disco?'

twenty three

nightclubbing

The man with the nails addresses the girl at the counter, then beckons Vix, Lee and Xiao Wen to follow him through another set of doors. Vix begins to get out her wallet to pay, but the girl waves her away.

The hall beyond is big and dark, illuminated with a few yellow and blue filtered lights at the side. Around a hundred people are dancing in the centre of the room to a simple beat that throbs out of speakers at the far end. The rest are standing around a bar at the near end of the room, or sitting on wooden stools and tables near it.

The scene reminds Vix of school discos, but the strangeness of the detail makes it seem dreamlike. The DJ stands behind a wooden desk at the far side of the hall. On a small platform raised on metal struts above him a slim girl in a miniskirt moves her hips from side to side and swings her arms. She wears blue nail varnish and has long permed hair, she wears a silver mac and sucks beer through a

>>>import export

straw. A man in a vest smokes two cigarettes, tweezered side by side between his fingers. Five policemen stand evenly spaced around the edges of the dance floor, watching the dancers, their faces shadowed by their peaked caps.

The man with the nails strides off towards the centre of the room. Vix steps into the shadows, her back against the wall.

'He will go and get the tickets,' says Xiao Wen. 'We must wait.'

'I'll get the beers in, then,' says Lee. He strolls towards the bar.

Xiao Wen and Vix move along the wall and sit down at a free table. The people around them smile at Vix and raise their bottles in greeting. Vix smiles back and nods. She watches the man with the nails approach one of the policemen.

'What's going on?' she asks.

'Those are his friends. They have the tickets to sell.'

'Why are there policemen in here?'

'So no problem.'

'Why does he have long nails?' asks Vix. 'In my country only women do that.'

'It is a fashion,' says Xiao Wen; 'it shows he is not working in fields.'

'Just to show he has money?'

'Yes. And in old days in your country, people wanted to be white, yes? To show they did not have to work in fields. Now a suntan is better. Because only rich people go and lie on beaches in foreign places. Beauty and money are always in a married state, I think. Oh, this is wrong. My English is too terrible.'

The way she says terrible, with a heavy stress on the second syllable, makes Vix smile and want her to say it again.

'No, it's really good.'

'You cannot speak my language so I have to speak yours. And I look like a fool.'

'No, no, I think it's amazing. You taught yourself. You must be very clever. And dedicated. I can't imagine someone in my country doing that.'

'I like to study. Nothing else to do.'

Lee returns with three bottles of Tsingtao beer, held in a triangle in front of him. 'One thing I'll say for this country,' he says, 'cheap beer.' He plonks the beers down on the table and draws up a stool. 'So,' Lee grins at Xiao Wen, 'do you come here often?'

'You should know,' replies Xiao Wen, raising her voice to be heard over the music, 'I never do this.' Xiao Wen holds up her bottle. 'This also I do not do.' She takes a swig, then coughs, holding her hand over her mouth. 'But now I celebrate to meet new friends.'

'I'll drink to that,' says Lee. 'Cheers.' He holds up his bottle and clinks the base against Xiao Wen's, then Vix's. Vix smiles a slight smile.

'You have to have a drink now,' he tells Xiao

Wen, and she swigs again and pulls a face.

'You'll have to learn to get used to the taste,' says Lee. 'Practise.'

'Is this like the place you work?' asks Xiao Wen.

'My club's a bit more . . . recent,' says Lee, looking around. 'More lights. More decoration.'

Lee points at the platform with the dancing woman on it. 'But we don't have that.'

Vix looks at the girl on the platform, then at the crowd, and realizes they are all facing her, and most of the dancers are copying her movements.

'It must be very modern, not like here. I would so much like to see this place,' says Xiao Wen.

'I'd like to show you,' says Lee. Vix looks at him catching Xiao Wen's eye and raising his eyebrows.

'What's it called?' asks Vix.

'Dazzlers. In Deptford. I own it, actually.'

'Your life sound very exciting,' says Xiao Wen. 'Not like mine.'

'What do you normally do at night?' asks Vix.

'I study.'

'Don't you go out?'

'No money. Factory work not good money.'

'How much?'

'Three hundred yuan one month.'

The tune finishes. The dancers stop moving. Then another, faster beat swells out of the speakers. Vix recognizes it as soon as the vocals start: '*There's No Limit*,' an old chart hit. For a moment she experiences a strange sense of vertigo from the unexpectedness of the well known.

'Wah!' says Lee. 'Cheesy techno! I haven't heard this for ages.'

'While we are waiting,' Xiao Wen says shyly, 'let us dance. This I would like.'

'Yeah,' says Lee, nodding his head to the beat. 'Yeah.'

They get off their stools and head into the centre of the crowd on the dancefloor. A space clears for them, and the dancers around grin, and a few raise their thumbs. Many stop to watch. Vix begins to move self-consciously, imitating the way they sway and pump their arms up and down, elbows tight against their waists. Beside her, Xiao Wen begins dancing in a similar way. Though her movements are simple, she moves with grace and style; Vix acknowledges that she looks good, feeling a little envious of her slim, shapely frame. Lee dances next to Xiao Wen. A circle of observers form around them, and some of them begin to clap in time. Vix feels awkward, and slows almost to a stop. The attention seems to have the opposite effect on Lee; his movements become bolder and he begins to throw himself around in a jerky frenzy. The crowd around them swells, the clapping gets louder.

'Uh uh, uh huh huh huh, there's no limit!'

The tune kicks into a faster section. Lee's eyes are closed and his mouth open. Legs planted far apart and knees bent, he bounces on the balls of his feet while his arms chop and windmill. Xiao Wen and

Vix move aside out of reach of his swing.

'He is funny man,' says Xiao Wen, leaning close to shout in Vix's ear.

'This is how we dance', says Vix, 'in my country.' She admits to herself that Lee's movements, pretty standard for 4 a.m. in some British field or warehouse, look pretty bizarre here.

Fingers splayed, Lee makes stabbing motions with his hands while jerking his torso from side to side. Some of the observers are open-mouthed; applause breaks out, people start whistling and Lee's space contracts as others stop dancing and join the observers, who jostle each other for a view.

Two girls step forward and begin pulling on Lee's arm and pointing to the platform above the DJ. Lee slows, grins, then lets himself be led off.

'*Kan laowai!*' shouts the DJ over a microphone. Vix looks at him and guesses that he is the only man in the place with long hair. '*Kan dabizi!*'

Vix turns to Xiao Wen. 'What did he say?'

'He says to look at the big nose.'

Lee stands spotlighted on the platform. The crowd below watch expectantly. A new tune comes on, more simple techno, and Lee starts working himself up, jogging and jerking, his head low and ducking from side to side.

Vix and Xiao Wen watch Lee's movements get faster and more complex. He stands up straight and sketches oblongs in the air with chopping hands. Beneath him, they all start doing it.

Xiao Wen turns to Vix; Vix bends down to hear her.

'Xiao Vix, I want to ask you a thing.'

'What?'

'Will you sponsor me to go to your country?'

'What do you mean?'

'You sponsor me and I can go to your country.'

'I'm sorry, Xiao Wen. I can't.'

'No matter,' says Xiao Wen quickly, 'no problem.' Both turn to watch Lee, who now looks like a human graphic equalizer, his hands drawing levels in the air. Xiao Wen raises her voice. 'He is an interesting dancer.'

The tempo of the music changes, and Lee starts bouncing about, first on one foot, then the other, and making pistol shapes with his stabbing hands.

'I dance now.' Xiao Wen takes a couple of steps to the side. She looks up at Lee and begins bouncing about, first on one foot, then the other.

Vix hops about a little herself, then slows to a stop, unable to get into the music. She wonders what Sol would think of this place, then starts worrying about the tickets. She heads off, sits down and watches Xiao Wen, who is trying to copy Lee's hand movements, biting her bottom lip in concentration. The tune finishes. Lee stops, waves to the crowd and clambers down off the platform.

'What did you think?' Lee sits down. He's glowing with sweat. He wipes his forehead with the bottom of his T-shirt.

'They like you.'

'I wiggle my foot, a hundred people wiggle theirs. Mad.' Lee slugs heavily on his bottle. 'Fag?' he asks, flicking a new pack of Flying Panda onto the table.

'No. I told you, I've given up.'

He strips the packaging and slides a cigarette out.

'Getting off on the power?' says Vix.

'Yeah, I felt like techno Jesus. Showing them the way forward. They haven't got a clue how to dance.' Lee taps a passing man for a light.

'They just do it differently.'

'Dragging them out of the Fifties. Best laugh I've had since I've been here.'

'What do you think of Xiao Wen?'

'She's cute.' He smiles a lopsided smile. 'Nice to meet some locals. You know, learn about each other's cultures and that.'

Xiao Wen joins them. Behind her stands the man with the nails and one of the other policemen.

'He has tickets for you,' says Xiao Wen.

'Yes?' says Vix. 'Brilliant.'

The policeman holds two cardboard stubs out. Vix grabs them from him and holds them up close to her face to scrutinize the tiny characters.

'Are they OK?' she asks Xiao Wen, leaning over so she can see them, too.

'Yes, they are good.'

'Excellent.'

'See,' says Lee, getting out his wallet, 'they'd

have tried to rip us off if we hadn't come.'

'But', says Xiao Wen, 'they are for two days' time.'

'That's no good,' wails Vix.

Xiao Wen talks to the two men a moment, then turns to Vix. Her tone is soft and sympathetic. 'Tonight no possible. Sorry.'

Vix unzips the money belt inside the waistband of her jogging bottoms and gets out five hundred yuan. The policeman takes the money from her and Lee. The man with the nails nods at the three, winks, then walks off, his arm around the shoulder of his colleague. Vix zips her ticket into the pouch. She feels quite calm. Well, she tells herself, that's it. She has another face to fit into her catalogue of people she'll never see again. She feels oddly resigned about it, and realizes that knowing about it is better than the uncertainty. Well, she tells herself with a mental shrug, it probably wouldn't have worked out anyway.

The music changes abruptly. A slow love song comes on. Vix recognizes it, an old Andy Lau, familiar from her time in Hong Kong. It's not the sort of tune Vix wants to hear right now.

Lee is looking pleased. He taps Xiao Wen on the arm. 'Hey,' he says, 'let's dance.'

'Yes,' she replies. Xiao Wen pops to her feet.

'I'll sit here for a bit,' says Vix as they step off together.

On the dance floor, about half the dancers

migrate to the sides of the hall. The others pair off and begin to dance face to face, arms around each other.

Vix starts shredding her bottle label, watched by a nearby group of men. They have short, bristly hair and all are smoking. She stares straight back at them, frowning, and they meet her gaze and smile. She wishes she was surrounded by friends. She wishes Sol was here. She watches the couples on the dance floor.

Lee faces Xiao Wen, his left hand on her waist, his right held in hers. Other couples glide around the floor, but they just shuffle a little from side to side. Lee looks uncomfortable; he is obviously unfamiliar with this style of dancing.

Lee steps on Xiao Wen's foot. They stop moving and stand, and the distance between them decreases. They look into each other's faces, and Vix can see what they can't: two men at the side of the dance floor are staring at them with expressions of distaste.

One steps forward, a bottle in his hand, walking a little crookedly out of the shadows. He taps Xiao Wen on the shoulder, then bends down to speak to her. She turns, says something back and disengages from Lee. The man steps up to Lee and stands directly in front of him, very close, leaning forward, his face hardly a foot from Lee's. His arms are held out straight and slightly back. The bottle catches the light. The couples near them stop moving. Vix stands up.

The man says something and leans closer, his face now inches from Lee's. Lee takes a step back. The man pushes him in the chest with both hands. Lee stumbles, almost falls, then lurches back upright and pushes him back. The man swings his arm around and catches Lee on the forehead with the bottle. Vix hears the smack of impact. Someone shouts, someone screams. Lee grabs his head and staggers back. From the side of the dance floor, men rush out and, in a mass, fall on Lee's attacker and haul him away.

Xiao Wen rushes over to Vix.

'Terrible, terrible. Quick, we should go.'

Lee walks over, one hand held against his fore-head. They step quickly to the exit, the crowd around them suddenly still, their faces shocked, apologetic or just interested.

Outside, four taxi drivers lean on the sides of their parked cars, smoking. The air is pleasantly cool. It has stopped raining.

'Are you all right?' asks Vix.

Lee removes his hand. She holds his head and peers close.

'Fucking hurts.'

Xiao Wen talks rapidly in Mandarin, holding her cheeks with her hands.

The club doors swing open and five youths come out, dragging Lee's attacker. Shouting, they throw him onto the pavement a couple of metres away and huddle around him. He curls into a ball, hands over his head, and they kick his side, back and arms.

Xiao Wen starts talking even faster. Four policemen come running out of the doors, and the youths scatter down the road. The man on the ground raises his head and starts to get shakily to his feet. The policemen cluster around. One hits him with both fists on the back of the neck and he slams back down to the pavement. The policemen continue where the youths left off, striking out with their green trainers. The taxi drivers watch and puff.

'Let's get out of here,' says Vix.

twenty four

world people unite

Vix is in the front passenger seat of a taxi, Xiao Wen and Lee are in the back. Lee holds his forehead and groans. Xiao Wen, obvious distress on her face, squeezes his elbow. He groans again and she puts her hand on his face.

'Oh, Mr Lee, I am so sorry.' Xiao Wen takes his hand and strokes it. 'So sorry, so sorry.'

'I'm all right. I'm all right. You're very good to me. It's not your fault.'

'It is. I should not have let you go that place. Not such a good place.'

'Never mind.'

'This town, small town, ignorant people all around. This place cold like a stone.'

Vix turns back round and watches the buildings flash past as they barrel through the empty streets. The driver, a short man with yellow teeth, is hunched low over the wheel, going as fast as the uneven roads will allow. It's a bumpy ride. He grins

>>>import export

at Vix, picks a packet of cigarettes off the dashboard and waves them over his shoulder.

'Cheers,' says Lee, and takes one.

'What did they say to you?' Vix asks Xiao Wen.

'They say not a good thing. A not-true thing.'

'What?' asks Lee.

'They stupid people.' She grins widely, stroking Lee's arm. It strikes Vix that Xiao Wen seems more disturbed about the incident than either herself or Lee.

Vix deliberately looks away from the train station as the car pulls up outside the hotel.

'I'm hungry,' says Lee. 'I want to go and eat.'

'I can take you to a restaurant,' says Xiao Wen. 'A very good place.'

'I'd like that,' says Lee.

'You will come with us, Vix?' asks Xiao Wen.

'I'm tired. I'm just going to go and sleep or some-thing.'

'I will see you again?' says Xiao Wen.

'I guess so,' says Vix.

Vix has no desire to talk to anyone, or cope with anything. She wants to be under a duvet. She climbs out, says goodbye as the taxi accelerates away, and enters the hotel.

She buys a pot noodle from the reception shop and goes up to her room. The room is too quiet for her, too dingy, too full of angles. She puts the pot on the bedside cabinet after a few mouthfuls. It's got prawns in it; she'd assumed it was vegetarian,

go>> simon lewis

like British pot noodles, and hadn't checked the ingredients before she'd bought it. She lies down and cries softly. It gives her a headache. She closes her eyes and sees hypnagogic shapes bubbling and morphing. She has a sensation of sinking, and then she slides into darkness.

Vix sits alone in a hut made of coconut matting, with a floor of dried buffalo dung. She leaves, and walks into a wooden room with blue walls and a short, wooden bed, with a poster of Shiva tacked to one wall. A door leads into a brick room which has a thin mattress on a mat on the floor. She walks out of that into another guest-house room, with three beds under mosquito nets and a door that leads into another guest-house room, which leads into another, and then another. She lies on the bed in the room in Hong Kong, looking up at the fan. There's a knock on the door. Fred will be wanting the rent again, and she starts to worry; she hasn't got any money.

She wakes with a start and the dark room slams into place around her. For half a second she has no idea where she is. She blinks and stares at the grey shape of the thermos, forcing the dream images out of her mind.

Someone is knocking on the door. She gets up groggily, wipes dried spit off her lip and slaps on the light switch.

It's Lee. His hands are thrust into the pocket of his top, his head is low, his voice an urgent whisper.

'Vix, listen.'

'What time is it?' she mumbles.

'I don't know. About half-ten, maybe.'

'Oh.'

'Vix. I want to ask you a favour.'

'What?'

'Xiao Wen's getting a room here.'

'What? Why?'

'I want you to distract the woman at the end.'

'What?'

'I want to go and see Xiao Wen, see? In her room. Only you're not allowed. Apparently. I mean foreign men aren't allowed in Chinese women's rooms, and the other way around. Very bad, apparently.'

'Yeah?'

'So I want to ask you to go up to the end of the corridor and distract the woman's attention while I scoot over to her room.'

'I see.'

'Please? She'd ask you, only she's shy.'

'Why should I?'

'I'd do it for you. You can take her the thermos. Ask her to go and fill it up.'

'So you're not coming back tonight?'

A grin spreads over Lee's face. 'Maybe not.'

The thermos is capped by a cork stopper. She takes it out and empties the hot water down the sink in the bathroom. Lee stands just inside the doorway.

Vix walks down the corridor towards the desk by the stairwell, where a girl sits, slumped forward, arms on the desk, head rested on her crossed wrists. Vix realizes that though she's seen a lot of staff, she has yet to see or hear another guest in the hotel. Perhaps all the other rooms are empty. The thought, combined with the gloom and the institutional feel given by the wide corridors and bare walls and high ceilings, unsettles her.

The girl raises her head as Vix approaches. She sees the thermos and sighs dramatically, then slides off her chair, yawns and scratches her head. Vix holds out the thermos. Looking levelly at Vix, the girl takes it. She turns and shuffles to a small door Vix hadn't previously noticed in an alcove behind her.

The girl opens the door, and Vix peeks into the room beyond. It's about five metres by four. With unpainted, windowless walls, and lit by a single bare bulb, it reminds Vix of a garage. It's dense with signs of habitation, and has a male tang to it. Metal bunk beds line the longer side walls; eight beds in all, a couple of them occupied with prone figures, sheets over their heads to cut out the light. A boiler stands against the far wall. The pipes that cross the ceiling are draped with clothes. The unoccupied beds and the narrow space in the centre of the room are scattered with towels, books, shoes, newspapers and underwear. Three men sit playing cards on a bed by the door. One is cross-legged on the thin mattress, his back curved low to fit in the narrow space. The other two perch either side on the edge of the bed, bent forward and twisted around to look at the cards on the sheet between them. They all have vests on, and blue trousers with a red stripe down the side, and they are barefoot. Blue jackets hang on the ends of the beds. She recognizes the uniform; they're hotel security guards. This must be where they live.

The girl shuffles past the men to the boiler. One of the card-players scratches his armpit, looks up, and catches Vix's eye. She steps back, out of view.

Vix looks behind her and sees Lee leave their room and step quickly down the corridor and into a room four doors further down.

Being involved in his little adventure doesn't interest her. She wants to get back to her room, get under the covers and set herself a good dream to take away the aftertaste of the bad one.

The girl comes out and returns the thermos, and Vix goes back to her room. She sits down on the bed and tries to order her thoughts. Going to miss the train. Sol. Her mind keeps tediously returning to the same subjects. Should get ready for bed, she thinks, and continues sitting where she is.

The packet of cigarettes and the matches are still on the bedside table. She stares at them. They stare back at her. Just one, she thinks. She imagines what it would be like to smoke a fag, to breathe out and feel her body unwind. She sees an image of herself from the outside – sitting on the bed in the dingy room with the cigarette, a shadow across her uplifted face as she breathes out an aimless cloud. The picture is romantic and glamorous; it has a melancholy poetry. Herself as existential hero.

She lights a cigarette. It tastes bitter and rough and makes her cough. She sits on the side of the bed smoking and feels ill and sad. For five drags she looks at Lee's bed, covered with clothes.

There's a pair of striped trousers there, patched on both knees. She wonders why she's looking at them so hard, then realizes that they are naggingly familiar. She stubs the finished cigarette out and crouches down beside his bed and fingers the material, running her thumb along the edges of a patch.

In her mind she sees the collage of photos on the wall of her room in Hong Kong. She sees a black-and-white image of a bare-chested man standing beside a hammock. The world seems to grow suddenly strange and small. A man wearing these trousers. Lee. Sol knew Lee. They were together in India. Now she thinks about it, Sol actually mentioned someone called Lee a few times. Sol said the guy was OK; he'd lent him money.

Vix sits down on the bed. It feels like a childish cosmic joke: you can't have Sol, but you can meet one of his mates. She feels cheated, almost angry. And then she thinks, maybe Lee has Sol's address. The idea makes her catch her breath. She casts her

323

eyes over the stuff on the bed, looking for an address book. Among the clothes sit a toothbrush, tapes, Walkman, an empty soapdish – all of them dirty or cracked. Nothing. She turns the clothes aside to look underneath. Nothing. She reaches down for the sports bag and pulls it towards her. The bag is frayed around the bottom corners. The white lettering on its side is cobwebbed with cracks. Lee's necklace still hangs from the open padlock on one of the double zips. She unzips it and reaches in. Past a layer of clothes, she feels something thin like a paperback, but a little longer and wider. She pulls it out. An uneven dark-brown slab, heavily wrapped in cellophane and smelling of aniseed. Funny thing to have. She lays it aside and digs further, and finds a small black address book. Yes. She flicks through the pages and almost shouts when she sees the familiar big hand-writing. SOL, in capital letters. A flat in Brixton. Yes.

Trembling slightly, she copies the address down into her diary. She laughs out loud. Then she puts the address book back, and notices the brown slab a second time.

Thoughtfully she weighs it in her hand. Maybe it's medicine or samples, she thinks, or some weird herbal remedy or foodstuff. Maybe it's not what it looks like. She goes over and bolts the door, then sits back down on the floor, directly under the weak bulb, and examines the package. The stuff inside isn't solid, as she'd thought, but a tightly packed powder. It's maybe a kilo.

Looking closer, she sees the edge of a button embedded in the powder. That seems odd. She remembers with a start something she was told by a boastful smuggler in Thailand. Hash shows up orange on the X-ray machines used at airport and train station customs, the same colour as clothes. He'd described to her how he'd put zips and buttons in packages of hash to send abroad.

But this wasn't hash. Jesus. The crazy fucker. She puts the package down on the floor and sits down on the bed. She gets up and sits down again. She gets everything out of the sports bag. Two more identical packages sit wrapped in T-shirts at the bottom. The crazy fucker.

The handle of the door turns. Vix freezes, and fear lurches up her back and makes her straighten. Two soft, short raps.

'I'm in the bath,' she calls out. Her voice is strained and unnaturally high. She concentrates on maintaining a bright, unconcerned tone as she says, 'Hang on a sec.' Her hands hang in the air for a moment, then she begins to put everything back in the bag in the correct order, working quickly. Which corner did the book go in? Which was on top, the yellowing T-shirt or the cut-off jeans? How much is three kilos of smack worth? And how many years in prison would you get for it? Christ, you'd probably be shot here. Bullet

325

in the back of the head in a football stadium. She takes a sweater out and stuffs it in the other corner. That looks right. She hears another knock on the door – three raps, a little louder this time.

'Just coming,' she calls, cheerily.

She bungs the rest of the stuff in anyhow, zips up the bag and places it back at the foot of the bed, jumps up and reaches for the bolt on the door. Her hand freezes a few inches from it. She turns and sprints into the bathroom, wrenches the cold tap on and throws water over her face. She bends down and jams her head under the stream of cold water, wiggling it around until her hair is soaked. Back in the room, she grabs her towel. Pulling back the bolt, she realizes it was a stupid idea to pretend she was having a bath; the lie would be discovered if he went into the bathroom. She would have to run back in there as soon as she let him in. She opens the door a few inches and peers out.

Xiao Wen stands outside.

'Xiao Vix,' she whispers. Vix looks outside. The girl at the desk is slumped over it again, asleep.

Xiao Wen steps inside quickly and pushes the door to without shutting it. She murmurs so softly Vix can hardly hear. 'I am very sorry to disturb you. I want to ask you a thing.'

'Oh yes?'

Xiao Wen dips her head.

'A little thing.'

'What?'

Vix's head is uncomfortably cold. She shivers as drips run down her neck and she begins to dry her hair.

'I want a thing.'

'Yes?'

Xiao Wen looks out of the corner of her eye, staring at a point on the floor behind Vix. Vix turns; has she left some obvious clue? But there's nothing there.

'Little thing. Man wear it.' Vix realizes Xiao Wen is just embarrassed. 'Put it on. For love.'

'Oh,' says Vix, 'right, condoms.' She walks over to her bed, sits down on it, puts her washbag in her lap and unzips it.

'Mr Lee say no problem, but I make a worry. So I ask this thing.' Vix roots around in the bag. The bottom is full of odds and ends, mostly sanitary towels; she stocked up in Hong Kong. She picks out three foil squares. They're dirty and crumpled, and she checks each to see that the wrapping is still intact.

Vix glances at Xiao Wen's delicate hands, twisted together in front of her.

'Are you sure about this, Xiao Wen?'

'Yes.' She bends over slightly and stretches her hand out full length to take the condoms, then

327

straightens and holds them tight. 'I in love. Mr Lee say he will marry me.'

'What?'

'He say he will take me to your country.'

'What?'

'I can see the sights.'

'No,' says Vix. 'No.' Vix shakes her head, and water droplets flick off her hair. She sees one land and glisten on Xiao Wen's pale neck. She stands up and steps forward. 'He doesn't want to marry you, Xiao Wen.'

'Very happy. I have a gentleman to step out with. This I never have before.'

'Don't believe him.' Vix puts a hand on Xiao Wen's shoulder. She looks hard into her eyes. 'Xiao Wen, Xiao Wen, he doesn't want to marry you.' She grips her shoulders with both hands. 'He's just saying that. He wants a shag. That's all. He'll go and never come back.'

Vix imagines Xiao Wen afterwards, alone, here, wondering and waiting, held hostage by an idea that grows bigger and more abstract every day. Well, she thinks, I should know.

Xiao Wen, smiling, takes a step back, and Vix's arms fall to her side. 'I no believe,' she says.

'Do you want to know what Lee is really doing here?' Vix crouches down on the floor next to Lee's sports bag, unzips it and reaches inside with her right arm. 'He's a smuggler. And he's a fucking idiot. He's got loads of heroin. Must have bought it in Pakistan. He's taking it to Europe. And he uses it himself.' She finds the package and pulls it out.

'What the fuck are you doing with my stuff?' Lee is standing in the open doorway. He is barefoot, with unzipped jeans on. His torso is leaner than it looked in the photograph.

He rushes forward, towards Vix. Instinctively, she moves away from him, head turned, right arm raised to block a blow. Xiao Wen screams.

'What the fuck do you think you're doing?' shouts Vix. Lee grabs her raised arm. 'Telling her you're going to marry her.'

He tears the slab out of her hand, and in the process her nails rake the wrapping; it rips. A stream of brown powder sprays out and drifts over the floor. Vix stands up.

'Now look what you've done.' Lee cradles the split package. He cries out as powder slips through his fingers. He moves the bag carefully around in his hands so the tear is uppermost. Vix and Lee face each other. Xiao Wen, watching, holds her hands on her neck and begins to rock slightly back and forth.

'Leave her alone,' says Vix.

'Fuck you.'

'I'll grass you up.'

The three card-playing security guards run into

329

the room. Now they have their blue jackets over their vests. The jackets are far too big; they have gold buttons, epaulettes and a number on the shoulder. One guard wears blue flip-flops, one wears yellow plimsolls, and the third wears a pair of novelty slippers designed to look like hedgehogs, covered in yellow fake fur, with a little nose, eyes and fluffy ears on the front.

Flip-Flops barks harshly in Mandarin and stops in front of Xiao Wen. Hedgehogs stops beside her, Plimsolls on the other side.

Lee's mouth drops open and his face pales visibly. Slowly, without looking at it, he shifts the bag of heroin into one hand, and lets the hand fall gently to his side.

Flip-Flops addresses all three of them.

'What is he asking?' says Vix.

'He wants to know what is going on.'

'*Bu hui shou* – cannot speak,' Vix tells the guard. She turns to Xiao Wen. 'You tell him. Go on, tell him.'

Xiao Wen talks rapidly to the security guards.

The hand holding the bag of heroin moves backwards slightly. Vix can see what Lee cannot; that the bag is spilling a stream of brown powder onto the floor behind him. It piles up in a little pyramid.

Vix stares at Lee, and he looks back at her. She listens to Xiao Wen's rapid speech, and recognizes the word '*peng you*', friend.

The girl from the desk stands in the doorway. She points at Xiao Wen and starts talking. Xiao Wen talks back at her; suddenly everyone is talking, a torrent of indignant Mandarin. Vix stands with Lee, baffled, watching the argument. She feels completely powerless, only able to observe and unable to understand. It dawns on her that the guards think Xiao Wen is to blame for something.

Hedgehogs barks at Xiao Wen, cutting her off, and takes hold of her elbow. She begins to talk louder, protesting, Vix assumes. Plimsolls grabs the other elbow. He spits out a phrase at her; calling her something, Vix guesses.

'*Wo bu shi!*' says Xiao Wen. A phrase Vix knows – 'I am not.'

'What's going on?' says Vix.

'They say I break the rules,' says Xiao Wen.

Plimsolls and Hedgehogs begin to frogmarch Xiao Wen out of the room. The girl from the desk follows them. She cries out again, ending a short phrase with 'Mr Lee.'

Flip-Flops moves towards Vix and Lee and stands between them, side-on, arms raised, a palm facing each. He looks from one to the other.

Flip-Flops looks hard at Vix and points at her with his finger. Then he turns his head and looks hard at Lee, pointing. He talks to them loudly and seriously in Mandarin.

'*Bu hui shou,*' says Vix.

Flip-Flops points down at Lee's feet. Lee looks back at him, his mouth slightly open and turned down. The guard wobbles his pointing finger. Lee's eyes open wider. His tongue darts out and touches his top lip. Now the man shakes his whole hand. He is pointing, Vix realizes, at the little pyramid of spilt heroin which is growing slowly behind Lee. Flip-Flops reaches out and takes Lee's arm by the wrist. Lee's eyes widen and his nostrils dilate as Flip-Flops pulls Lee's arm out from behind him. Both men look at the bag of heroin.

'I think he's trying to tell you that you're spilling something,' says Vix, levelly, staring hard at Lee.

Flip-Flops twists Lee's wrist gently, so the bag is rotated and the powder stops streaming onto the floor.

Lee looks down. 'Oh, oh, oh,' he stammers, and he turns his head away from Flip-Flops as he flushes fiercely.

Flip-Flops looks sternly at Vix, and then at Lee. Then he turns and walks out of the room.

Lee sits down heavily on the bed. 'I'm a jammy fucker,' he gasps. 'A jammy fucker.' He starts to pant, and the pants turn to gulping chuckles.

Vix goes to the door and looks down the corridor. Hedgehogs and Plimsolls are walking Xiao Wen towards the stairs. Flip-Flops walks behind. Xiao Wen is silent, and walks with her hands clasped in front of her, taking small, quick steps along the concrete. The yellow-uniformed girl is sitting back at her desk. Lee laughs harder.

part seven

another country

green channel

'This your luggage?'

'Yes,' says Lee.

'Put it on the table and take off the padlocks.'

The customs official is short and fat, with a juicy caterpillar of a moustache and a touch of London to his accent. Another man stands behind him, watching, leaning against the wall, his arms folded.

As Lee slips his necklace out from inside his T-shirt and unlocks his two bags, he speculates why they picked him out from the passengers streaming through the green channel. It seems so unjust; he looks, he reckons, as innocuous as anyone else.

He's wearing clean blue jeans, a white T-shirt from the Hard Rock Café and a black bomber jacket, an outfit he assembled in Beijing specifically for border crossings. His tangled nest of hair is tucked up underneath a blue baseball cap. He has taken his earring out, shaved and washed.

He was careful to fix a nonchalant, bored expression on his face as he walked through the

>>>another country

corridor, and not to let it slip as he went past the mirrored section of wall at the end. It was a two-way mirror, he imagined, through which they monitored the passing arrivals for any signs of relief or loosening of tension.

Despite all his routine precautions, Lee was called back by an official right at the end of the corridor, within sight of the airport concourse and the people waiting for other passengers, standing with signs saying, 'Intertech Technologies', 'Andrew and Maisie', 'International Marketing Ltd'.

The official reaches into the kitbag and begins pulling out its contents – mostly musty clothes – and dumping them on the table.

Lee orders himself to be settled, and thinks about all the other crisis points he has endured.

To start with, there was that little bit of nastiness in China. He spent two nervy days fretting in that grotty little town, terrified that one of the girls would grass him up. He avoided Vix as much as he could, spending his time wandering the streets clutching the sports bag, and only going back to the room when it got dark. When he did see her, she simply refused to speak to him. He never saw Xiao Wen again. That was something of a relief. There could have been a nasty scene. He chided himself for getting involved, and resolved in future never to mix pleasure with business.

Then there was the long, tedious journey to cope with, with its periods of intense, edgy boredom, punctuated by sudden bursts of fear and adrenalin when he came to a border crossing. At the Russian–Chinese frontier he hardly received a glance. The guards just looked at his passport, checked his visa, then left the compartment. It was easy to see why – half the people on the train were flagrant smugglers; why bother with a little Western tourist? There were Chinese women with jewellery all the way up both arms and furtive Russians whose compartments were so packed with boxes there was nowhere to sit down. Even the train guards, the provodniks, were in on it. The man in charge of his carriage had a stash of vases. He would get out at every little station they stopped in, and parade along the platform with one in each hand, offering them for sale. Siberians must be seriously starved of consumer opportunities, Lee reckoned, judging by the way they rioted on the platform for the chance to buy the golfing umbrellas, Mickey-Mouse T-shirts and shell suits sold off the train.

It took six days to get to Moscow. The sense of confinement and the crap food reminded him of being in hospital. He had nothing to do all day but watch the repetitive landscape of hills and birch trees scroll past the windows, or hang out in the dining car eating pickled gherkins the size of potatoes and drinking watery soup. Consequently, his drug use escalated from the odd toot to a daily habit. He spent a lot of time cooped up in the toilet with tinfoil and matches. He didn't consider himself addicted, though; he told himself he was OK so long as he didn't inject.

He didn't dare get his stash out in Moscow, however, or on the onward Berlin train, so he was nervy and tense by the time he got to the Polish frontier. The guards there questioned only a few of the passengers, and again they passed him with hardly a glance. The German frontier was the worst; by then he was feeling shivery and cramped with withdrawal. Despite his taut, sweating face, the customs officials again paid him no attention. They were more interested in querying the papers of the Russians, looking, he assumed, for illegal immigrants.

It seems a cruel irony to be stopped here, on the very last leg of his journey, in his own country.

'You have a good time?' asks the official. He looks up and smiles thinly at Lee.

'What?'

'In Germany.'

'Oh yeah.'

The official shakes the bag to make sure it's empty. He sifts through the pile of stuff on the table, briefly holding up a yellow T-shirt for further inspection. He shakes Lee's battered Walkman and checks in the battery compartment.

'OK,' he says, 'that's fine. Would you pack it up again? And I'll just have a quick look at this one.'

Lee begins stuffing clothes back into the kitbag as the official unzips the sports bag. It's looking pretty battered now, and the design on the side has started flaking off; now it says 'Worl Peple Unit', and of the globe, only the poles and South America are left intact. The other continents are flecks of green.

The official reaches in, and Lee imagines his hand squirming around inside. He pulls out Lee's address book and sets it down on the table. Then he takes out a wooden Russian doll. The first compartment is an image of Yeltsin. The official unscrews it to reveal Gorbachev inside. He unscrews Gorbachev, and continues until he has unpacked all the layers, down to the little wooden Marx, which he shakes to make sure he's empty. Then he takes out a set of chopsticks, a penknife, a plastic bag of about thirty motorway-service-station sugar sachets, a foil pack of Aspirin, a roll of toilet paper, a half-eaten sandwich wrapped in silver foil and two zipped-up black bags. He unzips the first bag, and pokes around the grotty cake of soap, rusty razors, yellowing flannel, uncapped tube of toothpaste and flayed toothbrush inside. He unzips the second bag.

'Hello,' he says, peering at the four thick wads of American dollars inside.

The other man uncrosses his arms and leans forward.

The official looks at Lee and raises an eyebrow, then takes out the wads of money and puts them down side by side on the table. Each is about the size and thickness of a cigarette packet, and is bound

341

with a green rubber band. He picks one up and flicks through it. It's made up of hundred-dollar notes.

'Have you robbed a bank?' asks the official.

'My savings,' says Lee.

'How much money is here?'

'About forty thousand dollars. I've been working in Berlin.'

'Doing what?'

'Rigging.'

Lee tells himself they can hardly arrest him for carrying too much money. Could they? He resists the temptation to look away or lick his lips, or scratch the side of his mouth.

'You didn't make all this rigging.'

'No. I'm a DJ as well. And I bought a car, then sold it.'

The official scratches his moustache, as if to tickle it awake. He turns to look at his colleague.

'What d'you reckon? Give him the treatment?'

'I've got nothing,' says Lee. 'You can X-ray me and root around up my arse all you like. I'm clean. Sir.'

'On your bike. Pack all this up quickly; we don't want it stinking out the whole corridor. I hope you don't get mugged on the way home.'

The most problematic part of the whole operation had been getting rid of the fucking stuff. He could have sold it much easier, perhaps, in Amsterdam or London, but he knew better than to try to get it across any western European borders; he wasn't stupid. For a month he stayed in a hostel in Berlin, discreetly making contacts. Then his money ran out, and he spent a couple of nights sleeping rough, and for two days he went for free meals to a Hare Krishna centre. At that point he decided just to get rid of it as quickly as possible. He sold the stuff at ridiculous prices to a group of Autonomen, some Danish bikers, and a conglomerate of investment bankers and insurance salesmen. But now he had his wad – changed into hundred-dollar bills to make it less bulky – and he was, he reckoned, set up.

Lee finishes packing his stuff, gives the customs officials a nod and strolls cheerfully out onto the concourse. He removes his baseball cap, tosses it in a bin and looks at place names on the arrivals board.

Lee begins to fantasize about the places he will go now that he is a man of independent means. He sees himself sitting in a deckchair on some palm-fringed beach, surrounded by half-naked women. No, naked women, eager to fulfil his every desire. Sipping a pina colada – whatever that is – or some posh Martini thing. No, come to think of it, he wouldn't want to drink cocktails, would he? Lager. He'd be sipping a pint of chilled lager. And he would be eating something flash. Lobster. As he had no idea what that tasted like, he reconsidered. Prawns? Shark. Shark was nice; he'd had it in India. Actually, he decided, what he really wanted right

343

now was a cheese-and-pickle toasted sandwich. Right. He saw himself sitting on a palm-fringed beach, surrounded by naked women, drinking lager and eating a cheese-and-pickle toasted sandwich.

Later. First, unfinished business.

Reminding himself that these are his first steps on English terrain for eight months, Lee examines his feelings. Nothing, though the sight of familiar brand names and adverts in the shops is somehow reassuring. He treats himself to a multipack of crisps and heads down to the tube, munching his way through them as he goes. Barbecue beef! Of course, here you queue up in an orderly line to buy tickets. Smoky bacon! On the platform everyone seems very quiet, a little withdrawn and they stand far apart from one another. Roast chicken! No-one on the train looks at anyone else, and he's struck by the racial mix of his fellow passengers. Prawn cocktail! Some of the journey is on the surface, and Lee turns his head for a view of the London landscape. The weather is overcast, and all he can see – the little trees and houses and streets – looks washed-out, the colours all muted pastels. After the primaries of Asia, it's like he's looking through tissue paper. Shit, cheese and onion.

He gets off at Stockwell and starts walking, noting sights which serve as forceful reminders that he's home. The colour and texture of the pavement. Pub signs. He has to ask three pedestrians the way before he reaches the estate, and three more

344

before he finds the right block – one of fifteen or so. Tall people, litter, pint glasses. The estate, with its dull parade of blocks, its patches of grass, its car parks, looks like it was built by a limited imagination. Public drunkards. Bollards. The lift smells of chips and piss. He gets off at the top floor. Good view. He knocks on a door.

Sol answers, holding it wide open and grinning.

'Lee.'

'Sol. All right mate?' They hug, then Sol leads Lee into a hallway, where he dumps his bags, and through into a kitchen.

'It's good to see you again, mate. I couldn't believe it when you rang.' Sol fills a kettle from the sink. 'So, did you get homesick in the end?'

'Just fancied a change of scene. Remind myself why I fucked off in the first place.' Lee sits down at the kitchen table. 'How are you?'

'I'm all right. Surviving. Got back about a month ago.' Sol plugs the kettle in and switches it on.

'What's it like being here?'

'It's all right.' Sol shrugs. 'It's easy. Bit boring. You know.'

'What about that . . . you know, that business you were worried about? The dead pimp.'

'You haven't told anyone else, have you?'

''Course not.'

'I was mad telling you. Never told anyone else.' Sol rinses two mugs. 'Nothing. Nothing happened. My flatmate's mates, they know their stuff. The

345

body's never been found. I think maybe I got away with it.' Sol raises his voice. 'Hey, I got a job.'

'Yeah?'

'Pho-toh-graph-er's assistant. Sounds good, huh?'

'Nice one.'

'I'll have to show you all my pictures from India.'

'Yeah,' says Lee, a little uncertainly, 'for sure.'

Sol grins. 'No I won't. Not unless you really want to see them.'

'No, I do. Really.'

'Really?'

'Yeah, really. Totally.'

'OK, OK, if you insist. I'll get one together first, yeah?'

'You got some weed?'

'Skunk.'

'Yes. Now I feel like I'm home.'

'Tea or coffee or herbal shit?'

'Tea. Two sugars.'

Tea! Spliff! Sol! Lee drums his fingers on the table and sits forward. He finds himself getting absurdly excited; he can't stop himself grinning. He feels like a hyperactive child, bursting with sudden, unfocused energy. Unexpectedly, he feels full of boundless warmth towards Sol, his mate, and he feels the urgent desire to communicate what has happened to him, to tell it all – well, nearly all – in a big rush. He swallows it down; there'll be time.

Sol picks a couple of teabags off a packet on the

table and drops them into the mugs. 'So what are you going to do with yourself now?' he asks.

'Thought I'd hang about here for maybe a week or two. Then head off again.'

'Yeah? Where?'

'I don't know. Quite fancy Ibiza. Amsterdam, maybe. Bangkok. Or Greece, or—'

'Shut up, you flukey git.'

Sol is waiting for the kettle to boil. His back is turned to Lee as he says, 'Um, I know I owe you a lot of money, but, like, umm . . .'

Lee waves a hand in the air.

'Forget it.' Sol turns around to face him.

'What?'

'Yeah, no problem. It was a gift. Just let me stay a while, all right? And think of it as rent.'

'Cheers. Cheers. Hey, you've been pretty lucky for me.'

'How's that?'

'I'm three hundred quid richer thanks to you. Well, sort of.'

'What are you talking about?' The kettle boils and Sol makes tea, then chucks the dripping teabags in a shopping bag hanging from the door handle. He puts Lee's cup down in front of him.

'Hang on, I'll show you. Wait there.'

Sol dives out of the room, and Lee smiles; it's exactly the same Sol he remembers, the same restless manner.

Lee sips, then leans back and closes his eyes. The

347

tea's hot and milky. He feels comfortable and secure for the first time in a long while.

'Some mate of yours rang.' Sol shouts from the hallway. Lee hears him going upstairs, taking them a couple at a time.

'What?'

'I told them you were coming here today.'

'Who? Was it a girl?' But Sol is on the flat's upper storey now, and too far away to hear.

Lee feels his happiness move up a notch. It's Hell, he knows it; it couldn't be anyone else. He wrote to her from Berlin, a month ago. And she wrote back, sending a postcard to the hostel. On the front was a picture of a group of dancers in soft focus. He has read the back so often, he knows her words by heart. 'Dear Lee. Good to hear you're OK and having a good time. I still think of you sometimes. If you're ever in the country, look me up. I work in a body-piercing studio now, and I'm very happy.'

Dancers in soft focus, 'I still think of you sometimes', 'Look me up'. It was an invitation, surely; even after all this time, she has feelings for him that she can't deny. He wrote back immediately, giving her Sol's phone number. He would buy some decent clothes tomorrow, then go round to see her. With his pride, his money, his casual confidence and his tan, she would find herself irresistibly drawn to him. He would talk to her of foreign lands and strange peoples – without mentioning unfortunate incidents like the motorbike accident with the cow or the smuggling operation, obviously – and he certainly wouldn't tell her he had come back to England just to see her.

Lee sips his tea and lets himself slip into fantasy. A body-piercing studio! It sounded deliciously erotic.

There's a rap on the door.

'I'll get it,' shouts Lee, and strolls out into the hallway.

Lee opens the door.

Marlowe stands outside in jeans and a bomber jacket, with slightly less hair than Lee remembers. Danny stands behind him. He catches Danny's magnified eyes.

'Fuck,' says Lee, feeling the blood drain from his face.

Marlowe lunges forward and shoots out a giant Neanderthal hand that closes around Lee's mouth. He slams Lee against the wall by the door, and stands close, holding him hard, breathing hot oniony breath in Lee's face.

'W–W–Well, well,' says Danny. 'Here we all are, then.'

'Who is it?' Sol shouts down from upstairs. The pressure of Marlowe's sausage fingers hurts Lee's jaw, drags his skin down and makes his eyes widen. He kicks out and flails his arms. Trying to scream, the noise squeezes out as a squeaky whine, like the cry of a sad dog. One hand tight around Lee's chest,

349

Marlowe hauls him out the door. Thrashing around, Lee kicks the door, which bangs against the wall.

'Who is it?' shouts Sol. 'What's the noise?'

Marlowe slams Lee's head into the concrete balcony of the walkway outside. Danny pulls the door closed. He grins.

'R—Right, mate,' he says, 'you're coming with us.'

twenty six

last of the snail kites

Pug and Sol sit in the armchairs in the big room, watching a nature documentary. Pug leans back, his feet planted wide apart on their heels on the rug, his head sunk deep into the back of the chair, as if it's sucking him down into the space behind the cushion, where so many coins, lighters and biros have gone before. Sol sits perched on the end of his, leaning forward, staring glumly at the screen.

'Is there anything on the other side?' he asks.

Pug consults his *TV Quick*.

'It's all anniversary, tribute stuff. All channels.'

'Tributes to what?'

'It's fifty years since Elvis became independent, and twenty years since India overdosed on cheeseburgers.'

'Put India on.'

'What you want to watch a program about India for? You been there already. This is interesting.' Pug tokes hard on a spliff, then puffs out a

>>another country

351

languorous smoke dragon and points the spliff at the screen.

'See that bird,' he says, 'A Snail Kite. I want to be one of those. What a touch.' Pug jabs and waves the spliff, using it for emphasis. 'You're a big, nasty-looking bird, so nothing fucks with you, and you get to bum around Florida eating five-inch snails. They're big and juicy, they don't bite back and they're not hot on evasion.' He tokes again. 'Yeah, I'll be one of them next time around.'

Pug swings his hand across, spliff cocked.

'No ta,' says Sol.

'What?'

'I don't want any.'

'Come on, it'll relax you.'

'I've got to have a clear head.' Sol is slowly rubbing his sweaty palms together.

'And this'll clear it.'

'No it won't.'

'Suit yourself. More for me.' Pug looks across. 'It'll be all right, all right? Rule seven, don't get vexed over cunt. Relax. You'll feel great afterwards, anyway. I always do.'

'I'm not like you.'

They sit in silence. Sol can't concentrate on the screen; his gaze wanders restlessly around the room. It's a lot tidier than it used to be. There are pot plants now and the carpet has been hoovered.

'I've decided what happened to your mate,' says Pug. 'It's the only explanation. Alien abduction.

They're going to experiment on him, put a little computer in his head and send him back. You see him again, you check him thoroughly. There'll be a little scar on his neck. He'll seem normal, but—'

'Yeah, yeah.'

'What? What is up with you?'

'I don't need this now.'

Pug stares moodily at the screen, mashes the last inch of the spliff into an ashtray on the chair's arm, grunts and wriggles his bum. Sol runs his hands over his smooth head, brings them down around his neck, over his jaw. He looks at the floor and studies his fingernails – they need cutting – scratches an itch on his arm.

'Their habitat, though, is endangered', says David Attenborough, 'by the needs of human civilization.'

There's a rap on the front door.

'Shit,' says Sol, 'shit, shit, shit.'

'Just tell it like it is,' says Pug.

Sol gets up. 'You stay out of it, stay in here, and don't say a thing.' He becomes aware of his breathing as he walks to the door and he wills it to slow down. In the moment it takes to reach for the handle, pull it down and pull it towards him, he examines his confused feelings. They're so mixed up, he can't get a grip on anything, except wishing he was somewhere else. He opens the door.

'Hi,' says Vix. Seeing her stuns his system; inside he feels hollow, and a wind rushes round his empty

353

body. She is beautiful. There's a slight blemish on her cheek, her eyes look tired, the eyeliner is a little thicker on one eye than the other. But it doesn't work; the details just make her seem more real. A voice in Sol's head is shouting; Oh God, oh God, oh God.

She's wearing her jogging bottoms, a blue cotton shirt with a grandad collar over a black T-shirt, a khaki army-style jacket and green plimsolls he hasn't seen before. Her hair is a slightly lighter brown than he remembers.

Behind her stands a thick-set middle-aged man with a trim beard, carrying her green army ruck-sack in one hand.

'Hello,' says Sol.

Vix cocks her head to one side, girlishly. 'Give us a kiss, then,' and she rushes forward and puts her arms around him. Hands at his side, he kisses her on the cheek, and he catches the smell of the shampoo she uses. She plants her lips on his, and he thinks how good it would be just to open his mouth and fall and let it happen. No, no. She hugs him, making a contented humming sound, releases him, then steps back, her hands on his shoulders.

'Don't be shy,' she says. 'This is my Dad.'

Sol looks over her shoulder.

'Hello.'

Sol is glad of an excuse to disengage from Vix. He steps aside and shakes the man's heavy hand, remembering to try to be firm, but not too firm.

'Owen,' says the man, in an accent thicker than Vix's. He puts the rucksack down in the hallway.

'He picked me up at the airport,' says Vix, 'and then we went and had a meal. He took me to a Chinese!'

'Well, I thought you'd like it.'

'The last thing I want is more Chinese, isn't it, Dad?' They're both smiling; playing out for his benefit, he imagines, a discussion they've had before. 'Can we come in, then?' says Vix.

Sol leads them through into the kitchen and they stand there, looking around, like the people who don't know anyone at a party. Vix looks about with wide, curious eyes. He feels a surge of desire for her and wills it away.

Owen leans against the sink.

'Traffic was a nightmare,' he says. 'I hate driving in London.'

'You found somewhere to park all right?' says Sol.

'Oh yes. Don't want to leave it too long, though. You know what they're like. I forgot to take the stereo out, didn't I?'

'What . . . what do you plan to do now?' Sol asks Vix, tapping his hands against his thigh.

'I've been asking her that all afternoon,' says Owen. 'She changes her mind every ten minutes.'

'I thought I might get some cash together. Maybe go to college, or something. I don't know, I've only just got back, haven't I?'

>>>another country

'About time you got a job,' Owen's voice is rich and deep. 'Really. Once you find your feet.'

'I mean right now,' says Sol.

'Right now I need a cup of tea, and a bath, and a pint. You can show me those Brixton pubs you've been going on about.'

'Yeah.' Sol feels like running out of the room. He looks everywhere but at Vix; he can't catch her eye, and for a moment they stand in silence.

'Well, I'm sure you two have got a million things to talk about,' says Owen. 'So I'm going to leave you to it, and I'll come and pick her up in a couple of hours. Got to answer a call of nature, then I'll leave you alone. Where is it?'

'Upstairs,' says Sol, 'head right, end of the corridor. You have to pull the thing hard to make it flush.'

Owen pushes himself off the sink and leaves the room. Vix jumps forward and wraps her arms around Sol, putting one hand round the back of his neck. He stands still and cold, arms at his side. She brings her face up to his and he turns his head away. Vix steps back and bites her bottom lip.

'What's that?' asks Vix, pointing at the kitbag and the blue sports bag sitting in the hall beside her rucksack and visible through the open door.

'A mate was here earlier,' says Sol. 'He left it. It was weird. He came round, then just disappeared. Um, listen, Vix . . .'

'What?' But Sol can't think of anything to say.

The words form in his head but don't reach his mouth.

'Sol?' says Vix, her smile dissolving. 'What's wrong?'

'Your Dad seems really pleased to see you,' says Sol. 'I'm glad you're getting on. That's good. Family.' He feels the words trail out of his mouth. He's rambling; the volume of his voice decreases as it tails off. 'Very important.'

'I thought,' says Vix, 'I thought you wanted to see me.'

'I do. Sort of.'

'I came all this way. I wouldn't have come back if . . . I thought. You said, you said . . .' Sol looks at her. Her face is beginning to redden. 'What's going on?'

'Vix,' says Sol, 'you've got your life, and I've got mine.'

'What?'

'Travelling, yeah, that was great. I'm not saying it wasn't great. But now we're just two different people, you know?' Sol feels the prepared words slip out smoothly. If only he could look at her while he says them. He's compulsively running the thumbs of both hands between his second and third fingers. 'We had a brilliant time, it was great, but now it's different. We're in a different place, and things are different.'

'What?'

Sol looks her in the eye. The expression on her

357

face is crumbling; she doesn't look so pretty.

'Are you telling me you don't want me here?'

'I'm saying that what we had was a holiday thing. You know, no beginning or end, just a middle.'

'I thought you wanted to see me.' She puts her hands on her head. Her face is red, two vertical lines appear at the top of her nose, her mouth widens and turns down. It's a gaping hole, a wound; Sol wants to make it better. He wants to make it all right. He doesn't want to hurt her like this and he hates himself.

'I'm sorry. I'm sorry. I'm sorry.'

'Say it, Sol,' says Vix. She's angry now, and somehow that makes it easier for him.

'It was a fling.'

'Say it, you cunt.'

'We're finished.'

'Cunt!' she shouts. 'You stupid fucker.' She lashes out and kicks a kitchen cabinet door. She hits him in the stomach, not hard; the blow is inept. He grabs her wrist. It would be so easy now to pull her towards him, to hold her in his arms. No. He lets her go. She slaps him on the cheek. The sound is sudden and final. A full stop. He just wants her out, out.

'Vix, don't be stupid. Come on, your Dad's here.'

'Fuck my fucking Dad!' shouts Vix.

'I think we'd better be going now.' Owen stands in the doorway, jangling his car keys.

'Yes,' says Sol.

'Fuck you,' shouts Vix. 'Fuck you!' She lashes out at him once, a swiping blow that catches him on the shoulder.

'All right, love, that's enough.' Owen steps in and grabs hold of Vix's upper arm. 'You don't change do you? Christ.'

He starts to drag her out. She shrugs him off.

'All right,' she says, 'I'm going.' She turns and points herself at the door.

'Sorry about this,' says Owen.

'Yeah,' says Sol.

Vix turns round suddenly and spits at Sol. The gob of spittle lands on his thigh. He watches her stalk out into the hallway. Her father opens the door.

'It's always a fucking scene with you, isn't it?' he says. 'Christ. You haven't changed.' Then Sol hears his voice soften. 'OK, love, OK. I'm not going to say anything. It's going to be different. Come on. What are you farting about for? Let's go.'

Sol wipes away the gob of spit and sits down at the kitchen table. He puts his head in his hands and tries not to listen to Vix in the hallway, picking up her luggage, and her father pacing about and swearing to himself outside the door. He presses his fingers into his eyes, and the pain stops the shouting in his head. He hears the front door slam shut, and suddenly there's a terrible silence.

Sol stands and stares at the closed door. An initial

359

rush of relief is replaced by a feeling that he's dirty and soiled, a feeling of shame. He shakes his head, tells himself that he has done the right thing, and stares at a section of the grimy white wall. The words keep repeating in his head, 'The right thing, the right thing.' A couple of minutes pass.

Pug comes in and heads for the fridge.

'Could have been worse,' he says. 'I've had worse. Did she slap you or did you slap her?'

'She did.'

Pug pulls out a can of Stella and a Twix. 'Does it sting?'

'Yeah.'

'Give it a minute. Beer?'

'No.'

'Nasty, turning up with her Dad, though. Lucky he didn't have a go. I was ready, you know. I was poised. I was going to take action on your behalf. If things got, you know, serious.'

'Cheers.'

'I did have a little peek. Tell you what, she was fit. You should have let her stay the night, shagged her brains out, then dumped her in the morning. That's what I'd have done.' He opens the can.

'I could hardly do that, could I?'

'No, course. You'd have to take her out. Go to a hotel, or a park. I'd have covered for you.'

'I've made my choice.'

'Fair enough.'

'Pug?'

'What?'

'We're going to move out.'

'Oh.'

'You understand, don't you?'

'Thought you might.' He slugs on the can. 'Who am I going to take the piss out of when you're gone?'

'I want to say thanks for, you know, everything. I mean for all that you've done. While I was away. I didn't expect it. You're a good mate.'

'Stop it, man, I'm going to cry.'

'You're a bit of a tosser, though.'

'You're a tosser, too. You coming in? I'm rolling, if you're smoking.'

'In a minute.'

'I'll put India on.' Pug ambles out of the room.

Sol lights a cigarette and inhales deeply. He looks around him at the bright room. What a lot of stuff we own, he thinks. He looks at the fridge, and for the first time he wonders how it actually works. He has no idea. The microwave – what's that all about then? All the stuff around him – mostly he has no idea what it's made of or how it works, why it works, and he's never met the people who made it. The milk sitting on the table – where was the cow that did that? What does pasteurized mean? Who put it in that carton? How did it get here? He's sitting in an oblong-shaped space, part of a network of oblong spaces, which are surrounded by a bunch of other oblongs going way up high into

>>another country

the sky. Why? How? What for? And the clouds he can see through the window, the darkening sky – what's going on there? Himself – the veins and the blood and the brain, all that, the breathing lark, how does that work? Why? What for? He feels like an infinitely mysterious system inside an infinitely mysterious system inside an infinitely mysterious system. He hasn't got a clue about anything. Nothing is certain. No, one thing is certain, he tells himself. He has done the right thing.

The front door opens. Sol stubs out his second cigarette, and sits up straight. Femi comes in, carrying a plastic shopping bag and a ring binder.

'Hello, darling,' she says, putting the shopping and the folder on the table. She kisses him on the top of his head. She's wearing a brown dress with a batik design, which tightens over her swollen stomach, and her hair is straightened, scraped back and clipped. 'How are you?' She starts taking the shopping out of the bag and putting it away in the cupboards.

'I'm OK. How was class?'

'Easy. I'm the best. Today, irregular verbs. I ran out of the house. He held her tight.'

'I told Pug we wanted to move out.' Sol watches her moving busily around the room. 'You know the money I won?' says Sol. 'I've been thinking. Why don't we go on holiday?'

'Sol, Sol, you just come back. How we go holiday with baby soon?'

'After then.'

'How we go holiday with baby? Come on. Hey.' She stops, shuts a cupboard door and sits down next to him. She takes his hand in hers and strokes his cheek. Her voice is soft and low.

'It will be OK, Sol. You will see. Come on, you will see.'

It's his baby. It's that simple. He pats her hand. Yes. She's right. It will be all right. He'll make it right. He knows for sure he's done the right thing.

twenty seven

the children's home

Vix sits on her jacket, leaning against a wall at a party. Shell sits next to her. Vix shouts to be heard over the music.

'I keep expecting men to act like human beings, and they keep on disappointing me.'

Shell makes no reply. With her feet tucked under her, her arms around her legs, she moves to the pounding beat, rocking back and forth like an autistic child. Vix wonders if she's heard.

In front of them twenty or thirty people are gyrating to the music booming out of a system set up at the far end of the room. Near the centre of the storm of bodies a bemused-looking dog – a big Alsatianish thing – stands still, swinging its head around. Vix wonders if it's looking for its owner. She hopes it's all right; she worries for it; the music must be deafening it.

The windows are blacked out with sheets, painted with pictures of aliens in UV colours. The only other decoration is the graffiti – 'A's in circles, mushrooms, trees, circles with a jagged arrow running through them – daubed and sprayed on top of peeling wallpaper which shows a repeated design of cartoon bunny rabbits. Shell has told her the place used to be a children's home, and despite the marks of the squatters it still has an institutional feel to it, conveyed by details like the rough grey carpet and the criss-cross wires that run through the glass in the doors.

'What you need,' yells Shell, 'is a snagbob.'

'A what?'

'It's my new theory. Sensitive men are sweet to you, but they're boring. Bastards are sexy, but they treat you like shit. So what every nice girl needs is a snagbob. Sensitive New Age Guy but a Bit of a Bastard.'

'What I need', shouts Vix, 'is my head examined for going out with the shits I go out with.'

'We all need that.'

They lapse back into silence. The dog barks once, then pads off sheepishly out of the room towards the stairs.

'Ah, it's nice to see you again, Shell,' says Vix, and squeezes her friend's arm. Shell has changed a lot since Vix last saw her. Her hair is a short, chic shock, her clothes trendily baggy, her accent less pronounced. She calls herself Michele now. It must, Vix reflects, be the effect of coming to live in London; you get the chance to reinvent yourself.

'And you.'

'Cheers for taking me in hand. I know I was a state.'

'It's a pleasure. Stay as long as you want. Longer. The problem with London is everyone's too up their own arse to really know how to have a good time. What I need round here is a friend who knows how to drink. Do you know what I mean?'

Shell takes a big slug of her can, and Vix takes a slug of hers. A sweating crusty in a vest asks, in a thick southern European accent, if they've got any skins. They haven't.

Vix reckons that about half the people here, and almost all of the really whacked-out ones – the ones with the most ostentatious hair, tattoos and piercings – are from Italy or Spain. Shell says Hackney has a big reputation abroad.

'Your Dad didn't seem too bad,' yells Shell. 'I think he was really happy to see you.'

'Yeah. He seems really different. I think it's this new job he's got, working in the heritage centre. I'm not going to believe it just yet, though. I'll give it six months.'

'You going to live with them again?'

'I can't, I can't face it, not any more. I thought I could maybe go and live with fucking bastard-features in Brixton.' Vix holds her can tightly in both hands and looks down at the carpet, peppered with cigarette butts, roaches, crisp packets and chocolate wrappers, and blotchy with spilled beer. Her hand shakes a little.

'Vix, Vix, don't get upset, I won't allow it. Repeat after me: he wasn't worth it.'

'He wasn't worth it.'

'It was bound to happen sooner or later.'

'It was bound to happen sooner or later.'

'It's his loss anyway.'

'It's his loss anyway.'

'I've sat on bigger toothpicks.'

'But—'

'Say it.'

'I've sat on bigger toothpicks.'

Vix starts giggling and Shell joins in, banging her feet on the ground. Vix falls sideways into Shell's lap and Shell slaps her lightly on the cheek and musses with her hair.

'Bring on the next one,' says Shell.

'Next!' shouts Vix. 'Next!' as if she's at an audition. Still lying in Shell's lap, she waves her can in the air, and lager splats over the two of them. Shell leans down and talks in her ear.

'Check out the DJ,' she says.

'What?'

'Check him out.'

Vix climbs awkwardly to her feet, and peers through the bodies at the dark shape behind the decks in standard I'm-a-DJ pose; hunched over, a little to the side, one shoulder down, one headphone held to one ear. She recognizes the silhouette instantly: Dean.

'Oh, Sh-ell,' she says, 'She-ell.'

Shell stands up.

'You cow,' says Vix, not amused. Her shoulders drop. 'You knew he was going to be here, didn't you?'

Shell smiles sheepishly and a grin flickers round the edge of her mouth.

'Might have.'

'You think that's who I need to see right now? Bollocks.' She gets out a pack of B&H, gives Shell one and slots one between her lips with an irritable stab. 'There should be a rule. Exes should live on different planets.'

'Aren't you going to say hello?'

'No,' states Vix, 'I'm going to hide.'

'Come on,' Shell takes hold of Vix's arm. 'He's really sorry.'

Vix pulls away and steps back.

'You know him?'

''Course. He invited me. He lives here.'

Vix takes another step backwards, and is almost clouted round the ear by a bare-chested man dancing like he's having a vertical epileptic fit.

'No,' says Vix. 'No, no.' She picks up her jacket, shrugs it on, turns and heads into the throng of dancers, making for the stairs on the other side of the room. Shell doesn't follow. The winding stairs are lit by naked bulbs. She pushes past a man sitting with a broken guitar, two girls snogging and a swinging drunk.

Feeling the need for some air, she heads on up,

and begins to wonder if she's being a little stupid. She can't just compulsively run away from things all the time. The complex is large: there are three other dance floors, one on each level. She looks in on them briefly as she passes. Her mood is of calm detachment. She notices details that would once have passed her by, the conventions that govern dress and behaviour.

She feels like a researching anthropologist. These people – who are they? Why do they do what they do? When she was away, she had fantasized that on her eventual return she'd be cool and self-possessed, distinctive in exotic clothes and jewellery. Instead, here she is, scruffy and nondescript, an outsider observing.

She continues upwards to the fourth and top floor. There is no sound system here, and no lights – she assumes it's not wired up – and old, rotting institutional furniture; beige sofas and broken metal chairs, are strewn around the corridor at the top of the stairs. There's no-one here. At the end of the corridor, through a door's broken glass pane, she sees the night sky. The door leads onto a flat roof about ten metres square, bounded by a waist-high wall. She stands and looks at the lights of the city, spreading out as far as she can see. There are no stars in the sky, just the twinkling lights of aeroplanes. The music is distant and tinny. She perches on the wall, cries a little, walks around, smokes a cigarette and sits on the wall looking up.

A dog lopes through the open doorway and heads straight for her, wagging its tail. Stimpy. He snuffles at her legs and she strokes his head. He rolls over and she rubs his eager belly.

'Hi.' Dean stands in the doorway. 'Knew he'd sniff you out.'

Vix stops rubbing and stands. She can hardly see his face, but a line of reflected light defines its left side, showing a shape she knows well: the sharp, jutting cheekbone.

'You. Hello.'

He walks towards her and his boots crunch broken glass. He stops a couple of metres away. 'Be careful,' he says. 'It's not safe up here.' She looks at him, at the sky. She feels very calm.

Stimpy begins to explore the rooftop, his angular muzzle sweeping like a metal detector.

'So you're a DJ now. How glamorous. I thought you didn't like parties.'

'Not much else to do in the city.'

'No?' A silence follows, and Vix realizes that it bothers Dean much more than her. She doesn't care; she's content to let it hang.

'Vix, I'm sorry about what happened. Me running away like that. It wasn't right. But we knew we had to go, quick, and I didn't think you'd really want to come with me and—'

'Forget it. It's ancient history. So you live here then?' She feels very calm and adult, not at all as she'd expected; it's as if she's just chatting to a mate

'I used to live here.' He comes over to the wall. 'In that.' He points down at the scrub around the building, the garden, where a few vans and trailers are parked.

'Which one?'

'The amby.' An old ambulance, painted dark green. 'Now I've got a flat.'

'You? In a flat?'

'I got tired. I'm getting on. Good to get settled.'

'What about the amby?

'I'm selling it.'

'Is it taxed, MOT, all that shit?'

'Yeah, it goes, I've kept it nice.'

'How much?'

'What?'

'What do you want for it?'

'Two hundred quid.'

Vix reaches into the bulging inside pocket of her jacket and pulls out one of the four thick wads of bills inside. The green elastic band around it twists up as she peels off three notes.

'Is American dollars OK?'

twenty eight

harry kiss me

The Range Rover does a steady forty-five in the middle lane of the M25. Lee sits on the back seat, between Danny and Marlowe. He doesn't recognize the driver, but he comes from the same factory as Marlowe; the same basic model with a few optional styling extras. His head is shaved and there's a tattoo of a swallow, blue with age and losing definition, on the side of his neck.

Lee's ankles and wrists are wrapped and lashed together with silver duct tape, keeping him hunched forward in the seat, elbows by his knees, like an eager child. It's the kind of tape he used to see a lot of in the club, on bulky black equipment around the lighting rigs. Another strip seals up his mouth. He's dressed in the same clothes he had on the day before – the day of his arrival – only now they're dirtier. Damp sweat-stains the size of dinner plates hum beneath his armpits. His jeans are crusty with dried piss. He pissed himself in the night, while locked in the trunk of the car, parked in the alley beside the club. On his retrieval this morning the driver complained that it would take ages to get the stain out of the floor covering, and they escorted him to the loos in the club, pulled down his trousers and sat him on the toilet for five minutes, to make sure, Danny said, that such little accidents didn't happen again.

Lee isn't used to breathing through his nose; and it seems to be requiring all his concentration. In and out. In and out. If he stops thinking about it, he begins to take shallow, rapid breaths, and he feels himself start to hyperventilate, his heart dancing about inside his chest, the blood drumming in his head.

'Mint?' Without turning round, the driver holds up a tube of Polos. It's the first time anyone has spoken since they got in the car. Danny takes them, slips one out and hands the tube to Marlowe, who pops a couple in his mouth before handing it back. Danny sucks noisily, but Marlowe crunches straight away.

'They don't t–taste nice if you do it like that,' says Danny.

'I don't like them. I want to get them over with.'

'Why did you take one then?' says the driver.

'For my breath, make it smell nice,' says Marlowe.

'Should g–give him a few,' says Danny, nodding his head at Lee. 'He don't smell too good.'

'Need a lot of mints to sort him out,' says

Marlowe. 'Need twenty packets.' Marlowe puts a hand on Lee's chin and wiggles it around.

'Leave the lad alone,' says Danny, and pats Lee's knee.

Everything Lee can see seems charged with mysterious extra significance, as if he's tripping. There's something hyper-real about the green digits of the clock on the dashboard, saying 11:37; about the sheet of the sky, blue-grey through the tinted windows; about the green verges, the fences and the strips of land he can see beyond the road; about the road signs with their succinct codes. 11:38.

To the side he sees other cars passing, or being passed, and the profiles of the other people sitting in them, in their other worlds. A sporty green number cruises by in the outside lane. A girl in the passenger seat is puckering her lips, applying lipstick, looking at herself in the mirror on the back of the pulled-down sun visor. Lee wonders if she's the last pretty girl he will see, then cuts the thought off, stares hard at the green digits and goes over his escape plan. He will throw himself forward, somehow, dive between the two front seats, get around the driver, somehow, hit the steering wheel, make them crash, and while his three captors lie stunned and bleeding, he'll wriggle through the broken windscreen, cutting through the tape on the jagged glass, and hop into the road, where a glamorous woman in a sports car will pick him up.

A bead of sweat is dribbling down his forehead.

He wants to raise his hands to wipe it. It's annoying him. It's making him nervous. If only it would go away. He closes his eyes and sees angry red blotches pulsing and feels the thudding of his heart. He feels sick and imagines chucking up and choking. The sweat hits his eyebrow and dissipates, and the small relief gives him momentary comfort, before panic and fear grip him again. Please, please, make it stop, make it OK. Breathe in, breathe out. He opens his eyes. 11:39. Amazing how long a minute can be.

'Fucking traffic,' says the driver. They're stuck behind a Sainsbury's lorry.

'B–Bank holiday weekend, isn't it?' says Danny. 'Everyone and his f–f–fucking dog is on the road. Take the next junction.'

Right, thinks Lee. Right, this is it. He calculates the distance in front and tries to judge his moment. Now! He closes his eyes and hurls himself forward, as hard as he can. His shoulders bash the sides of the front seats and he rocks back into position. He starts to thrash around, jerking from side to side.

'What's he doing?' says Marlowe.

'He's panicking,' says Danny, and he puts an arm around Lee's shoulders. Lee stops thrashing and breathes hard. 'There, there,' whispers Danny. With his other hand he brushes Lee's matted hair back from his forehead. Lee stares at his feet. High-pitched whining noises come from his throat. His chest is racked with sobs and his vision blurs as tears start.

He feels the car slow as it peels off the motorway and hears the driver change gear. Looking up, he sees they are at a roundabout; Danny points at one of the exits, and the car swings into it. He can't see the names on the signs through his tears, but he guesses they are headed north-east, further into Essex. The road is straight and quiet and the car picks up speed.

Lee sniffles, swallows, blinks away the liquid in his eyes and sits up as straight as he can. Danny takes his arm from around his shoulders. Lee will not give them the satisfaction of seeing him whimpering. It's a thought to hold on to, and he repeats it over and over in his mind as they drive on and on, with Danny directing. They turn into a deserted single-lane track between fields, bounded by high hedges, and suddenly Lee is distracted from his fixed thought pattern by the realization that Danny has no destination in mind; he's just pointing them to quieter and quieter roads, guiding them deeper into the countryside.

'F–Fucking beautiful, here,' says Danny. 'C–Cows and trees. Look at those flowers, Lee,' says Danny. 'Look at them.' The base of the unkempt hedges are sprinkled with blooms. 'Fucking beautiful. You got to look at the flowers when you're going along.' He points to a gate ahead. 'There. That'll do.'

The car stops outside the gate, and Marlowe gets out and opens it, standing politely behind it as the car drives into the field. He heads back to the car, and Danny shouts at him to close the gate again.

'D–Don't want to piss off the farmer,' says Danny as Marlowe climbs back in.

The car drives slowly into the field, up a slight incline, and stops a few hundred metres beyond the gate. It's a large field, rising and falling gently, its grass is nearly a foot long, its edges defined by a copse, a stream and two more hedges. Lee can see more fields stretching to the horizon, and no buildings anywhere. The driver cuts the engine, leans back and sighs.

Danny opens the passenger door. Outside is still and silent, and the air smells fresh.

'Right then,' says Marlowe.

'H–Hang on,' says Danny. 'Be human.' He takes out a packet of Rothmans and points it at Lee.

'Cigarette?'

Lee stares at him, eyes wide.

'Cigarette?'

Lee nods.

Gently, like he's removing a bandage, Danny unpeels the tape from Lee's mouth. It hurts and he cries out. Then he opens his mouth wide and breathes great, greedy gulps of air.

Danny lights the cigarette and puts it in Lee's mouth. He sucks hard, rolls the smoke around, inhales deeply and lets it fill his lungs. Lee blows out smoothly.

'Thanks,' says Lee.

'That little st–stunt, Lee. With the car and the money. That whole palaver.' Danny is talking softly in his left ear. 'It was rash. It made me s–s–sad.' He reinserts the cigarette between Lee's lips.

'You want to know how we found you, Lee?'

'No.'

Danny takes the cigarette out.

'See, my wife, she reads the women's papers. Like this one.' Danny pulls a thin, folded magazine out of his back pocket. 'Take Five!' says the title, and under it, printed over the shoulders of a smiling model, MY HUSBAND'S PRISON HELL, HASTY PASTRY!, MY PARENTS TRIED TO KILL OUR LOVE. Danny pops the cigarette back, and flicks through the paper to an item on the centre pages. 'Thought this might tickle you.' He spreads it, and holds it out for Lee to read. The headline on one page reads BULIMIA: THE TRUTH, on the other, NOVELTY HOLIDAY-SNAP COMPETITION RESULTS!, and under it is a picture of a cow's head with Lee's face next to it. He starts to read the caption. 'Sol Thomas of Brixton, who snapped these two buddies in Goa wins . . .' Lee stops reading; he's getting smoke in his eyes.

'Oh, sorry,' says Danny. He drops the magazine on the floor, removes the cigarette and starts puffing it himself. 'H–Hello, I thought. He's supposed to be dead. What's he doing in Goa? So I made some enquiries. I got the photographer's ph–ph–phone number off a seccy at the mag. He told me you were going to pay him a visit.'

'Don't,' says Lee. 'Please.'

Danny pats Lee's shoulder. He takes the tape hanging off Lee's cheek and smooths it back over his mouth. Danny addresses Marlowe. 'No-one rips me off, Lee. No-one. Take everything out of his p–pockets. Remove anything that might identify him.' He gets out of the car and leans against the side, enjoying the view, as Marlowe snaps off Lee's thin leather necklace and delves about, with some difficulty, in Lee's jeans pockets. He pulls out his tatty canvas wallet and a tape. He gives them to Danny.

'We'll put this on,' says Danny. 'Least we can do.' And he leans in and hands the tape to the driver, who slots it in the stereo. For a moment Lee has no idea where he got the tape, then he remembers: those people in Berlin who gave him food. He promised them he'd listen to it. He hasn't, and he can't remember now why he didn't throw it away.

The music begins with a single drum beating, then others join in, and then a chorus of chanting, happy voices:

'Hare Krishna, Hare Krishna, Krishna Krishna, Hare Hare—'

'What the fuck's this?' says Marlowe.

'This is what those orange n–n–nutters sing,' says Danny, and he looks at Lee. 'I wouldn't think this was your sort of thing at all.'

379

'He don't look like one,' says Marlowe.

'Maybe he's undercover,' points out the driver.

To Lee, shaking silently, the things he can see and hear come to him vaguely, and nothing makes much sense. The hypnotic, rhythmic chanting he can hear could be coming from inside his head.

'Harry kiss me, Harry kiss me,' sings the driver, in time with the chanting. Marlowe laughs, and the driver continues, loud and tunelessly, swaying his head from side to side and tapping his feet. 'Kiss me, kiss me, hurry hurry, I'm all randy, I'm all randy, take your bra off, hurry Harry.'

The things Lee can see, and hear, and feel, they are so far away; he is somewhere else. He closes his eyes.

'Right,' says Danny, and slaps the side of the car. 'Get it over with and we can go home.' The driver turns up the volume on the stereo. The players are belting it out, the drum beats are getting faster, the chanting more frenzied.

'Hare Krishna, Hare Krishna, Krishna Krishna, Hare Hare—'

Marlowe reaches forward, hands outstretched, heading for Lee's neck. Lee is silent, his breathing is slow and deep. Nothing, now, there is nothing; get it over with.

'Hare Rama, Hare Rama, Rama Rama, Hare Hare—'

'He's going,' says Marlowe. 'Little fucker's going.'

'—Hare Krishna, Hare Krishna, Krishna Krishna, Hare Hare, Hare Rama, Hare Rama, Rama Rama, Hare Hare, Hare Krishna, Hare Krishna, Krishna Krishna, Hare Hare, Hare Rama, Hare Rama, Rama Rama, Hare Hare.'

THE END

NYMPHOMATION
Jeff Noon

The air of Manchester is alive with blurbvurts, automated advertisements chanting their slogans. But the loudest of all is for Domino Bones, the new lottery game. Every Friday night the winning numbers are illuminated on the body of Lady Luck, the voluptuous figurehead of the game. For the winner, it is unimaginable riches, for the losers another week to wait for the bones to fall again. But there is only one real winner, The Company, which plays the city's fragile expectations with callous ease.

A group of mathematics students are looking at the mind-numbing probabilities involved and searching for the hidden mysteries behind the game. They watch the city at work and at dangerous play and slowly uncover the sinister realities behind the mania. The Company is devouring Manchester – it has the nymphomation, an evolutionary process which has the power to take over the city's dreams . . .

0 552 14479 7

THINGS CAN ONLY GET BETTER
Eighteen Miserable Years in the Life of a Labour Supporter
John O'Farrell

'Like bubonic plague and stone cladding, no-one took Margaret Thatcher seriously until it was too late. Her first act as leader was to appear before the cameras and do a V for Victory sign the wrong way round. She was smiling and telling the British people to f★★★ off at the same time. It was something we would have to get used to.'

Things Can Only Get Better is the personal account of a Labour supporter who survived eighteen miserable years of Conservative government. It is the heartbreaking and hilarious confessions of someone who has been actively involved in helping the Labour party lose elections at every level: school candidate; door-to-door canvasser; working for a Labour MP in the House of Commons; standing as a council candidate; and eventually writing jokes for a shadow cabinet minister.

Along the way he slowly came to realize that Michael Foot would never be Prime Minister, that vegetable quiche was not as tasty as chicken tikka masala and that the nuclear arms race was not going to be stopped by face painting alone.

'VERY FUNNY AND MUCH BETTER THAN ANYTHING HE EVER WROTE FOR ME'
Griff Rhys Jones

'VERY FUNNY'
Guardian

'EXCELLENT . . . WHATEVER YOUR POLITICS *THINGS CAN ONLY GET BETTER* WILL MAKE YOU LAUGH OUT LOUD'
Angus Deayton

0 552 99803 6

A SELECTED LIST OF FINE WRITING
AVAILABLE FROM CORGI AND BLACK SWAN

99830 3	SINGLE WHITE E-MAIL	Jessica Adams	£6.99
99821 4	HOMING INSTINCT	Diana Appleyard	£6.99
99619 X	HUMAN CROQUET	Kate Atkinson	£6.99
99674 2	ACTS OF REVISION	Martyn Bedford	£6.99
99600 9	NOTES FROM A SMALL ISLAND	Bill Bryson	£6.99
99702 1	A WALK IN THE WOODS	Bill Bryson	£6.99
99808 7	THE LOST CONTINENT	Bill Bryson	£6.99
99805 2	MADE IN AMERICA	Bill Bryson	£6.99
99806 0	NEITHER HERE NOR THERE	Bill Bryson	£6.99
99690 4	TOUCH THE DRAGON	Karen Connelly	£6.99
99707 2	ONE ROOM IN A CASTLE	Karen Connelly	£6.99
99833 8	BLAST FROM THE PAST	Ben Elton	£6.99
99731 5	BLUEPRINT FOR A PROPHET	Carl Gibeily	£6.99
99679 3	SAP RISING	A.A. Gill	£6.99
99760 9	THE DRESS CIRCLE	Laurie Graham	£6.99
13937 8	THE FIRST FIFTY	Muriel Gray	£6.99
99609 2	FORREST GUMP	Winston Groom	£6.99
14681 1	CASTAWAY	Lucy Irvine	£6.99
99605 X	A SON OF THE CIRCUS	John Irving	£7.99
14474 6	IN BED WITH AN ELEPHANT	Ludovic Kennedy	£6.99
99037 X	BEING THERE	Jerzy Kosinski	£5.99
99748 X	THE BEAR WENT OVER THE MOUNTAIN	William Kotzwinkle	£6.99
99762 5	THE LACK BROTHERS	Malcolm McKay	£6.99
99569 X	MAYBE THE MOON	Armistead Maupin	£6.99
14136 4	THE WALPOLE ORANGE	Frank Muir	£4.99
14478 9	AUTOMATED ALICE	Jeff Noon	£6.99
14479 7	NYMPHOMATION	Jeff Noon	£6.99
99803 6	THINGS CAN ONLY GET BETTER	John O'Farrell	£6.99
99617 3	LIFE ON MARS	Alexander Stuart	£6.99
99666 1	BY BUS TO THE SAHARA	Gordon West	£5.99